WENDY MARKHAM

is a pseudonym for *New York Times* bestselling, award-winning novelist Wendy Corsi Staub. She has written more than fifty fiction and nonfiction books for adults and teenagers in various genres—including contemporary and historical romance, suspense, mystery, television and movie tie-in and biography. A small-town girl at heart, she was born and raised in western New York on the shores of Lake Erie and in the middle of the notorious snowbelt. By third grade, she was set on becoming a published author; a few years later, a school trip to Manhattan convinced her that she had to live there someday. At twenty-one, she moved by herself to New York City and worked as an office temp, freelance copywriter, advertising account coordinator and book editor, before selling her first novel, which went on to win a Romance Writers of America RITA® Award. *Slightly Single* was one of Waldenbooks' Best Books of 2002. Very happily married with two children, Wendy writes full-time and lives in a cozy old house in suburban New York, proving that childhood dreams really can come true.

To my beloved husband and our two beautiful children.
And, in gratitude, to "Will,"
without whom this book wouldn't have been possible—
and without whom I have lived happily ever after.

Slightly
Single

Wendy Markham

**RED
DRESS
INK**™

SLIGHTLY SINGLE

A Red Dress Ink novel

ISBN 0-373-81079-2

© 2002 by Wendy Corsi Staub.

All rights reserved. The reproduction, transmission or utilization of this work in whole or in part in any form by any electronic, mechanical or other means, now known or hereafter invented, including xerography, photocopying and recording, or in any information storage or retrieval system, is forbidden without written permission. For permission please contact Red Dress Ink, Editorial Office, 225 Duncan Mill Road, Don Mills, Ontario, Canada M3B 3K9.

This book is a work of fiction. The names, characters, incidents and places are the products of the author's imagination, and are not to be construed as real. While the author was inspired in part by actual events, none of the characters in the book is based on an actual person. Any resemblance to persons living or dead is entirely coincidental and unintentional.

® and TM are trademarks. Trademarks indicated with ® are registered in the United States Patent and Trademark Office, the Canadian Trade Marks Office and/or other countries.

www.RedDressInk.com

Printed in U.S.A.

This book wouldn't exist if it weren't for my
old and new friends at Silhouette, whose encouragement
and enthusiasm made the writing and editorial process a
pleasure. With warmest gratitude to everyone who played
a role, especially Joan, Karen, Cristine, Margaret and Tara!
I would also like to add sincere thanks to my agent,
Laura Blake Peterson, for her constant support.
And, of course, I must fondly acknowledge all the
fabulous city gals who crossed my path during my own
Slightly Single era, always there to share margaritas,
cigarettes, dance floors and wee-hour cabs to the
boroughs. Cheers to all, wherever you've landed!!!

One

Here's how my life will turn out: I'll marry Will. He'll become a big stage star and I'll give up my advertising career to stay home with our children. We'll stay in New York rather than going South or West (because I desperately have to have all four seasons), and someday we'll turn into the kind of senior citizens you see sharing the same side of the booth at Friendly's. Not that I've ever seen a Friendly's in Manhattan, or that Will and I have ever sat on the same side of any booth in any restaurant, ever.

Will, after all, needs his space.

In restaurants.

In general.

I, on the other hand, need no space.

Which is exactly what I tell my friend Kate, in response to her infuriatingly serene "Everyone needs space," over Tall Skim Caramel Macchiatos at Starbucks.

"I need no space," I tell Kate, who rolls her fake aquamarine pupils toward her dyed-blond hairline. Kate grew up in the Deep South, where it's apparently best to be a skinny blue-eyed blonde. Actually, speaking as a well-padded brown-eyed brunette New Yorker, it's probably best to be a skinny blue-eyed blonde any place.

"Yes, you do need space, Trace," Kate insists, with only a hint of the antebellum drawl she's worked so hard to lose. "Believe me, you *so* wouldn't want Will in your face every second of every day."

Okay, the thing about that is…

I so *would*.

Do I seem pathetic? I do, don't I? So I'd better not admit the truth to Kate, who has already declared that she's worried about me. She thinks my relationship with Will is one-sided.

"No," I lie, "not every second of every day. But that doesn't mean I want him blowing out of here for summer stock in the Adirondacks for three months without me."

"Well, I don't think you have a choice. I mean, it's not like you can tag along."

At that, I focus on my beverage, attempting to stir the sweetened foam into the darker liquid below. It refuses to harmonize, clinging in wispy clumps to the wooden stirrer like the cottony clusters of mealy bugs on my sickly philodendron at home.

"Tracey," Kate says in a warning voice, clearly on to me.

"What?" All innocence, I toy with my yellow plastic Bic cigarette lighter, flicking it on and off, wishing for the good old days when you could smoke anywhere you damn pleased.

"You're *not* thinking of tagging along with Will this summer."

"Why aren't I?"

"Mostly because—hello-o?—you're not an actress. You already have a career, remember?"

Oh, yes. The *career.* My entry-level job at Blaire Barnett advertising, where thanks to a glorified title and my tendency to pounce on new ventures before thorough investigation, I didn't realize I was a mere administrative assistant until a few weeks after I started, when my boss sent me a plant for Secretary's Day.

That would be the aforementioned insect-infested philodendron. Like my position at the agency, it seemed so promising that first day, all shiny-leaved and cellophane-and-ribbon-bedecked, with a card that read, *Dear Traci* (note the misspelling), *Thanks for all you do. Best, Jake.* I got it home, made it cozy on my lone windowsill…and, a week later, the mealy bugs moved in for the kill.

"I could quit," I tell Kate, still toying with my lighter.

"Smoking?"

"Good lord, no. My job." I toss the lighter on the table.

Mental note: Stop for more cigarettes on the way to meet Will.

"That's what I was afraid of." Kate, a refreshingly nonmilitant nonsmoker, smirks. Sips. Says, "So you'll just quit your job after less than two months—"

"*More* than two months—"

"More than two months," she concedes, "and— what? Follow Will to wherever he's going to be? What will you do there?"

"Build sets? Waitress at some coffee shop? I don't know, Kate. I haven't thought it through yet. All I know is that I can't stand the thought of spending the entire summer in this hellhole of a city without Will."

"Does Will know this?"

There is nothing ambiguous about her question, yet I stall. "Does Will know what?"

"That you're thinking of coming with him?"

"No," I admit.

"When is he leaving?"

"In a few weeks."

"Maybe he'll change his mind between now and then."

"No. He says he needs a break from the city."

She raises an eyebrow in a way that hints at her suspicion: that the city is not all Will is trying to escape. If she says it, I will tell her she's wrong.

But I won't be sure about that.

And that's the real reason I want to go away with Will this summer. Because ever since we got together three years ago, in college, our relationship has been about as stable as an Isuzu Trooper at eighty mph on a hairpin curve. In the rain. And wind.

When we met we were both juniors. Will had just transferred from a well-known Midwestern university to our upstate SUNY college. He had great disdain for the conservative, all-American mind-set that infused not just the school he'd left, but the family he was stuck with.

I could relate. Maybe that's what first drew me to him. The tiny western New York college town I had grown up in bore striking similarities to the Midwest Will was fleeing.

There was the accent—the flat, wrinkle-nosed *a* that gives *apple* three syllables (ay-a-pple) whether you're in the Chicago area or upstate New York.

There was my Roman Catholic religion, shared by every last person in my life but my friend Tamar Goldstein, the lone Jewish girl at Brookside High, who got to stay home while the rest of us went to school on the mysterious High Holy Days in October.

There was my sprawling extended Italian family, with its smothering traditions in which everyone was expected to participate: nine-thirty mass on Sundays, followed by coffee and cannoli at my maternal grandmother's house and then spaghetti at noon at my paternal grandmother's house. This is how every Sunday of my life began, and I continue to bear the scars aka cellulite everlasting.

Will is Protestant—his ancestors were from England and Scotland. He has no discernible accent; he has no cellulite. In his parents' house, spaghetti sauce comes from a jar.

But he, like I, longed to escape the stranglehold of small-town life and had wanted to live in New York City for as long as he could remember. The difference was, he saw the State University of New York at Brookside as a giant leap toward his goal. I didn't have the heart to tell him that Brookside might as well be in Iowa. He figured it out by himself eventually, and ultimately skipped graduation in order to get the hell out of town as soon as possible.

When we met that first semester of junior year, he had a girlfriend back home in Des Moines, and I was living at home three miles from campus, with my parents. Our coming together was a gradual thing, and the blame for that lies squarely with Will. In retrospect, I see that he was alternately torn between cheating on his girlfriend and dumping her—and me as well—in favor of screwing around.

He used to talk about her freely to me, in a maddeningly casual way that suggested he and I were friends. If I ever popped by his apartment unannounced and he was talking to her on the phone, he'd make no attempt to hang up and would tell me casually, when he finally did, "Oh, that was Helene." I figured that if he considered us more than *friends* (his word) who made out whenever we got drunk and ran into each other in a bar, he'd be a lot more furtive about his girlfriend.

So her name was Helene, and, naturally, I pictured her svelte and exotic.

Then Will went home for Christmas break and entrusted me with the keys to his apartment so I could water his plants. Yes, he had plants. Not marijuana plants, which were frequently grown in the frat houses near campus. Not a token cactus or one of those robust rubbery snake plants that you can pretty much shove into a closet and not water for a year and still keep thriving.

No, Will had regular house plants, the kind that needed sunlight and water and fertilizer.

Anyway, this key-entrusting episode was before we were sleeping together but after he'd gone for my bra clasp enough times for me to invest in something suitably flimsy. My usual was an industrial-strength closure with four hooks and eyes on an elasticized strip the width of duct tape.

I was dazzled that he trusted me not just with the plants he'd bought at the local Wal-Mart garden shop in September, but with the entire contents of the apartment he shared with two roommates. Didn't he suspect that I would spend hours going through the plastic milk crates he kept in his closet, reading letters from Helene and searching for photos of her?

I don't know—maybe he did suspect. Maybe he *wanted* me to snoop. The photos weren't hard to find.

They were tucked in the front cover of one of those cloth-bound blank books, along with a note from Helene that read: *Use this as a journal while you're away so that one day we can read it together and I'll feel like I was there with you.*

I gloated when I saw that the book was blank.

Not nearly as much as I gloated when I at last laid eyes upon the enigmatic Helene in a photo. I had known she was blond, a fact Will had mentioned more than once. And okay, I'll give her the hair. It was long and shiny and parted in the middle. But other than that, she was ordinary—even more round-faced than I was and wearing red plaid Bermudas that did nothing for her hips and even less for her thighs. She wore them with a red polo shirt, tucked in.

I have never in my life worn a shirt tucked in, but if I were so-inclined, I sure as hell wouldn't tuck it into red plaid Bermudas.

I stopped worrying about Helene when I saw that snapshot.

Sure enough, when Will returned from break to find his plants thriving, his plastic milk crates apparently undisturbed, and the plate of homemade cream-cheese brownies I'd left on his kitchen table, he informed me that he and Helene had broken up on New Year's Eve. I, in my not-just-friends-but-not-quite-more role, wasn't sure how to respond to that news. I remember ultimately acting sympathetic toward Will, and inwardly slapping myself a high five because I had won.

I had beaten out Helene. The shadowy hometown girl-friend had been eliminated from the competition.

A shallow, short-lived victory, because I soon discovered that I had a long way to go. Even now, three years later, the finish line eludes me.

Kate asks, "Don't you think you should tell Will you're quitting your job and going with him?"

"I didn't say I was definitely doing it. I just said that I wanted to."

Dammit. Kate's looking at me like I've just told her that I may or may not mow down everyone in this Starbucks with a sawed-off shotgun.

"I have to go now," I decide abruptly, picking up my white paper cup and my giant black shoulder bag.

"Me, too," Kate says, picking up her white paper cup and her giant black shoulder bag. "I'll walk you over to the subway."

Great.

One crosstown block and one uptown block of Kate's attempts to sell me on the many glorious pros of summer in the city. Laughable, because I've already spent enough steamy, putrid-smelling urban August days to last me a lifetime.

I'll have lived here a year Memorial Day, having spent the first few months sharing a Queens sublet with a total stranger courtesy of a *Village Voice* classified. Her name was Mercedes, and the few times I saw her in passing, she looked stoned. Turned out she slept all day while I was out temping, and was out all night doing God knows what—I tried to ask, but she was evasive. We both moved out on Labor Day when the actor who had sublet us the apartment returned from summer stock. I never saw her again, but I wouldn't be surprised if she shows up on an episode of *COPS* someday, vigorously denying something.

Thanks to my summer in a relatively affordable borough, I scraped together enough money to land a studio of my very own in Manhattan, in the East Village. *Way* east. Like, almost as far east as you can go and not be on the FDR Drive or in the river. The apartment has that kind of grimy and depressing thing going on. Like the Kramdens' place in those *Honeymooners* reruns on Nick At Nite, it seems to exist only in grainy black-and-white, no matter how I try to jazz it up. Not that I'm trying so hard.

Kate—whom I met temping on my third day in New York and who lives in a brownstone floor-thru in the heart of the West Village, courtesy of her wealthy parents back in Mobile—thinks I should splurge on a bright-colored cover for my futon. I tell her that I'm broke, which is always true, yet in reality I don't want to spend any money on my place.

Here's why: because if I make it more like a home, then there will be a permanence about it—a sense that I'm there to stay. And I don't want to stay alone in a drab East Village flat.

I want to live with Will.

Soon.

And forever.

"And just think," Kate is saying. "Shakespeare in the Park."

I shrug. "Maybe Will will do Shakespeare in summer stock."

"You think?"

I shrug. Probably more like *Little Shop of Horrors. Carousel,* maybe.

"Italian ices from sidewalk vendors," she pontificates. "Weekends in the Hamptons."

I snort at that.

"I've got a half-share," she points out. "You can visit me."

She goes on about summer, which is hard to envision on this gray May Saturday morning, cool and drizzly.

This stretch of lower Broadway is teeming with multi-pierced NYU types, stroller-pushing families, packs of suburban teenagers and the ubiquitous sales-flyer-thrusters.

Kate and I dump our empty cups into an overflowing trash can on the corner of Eighth and Broadway. I leave her admiring a pair of hundred-dollar fluorescent coral-colored mules in the window of a boutique and descend into the depths of the subway.

On the uptown-bound side I wait for the N train, standing away from the track with my back almost against the wall, yet not touching it because you never know what kind of filth is just waiting to rub off on your Old Navy Performance Fleece pullover. My eye is peeled on a scruffy guy who's pacing back and forth along the edge of the platform. First clue that he's not all there: It's forty degrees out and he's shirtless, wearing shorts and ripped rubber flip-flops. He's muttering to himself, something about lice—or maybe it's lights—and I'm not the only one giving him a wide berth.

Every once in a while you hear about some innocent New Yorker getting shoved in front of an oncoming train. My friend Raphael was actually on the platform when it happened once, but the pushee rolled off the track in the nick of time. The pusher looked like a regular businessman, Raphael said. He was wearing a suit and carrying a briefcase. Turned out when the police searched him that the briefcase was full of live rodents. The significance of this escapes me, other than proving that you just never know who you're dealing with in a crowd of strangers in the city, and it's best to keep your back to the wall.

Which I do.

Finally, the telltale rumble just before a light appears at the end of the tunnel. As the N train roars into the station, I move cautiously forward, positioning myself in advance exactly where the door will open, something that's possible only after several months of riding the same train every day.

The car is packed and too warm and smells of sweat and Chinese take-out. Hip hop music blares from the headphones of the guy next to me as I stand holding on to a germy center pole. As we lurch forward and the lights flicker, I keep my balance, thinking about

Will, wondering whether he'll be awake when I get to the studio apartment he shares with Nerissa, whom he met on an audition last fall. He likes to sleep past noon on Saturdays.

Does it bother me that he lives with another woman?

I want to say of course not.

But the reality is that I wouldn't mind if Nerissa got pushed in front of an oncoming N train tomorrow. She's lithe and beautiful, an English dancer in an off-Broadway show that opened a few months ago. She sleeps on a futon behind a tall folding screen from Ikea, and Will on his full-size bed…and never the twain shall meet.

Yes, I truly believe this. I force myself to believe it, because Nerissa has a boyfriend, a Scottish pro golfer named Broderick, and Will has me. Yet I've seen the way he looks at her when she drifts around wearing drawstring cotton pants over her dancer's leotard, with no hips to speak of and high, taut braless breasts.

I am all flesh, by comparison to Nerissa or not; all hips and thighs and buttocks. As I said, my bras are not wispy scraps of lace and underwire and skinny straps; my undergarments are not what you would readily call *panties,* a term that brings to mind slender sorority girls with Neiman Marcus charges. Sturdy, no-nonsense cotton underwear is necessary to keep my natural jiggle and sag from jiggling and sagging to an unfortunate extreme.

Will adores real lingerie, the kind that undoubtedly fills the top drawer of Nerissa's tall Pottery Barn bureau. This, I know about Will, because once, during our senior year of college, when we had been officially dating for a few months and I knew we were about to become lovers, he bought me a teddy. It was a champagne-colored satin-and-lace getup from Christian Dior, two sizes two small—which I didn't know whether to take as a compliment or a hint.

Every time I wore it, I put on a bra and underpants underneath. The bra because not wearing one would be obscene with my figure; the underpants because every time I moved, the teddy's crotch unsnapped because I was too tall or too wide for it, or, sadly, both. Finally, I replaced the snaps with a hook-and-eye combo. I had learned sewing in Brookside Middle School home ec, though back then never dreamed that I would use my skills for something so illicit as replacing the crotch snaps on a sexy undergarment presented by a man with whom I would have sex before marriage.

Anyway, it was hard to tell whether Will was ever truly turned on by the sight of me in that crotch-doctored teddy with my thick duct-tape-like bra straps peeking out at the shoulders and my sensible cotton Hanes riding lower on my lumpy thighs than the french-cut teddy. I like to think that he found me irresistible, but in retrospect, I'm not certain that's the case.

When we made love for the first time in college, it

was after drinking two bottles of red wine in the apartment he shared with two gay theater guys who were out rehearsing for the campus production of *Guys and Dolls,* for which Will wasn't cast. For that oversight he blamed Geoff Jefferson, the hetero-phobic (according to Will) theater professor. We drank wine and he verbally trashed Geoff Jefferson and we drank more wine and then we had sex on the nearest bed we stumbled to, which belonged to his roommate André. That's where I lost my virginity, on six-hundred-thread-count Egyptian cotton sheets imported from Italy, staring over Will's sweaty shoulder at a poster of Marilyn Monroe on a subway grate with her skirt blowing up around her.

Speaking of the subway, I get off at Times Square and emerge onto the bordering-on-garish family-friendly street filled with oversize theme eateries and warehouse chain stores where there were once peep shows, topless bars and porno flicks. Shoulder to shoulder with immigrants with complexions of various hues, overweight tourists with diagonal purse straps and a class trip group collectively gaping at the MTV studio across Broadway, I walk north and west: two short uptown blocks and two long crosstown blocks.

I buy my Salem Lights and a copy of today's *Post* from the familiar newsstand on the corner, where the Pakistani proprietor sometimes greets me like an old acquaintance and sometimes appears not to recognize me at all. It's unnerving.

Today, he gives me a big grin. We're long-lost friends again.

"Hello!" he pretty much shouts, as is his way. "How you today?"

I grin back. "Not bad. How about you?"

He shakes his head at the misty sky. "This weather. Too cold. Too gray."

I nod. I do trite conversation very well. "Seems like summer's never going to come." See?

"Oh, it's coming," he says with the conviction of a waiter at Smith & Wollensky vouching for the prime rib. "Then when it gets here, you complain."

I wonder whether he's employing the collective *you,* or if I'm supposed to take it as a sign that I'll be miserable this summer, not just because the city is so goddamned hot from June through September, but because Will won't be in it with me.

Two

Will's studio apartment is on the twenty-sixth floor of a high-rise doorman building with a marble lobby and three elevators. It's the closest thing to what my small-town upstate self used to imagine was a typical New York City dwelling. The building, I mean. The apartment is pretty much a letdown. But aren't they all?

Growing up in Brookside, I watched a lot of TV. Mainly sitcoms, and in most of them, the setting was New York. Thus I was weaned on Monica and Rachel's sprawling two-bedroom with oversize windows and a terrace-like fire escape, and the Huxtables' elaborate Brooklyn Heights brownstone with an actual yard and Jerry Seinfeld's spacious West Side one-bedroom complete with wacky neighbor.

Ha.

My place, you already know about.

Will's place, I'll describe as little more than a fairly large square room with square office-building-like plate glass windows along one end, and at the other, a separate kitchen the size of the stairway landing in my parents' Queen Anne Victorian. His bed is by the windows; Nerissa's futon and dresser are behind the aforementioned folding screen near the kitchen. In between are a semi-tacky black leather couch Will bought from the previous tenant whose fiancée wouldn't let him bring it to the marriage, Will's work-out equipment and a bookshelf crammed with CDs, scripts, *Playbills* and a few actual books, mostly paperback classics he couldn't sell back to the college bookstore after two semesters of American Lit.

Having buzzed me in, you'd think Will would be waiting with the door propped open, or at least somewhere near it. But I have to knock twice, and when he finally opens it, he's rumpled and yawning, obviously having just rolled out of bed.

He looks fabulous anyway. At least, he does to me.

Kate once announced, after two stiff bourbons at the Royalton, that she thinks there's something vaguely faggy about Will, and that she's not the least bit attracted to him. This disturbed me profoundly for reasons I can't quite grasp. Ever since, there are times when I look at Will and find myself searching for signs of latent homosexuality, half-expecting him to mince or sashay or toss a lusty leer at James, his strapping, too-beautiful-to-be-straight doorman. So far he never has, and I don't know what it is about him that Kate sees as effeminate. She doesn't even know about the plants in college, which, by the way, are still thriving years later on his windowsill.

Maybe it's just the musical theater thing—so many actors *are* gay, and she can't shake the stereotype because she's from the Deep South. Or do I blame too many of her hangups on that?

In any case, as far as I'm concerned, Will is masculinity personified. Think Noel from *Felicity* meets Ben from *Felicity* and that's pretty much Will. He's six-foot-one and clean-shaven, with a well-defined jaw and a cleft in his chin. He has thick dark-brown hair that has looked incredibly good with sideburns, or shaggy past his earlobes or close-cropped, as it is now. His not-quite-blue, not-quite-gray eyes are the precise color of my favorite J. Crew sweater, described as Smoke in the catalogue. He works out all the time, meaning he's lean and muscular. He frequently wears black turtlenecks, and he always wears cologne.

Where I come from, cologne, like jewelry, is worn only by Italian men—including my dad and brothers— or by Jason Miller, the local hairdresser of ambiguous sexual orientation. Okay, ambiguous only to my mother, who has speculated on more than one occasion how strange it is that such a sweet, handsome man isn't married yet. My mother also assumes without question that Lee Harvey Oswald acted alone, that O.J. is looking for the real killers and that all my adult life I've been going to weekly Sunday mass *and* Saturday confession.

In any case, maybe the cologne thing triggered Kate's comment about Will being faggy.

Even now, first thing in the morning—at least, what is considered first thing in the morning on Will's schedule and might be the brunching hour on anyone else's—he smells great and looks incredibly appealing in a rumpled, sexy way. Somehow, there is no morning breath; there is no Bed Head.

"Did I wake you?" I ask, tiptoeing to kiss his cheek, which is barely covered with stubble.

"It's okay." He yawns and pads to the kitchen area, where he fills a glass from the Poland Spring cooler that's jammed into the corner between the stove and fridge.

"How was last night?"

"Exhausting. A bunch of dowdy East Side dowagers and their philandering husbands. A martini bar and beef carpaccio, even though carpaccio's been over for years."

"What about martinis?"

"With this crowd they're always in."

I should mention that Will works for Eat Drink Or Be Married, a Manhattan caterer. He makes excellent money waitering at private events like weddings and charity dinners. Most of the guests are high profile, and sometimes he's privy to great celebrity dirt, which I find fascinating.

"Listen, Trace, I know we're supposed to go to your friend's party tonight, but I have to work."

"What?" Stabbing disappointment. "But we've been planning this for weeks! It's Raphael's thirtieth birthday."

I have to wait for Will to drain the full glass of water, something he does eight times a day, before he says, "I know, and I had asked Milos to let me have off tonight, but he got into a bind. Jason fell at the rink yesterday and twisted his ankle."

Jason, one of the other waiters, happens to be Jason Kenyon, the former Olympic figure skater. I'm not that big on following sports, but even I've heard of him— I think he got a bronze medal a few years ago in Japan. Now he's trying to make it as an actor here in New York, and he must be as broke as anyone else, because he's willing to wear a Nehru jacket while lugging monstrous trays around and clearing away rich peo-ple's plates. Not that it isn't worth it. They make twenty bucks an hour, plus tips.

"Can't Milos find somebody else to fill in?" I ask.

"He doesn't want just anyone. It's a big celebrity wedding out in the Hamptons, and he only wants a certain quality of waiter there."

"Flattering for you, but where does that leave me?"

Will puts his glass in the sink, then leans over and kisses my cheek. "Sorry, Trace."

I pout, then ask, "Which celebrity?"

"I can't say."

"You can't say?" I gape at him—or rather, his

back, since he's retreated to the other side of the room. I follow him. "Not even to me?"

"I'm sworn to absolute secrecy," he says blandly, removing his long-sleeved thermal T-shirt and tossing it into a nearby laundry basket. "You'll know tomorrow, though. It'll be in all the papers."

"So tell me now. I'm dying to know."

"I can't. Look, I don't even know exactly where the wedding is going to be held. They don't want anyone calling the press with the details. I'm supposed to give a code word to the car service driver who picks me up at the train station, and then he'll take me there. That's how undercover this whole thing is."

Pissed off at this whole ridiculous secret agent scene, I say, "Christ, Will, what do you think I'm going to do, tip off Page Six?"

He laughs, taking off his flannel boxers. "You'll know tomorrow."

"Along with the rest of the world," I grumble, watching him reach for the laundry basket again.

Unlike me, he's extremely comfortable naked. I could never walk around without clothes in front of anyone, even Will. *Especially* not Will. I'd be too conscious of him watching my thighs doing their Jell-O dance and my boobs swinging somewhere around my belly button. Then again, even if I had a perfect body, I don't think I could ever parade around nude.

Although everyone says that changes when you have a baby. According to my sister Mary Beth, who's had two, giving birth pretty much entails lying spread-eagled in some room with total strangers regularly coming along to stick their hands into your crotch up to their elbows. She says you don't even care who sees you naked after that. It must be true, because Mary Beth just joined a health club and started getting massages and taking steams. This from a girl whose mother had to write her a permanent excuse to get out of showers after fifth-grade gym because she was so traumatized by public nudity.

Naturally, I was traumatized about it, too. But by the time I hit fifth grade, my mother had already gone through my three brothers, who were so wanton that they would pull down their pants in front of me and my friends, bend over and fart for fun. So when I tried working the modesty angle for the gym shower excuse, my mother was in no mood to coddle. "You don't want to take a shower in front of everyone? Get over it!" was pretty much her attitude with me.

"Anyway, I really need the money," Will informs me. "I'm leaving in a few weeks, and I won't be making much over the summer."

"I thought they pay you."

"They do, but it's a fraction of what I get with Milos. I'm going to take a shower." Will heads for the bathroom. "Then we'll go out and get breakfast."

"Lunch," I amend, pulling out a cigarette and my lighter.

"Whatever. Hey, you know what? Could you not smoke in here?"

I pause with the butt midway to my mouth. "Why not?"

"It bothers Nerissa. She says her clothes smell like smoke whenever you've been here."

"Oh." I slowly put the cigarette back into the pack, trying to think of something to say to that.

I don't have to. He closes the door behind him.

No more smoking at Will's place?

Dismayed at this turn of events, I drift over to the couch and sit, grabbing a magazine from the pile on the floor. *Entertainment Weekly.* Will subscribes. I flip through it absently, stewing. It's not that Nerissa doesn't have a right to not smell like secondhand smoke. I understand where she's coming from. But I feel vaguely unsettled and, I guess, embarrassed. Like I have this dirty, disgusting habit that's infringing on other people's lives.

Which I suppose is the truth, but Will never seemed to mind me smoking at his place before. Sometimes he even bums cigarettes from me when we're out, and he says that if he weren't a vocalist, he would definitely be a smoker.

There's a part of me—granted, an irrational part— that wonders why Will didn't stick up for me to his roommate. He could have told Nerissa that I can smoke in their apartment if I want to, and that she'll just have to deal. After all, he moved in first. His name is on the lease, not hers. The more aggravated I get thinking about it, the more I want a cigarette.

I'm not one of those girls who started smoking behind the bleachers in junior high, or grew up in a smoker household. In my family, only my sister's soon-to-be-ex-husband Vinnie and my grandfather smoke butts, and my grandfather's had lung cancer for almost a year.

You'd think that would scare me into quitting, but the man is in his late eighties. I figure I'll quit in a few years, when I'm married and ready to get pregnant, because I don't think it's fair to expose a fetus to all the potential damages of tar and nicotine. But until then, my smoking is not bothering anyone.

Except, of course, Nerissa.

I had my first cigarette my sophomore year of college. My friend Sofia had recently started smoking to lose weight, and she claimed it worked. Of course, by our junior year she ended up in the Cleveland Clinic with a severe eating disorder, so the ciggy habit was the least of her problems. Not the best role model for me, but I thought she looked cool smoking, and as always, I was willing to try anything—except cutting back on food or exercising more—to lose weight.

What I wouldn't give to be thin, I think, gazing down at a two-page spread of Hollywood starlets at the Cannes Film Festival. Big boobs, teeny waists, no hips, no thighs. I don't get it. I mean, in my world, big boobs are a given. I come from a long line of women with racks. If you think I'm stacked, you should see my grandmother on my mother's side. She still wears this 1940s-style bullet bra, and you can see her coming from blocks away. She takes pride in what she coyly refers to as her "figure."

Not me. My figure, I could do without. I'd gladly swap everything between my ribs and clavicle for a flat chest if it came with the ten-year-old boy body I so covet—the one that supposedly went out of style with the waif models years ago. Yeah, right. As if Rubenesque is ever really going to be back in vogue.

I listen to Will in the shower. He's singing some Rogers and Hammerstein type song. He has a great voice, in my opinion. Sometimes I wish he would just scrap the whole Broadway scene and make a pop record. But he doesn't want to do that. His dream is to make it big on stage.

So far, he's only done a couple of off-off-Broadway musicals—one a revival of some obscure show, the other an original written by this guy he met in acting class. Both of them closed within a few weeks.

That's why this summer stock thing could be really good for him.

I just can't help wishing he were a little more wistful about leaving me behind. Or that he'd ask me to come with him, rather than making me wait for the right time to suggest it myself.

I haven't really thought it through yet—what I'd do if I actually did go along. I mean, I know I wouldn't be able to live with Will, who's staying in the cast house. But how hard would it be to find a small room to rent for the summer in some dinky little town almost an hour north of Albany? And there must be jobs

there, because it gets touristy in the summer. I'm definitely not fussy. I could waitress, or baby-sit.

I know what you're thinking, but look, I love the
thought of not having to take the subway to a nine-to-
five job in the hot, smelly city where I answer somebody else's phone and make copies all day. It would
be so freeing to do something else for a while.

As for the advertising career…well, I could always
find another agency job in the fall. Or something else.
After all, it's not like I have my heart set on becoming
a big-time copywriter. It just seemed like something I
could do with my English degree.

Other than teach.

My parents think I should teach. They think it's the
perfect job for women. My mother was a teacher before she married my father. My Aunt Tanya still is a
teacher at the middle school back home. My sister was
a teacher before, during and after her marriage to my
ex-brother-in-law Vinnie, who came home one day
last year and told Mary Beth he didn't love her anymore.

She was really broken up about it—they have a couple of kids, so I know it's a big deal—but if you ask
me, she's better off without him. He was always flirting with other women—especially after Mary Beth
gained a permanent twenty pounds with each of her
pregnancies.

Maybe not so permanent. She's trying to take the
weight off now. Hence, the health club. She doesn't
teach anymore. She lost her job about a week before

Vinnie dumped her. She was devastated about the job, but that didn't stop old Vinnie from kicking her when she was down. Shows you what a special guy he is.

The running water and the singing come to an abrupt halt, and moments later Will opens the bathroom door. Mist swirls around him as he comes out with a towel wrapped around his waist.

I find myself wondering if he does that when Nerissa's here. I guess it wouldn't surprise me, because he's so casual about nudity. Plus, like I said, she has a boyfriend, and he has me, so it's not like anything could happen between them. They're just roommates. Right?

Right?

"What are you doing?" he asks.

"Reading *Entertainment Weekly.*"

"No, I mean, you were staring at me funny. Like something's bothering you."

"I was?" Damn. I just shrug.

He does, too, and towels off.

I pretend to be fascinated by an article offering an update on the whereabouts of former *Road Rules* castmates.

Now is not the time to bring up the summer stock thing. Maybe over lunch.

Or maybe I should just drop the whole idea.

I mean, following Will to summer stock—that seems kind of desperate, doesn't it? Like I'm afraid that if he leaves New York, I'll lose him. Like I have to go along to keep an eye on him, and make sure he doesn't cheat on me.

But the thing is, there's a good chance that that's pretty much true.

Because maybe, in the back of my mind, I suspect that Will has cheated on me. It's nothing he's ever said or done, just a feeling I sometimes have. It comes and goes, so it could just be paranoia on my part. As Raphael always says, I'm not exactly the self-esteem queen.

I watch Will get dressed in jeans, a thick navy sweatshirt and sneakers. He combs his hair back into place after he pulls the shirt over his head, and turns to me.

''Ready?''

I nod and toss my magazine aside, grabbing my fleece pullover and black bag once again.

As we head out the door of his apartment, I reach for Will's hand. He's not big on affection—he says his family is on the cold side. Since my parents pretty much go around hugging everyone who crosses their path, I tend to stray into touchy-feely more often than I probably should. But Will is used to me by now, and gives my fingers a quick squeeze before releasing them to press the button for the elevator—something he could have done with his free hand, but maybe I'm just looking for reasons to be irked.

The truth is, I want Will to be as crazy about me as I am about him. Which I sometimes think he is— he just doesn't know how to show it.

For example, there was a time, a few years ago, when he used to call me *dear.*

Ew.

You know what I mean? With him it was *dear,* instead of hon, or sweetie, or babe or any of the usual boyfriend-girlfriend pet names. Maybe he had good intentions, but it just bugged me, because it seemed like something an aging spinster schoolteacher would call a prize pupil. *Yes, dear, you may go to the girls' room, but be sure to come right back for the social studies quiz.*

There was nothing remotely affectionate or romantic about it, and it just felt *forced.* I cringed every time he did it, especially when we were in public, and I wanted desperately to ask him to stop. Finally he did, on his own. Maybe he realized I never called him *dear* in return, or maybe it felt as unnatural to him as it sounded to me.

Naturally, as soon as he stopped, I missed it. At least it was something.

I wish he'd come up with some other endearment to call me, but I don't know how to bring it up. I can't just pop out with, "You know what would make me happy? If you called me Bunchkins or Sugar."

Which actually wouldn't make me happy, either. In fact, *gag.*

But you know what I mean. I just long for more, I guess, than we have. And now, with Will leaving, I feel this urgency, this need to establish our relationship more completely.

I suppose three years of going out is pretty established.

But I'm ready for more. I can't help it.

When Will needed a roommate and placed an ad in the *Voice,* I was stung. I had hoped that maybe he'd consider us moving in together. In fact, I had finally worked up all my nerve to broach the subject with him one night after much input from Kate and Raphael—but before I could open my mouth, he told me about finding Nerissa.

So let's take a step back and assess the situation as it now stands.

One gorgeous, buff, commitment-phobic actor blowing out of town.

One overweight, insecure, commitment-obsessed secretary left behind.

I just don't have a good feeling about this.

But that doesn't stop me from ordering the bacon cheeseburger with onion rings at the coffee shop around the corner from Will's building.

And it doesn't give me the courage to ask him if I can go with him.

Three

Raphael has a sprawling birthday party every year.

He always throws it for himself, and he always holds it at his apartment in the meat-packing district. A Manhattan Realtor or an optimist or a blind moron might call it a loft in a converted warehouse, but basically, there's nothing converted about the place. It still looks and feels like a warehouse—a cavernous, dank, virtually windowless, virtually unfurnished place that not even Martha Stewart, armed with a glue gun and yards of chintz and rolls of Persian carpet, could transform into anything remotely homey.

But it's a large dwelling, and in Manhattan, large dwellings are notoriously hard to come by. Raphael makes good use of his; he always invites everyone he ever met to his birthday parties, and he tells them to bring everyone *they* ever met.

According to Kate, who's known Raphael a year longer than I have and has therefore been to his birthday parties before, the crowd is typically comprised of incredibly gorgeous, hip, fashionable gay males and their incredibly gorgeous, hip, fashionable straight female friends.

This year, because it's a milestone birthday for Raphael, the crowd is expected to be even larger than usual, and also more gorgeous, more hip and more fashionable than usual.

Raphael told me that there's always a theme.

Last year, it was a jungle theme. Buff men in loincloths and animal prints.

The year before that, it was a beach party. Buff men in Speedos.

This year, it's an island theme.

Spot the trend? Raphael's motifs are designed to allow for minimal clothing—not to mention maximum alcohol consumption by way of fun, fruity drinks.

This year, he's rented fake palm trees. He wanted to have blazing tiki torches, but I talked him out of that one. His friend Thomas, who is a set designer for Broadway shows, created this shimmering blue waterfall and lagoon out of some kind of slippery fabric. Frozen cocktails are being served in fake plastic coconut cups.

I arrive almost two hours late, with Kate in tow. She's the reason we're tardy. She went to a salon to have her lip waxed shortly before the party was supposed to start, and we had to wait for the blotchy red swelling to go down.

Now, as we walk into Raphael's jamming party, she tugs my arm and asks, "Are you sure I look all right?"

Actually, she doesn't. In keeping with the island theme, she has what looks like a Hawaiian Punch mustache above her upper lip, despite her futile attempts to cover the welt with pancake makeup. The lighting in her apartment was so dim that I didn't realize how much it shows until we were on the subway.

"You look fine," I lie.

She cups a hand at her ear. "What did you say?"

"You look fine," I shout, to be heard above the blasting Jimmy Buffet tune and the din of voices. "I just can't believe you waited until just before the party to get your lip waxed. Why didn't you do it earlier in the day, or yesterday? You know you always have a bad reaction to the wax."

"I didn't realize my mustache had come back in until tonight," Kate shouts back. "I mean, what did you want me to do, show up here with five o'clock shadow? I can't believe you didn't tell me I had stubble when we were together this morning."

"I didn't notice, Kate. Guess I was too wrapped up in my own trauma."

"How bad do I look?" She takes a few steps toward the television set and strains to catch a glimpse of herself reflected in the darkened screen.

"Tracey!" Raphael materializes with a shriek, umbrella-bedecked frozen strawberry daiquiri in hand, and gives me a big kiss.

He's a beautiful man, with jet-black hair, mocha-colored skin and the longest eyelashes I've ever seen. People sometimes mistake him for Ricky Martin, and he invariably goes along with it, signing autographs and waxing nostalgic about the good old days with Menudo.

"Happy Birthday, honeybunch," I say, squeezing him.

"You didn't dress up, Tracey!"

"I didn't?" I feign horror and look down, as though expecting to find myself naked. "Don't scare me like that, Raphael."

He swats my arm. "I mean you didn't dress in keeping with the theme."

"What did you expect me to wear? A bikini? Trust me, Raphael, it's better this way," I say, motioning at my black turtleneck beneath a black blazer, worn with trendy black pants I splurged on in French Connection. Hopefully, the monochromatic effect is more slimming than funereal. "Great outfit on you, though."

"You like?" He does a runway twirl, modeling his tropical print shirt, short shorts and Italian leather boots. "You don't think it's too gay, Tracey?"

In case you haven't noticed, Raphael is a frequent name-user. He likes to think of it as his conversational trademark.

"Since when are you worried about being too gay, Raphael?"

"Since I saw the man Alexander and Joseph brought with them. Tracey, he's delicious, and incredibly understated. You'd never suspect he's a homo like the rest of us." He motions over his shoulder at the reasonably good-looking, straight-looking man deep in conversation with Alexander and Joseph, who tonight are wearing matching sarongs with their matching gold wedding bands.

"The rest of us? Speak for yourself," I tell Raphael, and add, eyeing the guy's not-in-keeping-with-the-theme blue crewneck sweater and jeans, "Anyway, maybe he's not a homo."

"Oh, please. Kate!" Raphael screams her name as she rejoins us. He grabs her and plants a big kiss on her—his standard greeting—then steps back, tilts his head and frowns, wiping at her upper lip with his thumb. "Sorry, I slobbered my daquiri on your face."

"Oh, hell." In her accent, which is suddenly full-blown, it comes out *hay-ell.* "That's not daquiri, Raphael. Tracey!" She turns on me, asking darkly, "It does not look okay, does it? It's still all raw and red, isn't it?"

I hedge. "It's not that bad."

"It's not that bad? Raphael thinks it's slobbered daquiri!" Kate rushes off to the bathroom.

In response to Raphael's questioning glance, I explain, "Lip wax."

He nods knowingly, and says, in his barely there Latin accent, "Poor thing. And with her complexion…

From peaches and cream to peaches and blood. Tracey, lip wax kills.''

"I wouldn't know. I'm a bleach gal myself.''

"Trust me. Wax kills.''

"Trust *you?*''

"I'm serious, Tracey.'' His eyes are big and solemn.

There are two basic Raphael moods: Giddy Enthusiasm, and Earnest Concern. He is not currently sporting the facial expressions that accompany Giddy Enthusiasm.

"You wax your lip?'' I ask incredulously.

"Tracey, *I* don't do it.'' He winces and shudders. "I have Cristoforo do it for me.'' Cristoforo would be his stylist and erstwhile lover who has since taken up with a well-known, supposedly straight soap opera actor who shall remain nameless.

"Cristoforo waxes your lip,'' I repeat, not sure whether to be bemused or amused.

"Not just my lip. My whole face. Believe me, Tracey, it's better than shaving every day.''

"I believe you, Raphael. So that's how you keep that boyish look.''

"You know it. Let's go mingle with Alexander and Joseph,'' Raphael suggests, promptly bouncing back to Giddy Enthusiasm as he links his arm through mine.

We make our way across the room to where they're standing. Along the way, I snag a daquiri from the tray of a passing waiter who's all rippling muscles and washboard abs, practically naked save for a tiny thong.

"You hired waiters?" I ask Raphael, who shakes his head.

"Tracey! That's Jones," he says. "You've met him before."

"Jones? Just Jones?"

"Just Jones."

"I don't remember him."

"Yes, you do."

"No, I don't."

"Of course you do, Tracey. He's the dancer. The one from Long Island? The one with the tutu fetish?"

Raphael has this annoying habit of insisting that you know people or have been places when you have no idea what he's talking about. It happens all the time. I used to argue with him.

Now I just shrug and go along, pretending to know Jones.

Note that Raphael's crowd, like the pop music industry, has more than its share of mono-monikered folks. Jones and Cristoforo. Cher and Madonna.

I don't know what to make of this, but it seems significant. I'm about to point it out to Raphael when he goes on with his explanation.

"Jones is going to be doing a chorus part in a summer stock production of *Hello, Dolly* in Texas, of all godforsaken places, so I told him to grab a tray and pretend he's rehearsing for the show. I thought he'd wear a tux, something classic with tails, but, Tracey, you know Jones and his infernal need to display his physique."

Like I said, I *don't* know Jones or his infernal need to display his physique, but I pretend to, rolling my eyes along with Raphael. Still, I have to ask, because I don't get the connection: *"Hello, Dolly?"*

"Yes, yes, yes, you know—the Harmonia Gardens scene with the dancing waiters."

I do know, but before I can tell Raphael, he rushes on, assuming I'm clueless, "You know, the dance contest and the stairway and 'so nice to have you back where you belong.' Shh, shh, we're almost there," Raphael says impatiently, wildly waving his hand at me as though I'm the one who won't shut up.

"Almost there" means that we're almost standing in front of Alexander, Joseph and the object of Raphael's latest crush. Maybe it's just that he's positioned beside two of the most flamboyant men in the room, but he seems awfully low-key and—well, normal. Too normal for Raphael's taste.

"Aruba…Jamaica…ooh, I want to take him… Tracey, isn't he adorable?" Raphael gushes in my ear against the opening bars of the song "Kokomo," which is blasting over the sound system.

"He's pretty cute," I agree. "But not adorable."

He looks aghast. "Tracey! How can you say that? He's definitely adorable."

I reassess.

The guy has short brown hair—just plain old short brown hair, rather than one of Cristoforo's statement-making "styles" or tints that are so popular with this crowd. He has brown eyes, and a nice nose, a nice mouth—the kind of guy you'd expect to find teaching sixth grade, or pushing a toddler in a shopping cart, or raking some suburban lawn. The kind of guy you'd expect to find pretty much anywhere other than here.

But here he is, an average Joe in a crowd of outrageous Josephs and Alexanders and Joneses—which is, I suspect, precisely the reason Raphael is so attracted to him.

"Joseph!" Raphael cries, moving forward. "I love the sarong! Yours, too, Alexander! And you... whoever you are, I love the sweater. Banana Republic?"

"I'm not sure," the guy says, wrinkling his nose a little.

He is pretty adorable. And I see that his eyes, which I assumed from a few feet away were brown, are actually greenish. He looks Irish.

Raphael is momentarily taken aback at his idol's lack of label awareness, but he recovers swiftly. "We've never met," he says, thrusting his hand forward. "I'm Raphael Santiago—the birthday boy. And this is my friend Tracey Spadolini."

"I'm Buckley O'Hanlon. Nice meeting you, Raphael. Hey, Tracey."

"Hey," I say, noticing a bowl of tortilla chips on a nearby overturned cardboard box serving as a table. I'm starving. I skipped dinner, feeling guilty about that massive diner lunch with Will.

I take a step closer and dive in, scarfing a couple of chips while Raphael manages to work into his next few sentences the fact that he's available now that he and his lover Anthony have broken up, that he works out at least five mornings a week and that he recently went to Paris on business. Until last August, he was an office temp. Now he's an assistant style editor for *She* magazine.

The job isn't as glamorous as you might think. Plus, the Paris trip was last September. But Raphael manages to make it sound as though he just blew into town on the Concorde with Anna Wintour.

"What do you do, Buckley?" Raphael asks.

"I'm a freelance copywriter."

"A writer? You're a writer! Buckley, what do you write?"

"Copy," Buckley says with a faint grin. "Trust me, it's not that exciting."

"Buckley is writing the copy for our new brochure. That's how we met," Alexander says, taking out a pack of cigarettes. He hands one to Joseph before putting one between his own lips. Raphael, a notorious butt-moocher, snags one out of the pack before Alexander puts it away.

I reach into the pocket of my blazer and take out my Salem Lights. Alexander clicks a lighter four times, and we all puff away.

Buckley shakes his head. "Guess I'm the only non-smoker left in New York."

"Oh, I'm going to quit tomorrow," Raphael announces.

"Since when?" Joseph asks.

"Since I turned thirty. Joseph, I want to live to see forty. That's not going to happen with a three-pack-a-day habit."

"Oh, please," Alexander says, and he and Joseph shake their heads and roll their eyes. They know Raphael well enough, as I do, to realize he's full of crap. Still, Raphael is trying to impress Buckley, and I think we owe it to him to play along. Or at least to change the subject. Which I do.

"So what's up with your new brochure?" I ask Alexander and Joseph.

Naturally, they jump right into that one. They love talking about their business—a gourmet boutique on Bleeker Street that specializes in organic preserves. They recently decided to design a Web site and add mail-order.

"If all goes as well as we expect," Joseph says, clasping his hands over his ribs in anticipation, "we're going to start looking at houses in Bucks County in the fall."

"That's great." I glance at Raphael.

He looks envious. I'm not surprised. That's the big thing in their crowd—for longtime lovers to buy a house in rural Pennsylvania, then spend years renovating and decorating and furnishing it.

I have to admit, even I'm jealous of Alexander and Joseph as I watch them exchange delighted glances, hauntingly similar to the expression I remember my sister Mary Beth sharing with Vinnie back when they were newly married and had just announced that they were expecting their first child.

I want to be in that kind of relationship.

Not the Mary Beth-Vinnie kind that ends in misery and divorce. The Alexander and Joseph kind, where anyone—except maybe Dr. Laura and the Reverend Jerry Falwell—can see that these two souls belong together.

According to Raphael, Alexander and Joseph, who must be in their mid-thirties, have shared a rent-controlled one-bedroom apartment in Chelsea for ages, since before Chelsea became overly ridden with celebrities and suburban-style superstores. Alexander is a tall, bearded, Ivy-league-educated African-American from a white-collar Westchester family, and Joseph is a short, community college-educated Italian from a blue-collar Staten Island family, but at this point they share so many mannerisms and inflections that sometimes I actually think they look alike.

Jones passes by and hands out fresh daiquiris all around. This batch is even rummier than the last, but it goes down just as easily and I'm feeling a little buzzed. Buzzed enough to find it necessary to either chain smoke or devour the entire bowl of tortilla chips.

I opt for smoking, lighting a new cigarette from the ember of the first.

"So what do you write besides brochures, Buckley?" Raphael asks coyly.

Usually, he does coy pretty well, but it's not working tonight. At least, not on this guy, who doesn't seem interested in Raphael. Or maybe he's just oblivious—although how he can overlook Raphael's breathless flirtation is beyond me.

The only other option is that he's straight. But somehow, I doubt that. I have to wonder—as a trio of newly arrived drag queens sporting grass skirts and coconut shell brassieres wander by—would a straight, reasonably adorable guy be at a party like this? In New York?

No way.

"I write jacket copy for books," Buckley says with a shrug.

"You're kidding! Buckley, that's wonderful!" Raphael screeches, as though Buckley just told him he's landed a walk-on on *Buffy the Vampire Slayer*.

"Trust me, it's really not that interesting," Buckley says, looking a little sheepish.

"What kind of books?" I ask.

"Everything. Suspense, romance, self-help, gay fiction, cookbooks—you name it."

"Gay fiction? Have I read anything you've written, Buckley?" Raphael asks, bubbly as a Brookside cheerleader doing high kicks at halftime.

"I just write the cover copy," Buckley points out again, squirming a little.

"I always remember cover copy. It's why I buy the book," Raphael tells him.

Kate joins us, toying with a strand of long blond hair. She's got it stretched across her upper lip, futilely trying to hide the blotchiness.

After Raphael introduces her to Buckley, she pulls me aside and says she has to leave.

"I don't blame you." I glimpse the slash of angry pink skin above the painstakingly applied pink lipstick that matches her pink tropical print sundress. "It looks like it's getting worse."

"You think?" she drawls sarcastically. "I look like I've been mauled. I can't believe you let me out of the house like this, Tracey."

I can't, either. But I didn't want to show up solo at the party after Will backed out. I've always had this thing about going places alone. Even after all this time living in New York, I'm still not over it. It's one thing to live alone and ride the subway alone and shop alone, but I don't think that I could ever go to a movie by myself, or a restaurant, or a party. The small-town girl in me persists in finding that vaguely pathetic.

What a lousy friend, huh? I don't blame Kate for being pissed.

"Do you want me to come with you?" I offer half-heartedly.

"No, thanks," Kate says.

"Are you pissed at me?"

"Nah." She tries to grin, wincing when the inflamed upper lip crinkles painfully. "It's not your fault I inherited sensitive skin. It's the Delacroix genes. That's what my mother always says."

"Good luck, Kate," I say sympathetically, giving her a hug. "I'll talk to you tomorrow."

When I turn back to the group, the group has dissipated. Joseph and Alexander are nowhere to be seen, and Raphael is currently being transported around the room on the drag queens' shoulders to a rousing chorus of ''Jolly Good Fellow,'' leaving only Buckley O'Hanlon standing there.

''You've been abandoned?'' I ask him. I drain the slushy remainder of my daiquiri in one big gulp that leaves my throat aching from the freeze.

''Raphael is…'' He motions with his head.

''Yeah, I see him,'' I say, watching Raphael hop down from his lofty perch just in time to toss back a flaming shot somebody hands him. Yes, flaming. As in, on fire. People clap rhythmically, chanting, ''Go, Go, Go, Go…''

Did I mention that Raphael's parties are wild?

''And Alexander and Joseph went to the kitchen to put the finishing touches on the cake. They said it's shaped like Puerto Rico, and there seems to have been some kind of mishap with Mayaguez.''

''What's Mayaguez?''

''From what I gathered, it's either a Puerto Rican city or an unruly houseboy.''

I laugh.

Buckley laughs.

Too bad he's gay.

Then again, I have a boyfriend. Will. Will, who should be here right now.

Doesn't he care that our days together are dwindling? Doesn't he know that we should be spending these last precious moments together before he heads off to summer stock without me?

That is, if I don't go along with him.

Which I still might do.

I pluck another daiquiri from Jones's passing tray and ask Buckley, "Ever been to the Adirondacks?"

"Nope. Why?"

So I tell him why. I say that I'm thinking of spending the summer in a resort town up there and I'm wondering how hard it'll be to find a job and a place to stay.

"Shouldn't you have lined that up before you made your plans?" he asks reasonably.

"You know, that's what I've always hated about you, Buckley," I say, jabbing him in the chest with a finger. "You're so damned practical."

He looks taken aback, then sees that I'm kidding, and he laughs. "Sorry. But I keep telling you, Trace, you've got to have all your ducks in a row. You can't just go around jumping into things headlong anymore. You're a big girl now."

"Buckley, Buckley, Buckley." I heave a mock sigh. "What am I going to do with you? When are you going to lighten up and learn how to live a little?"

"You're not the first person who's asked me that," he says ruefully, and I get the sense that he's only semi-kidding now.

"Really?"

He shakes his head. "I just got out of a relationship with someone who thought I wasn't impulsive enough.

But let me tell you, I'm impulsive. Just tonight, when I was getting dressed to come here, I almost wore a beige sweater. At the last minute—I'm telling you, the very last minute before I walked out the door—I switched to the navy.''

I stagger backward. "Good God, man! How positively madcap of you!"

We both dissolve into laughter. I'm impressed by his deadpan skills. And he really is cute. He would be great for Raphael, who usually tends to go for self-absorbed pretty boys or eccentric artist types.

As we chat, I make sure to work in some of Raphael's better qualities—how generous he is, and how funny, and how he knows more about pop culture than any other living human. I tell Buckley that Raphael has heard every new CD before the singles hit the airwaves; how he sees every Broadway show in previews; how he goes to every single movie that's released, whether or not the critics trash it.

"He saw *Flight of Fancy* almost the second it came out, before all this hype," I tell Buckley.

Flight of Fancy, of course, is the hugest blockbuster to hit the multiplex in ages, and it supposedly has a shocking *Sixth Sense*-like twist at the end. That was all I needed to hear. I can't take suspense. No matter how hard I try to wait, I always end up reading the last pages of Mary Higgins Clark novels before I'm halfway through. I just have to know whodunit.

"Did Raphael tell you the twist before you saw it?" Buckley asks.

''No, he wouldn't tell me! And I still haven't seen it.''

''You're kidding. I thought everyone had.''

''Not me. There's no one left for me to go with.''

Like I said, Raphael went without me, and so did Kate, who went with a blind date, and so did all my friends at work. But the thing that really gets me is that Will went with a couple of people who work at the catering company one night a few weeks ago when a gig ended earlier than they'd expected. I was really irritated with him when he told me he'd seen that movie without me. He knew I wanted to go.

''So now what? You're going to wait until it comes out on video?'' Buckley asks.

''Yeah, and believe me, I can't stand the suspense. I'm trying to get someone to go with me. But everyone I've asked says you can't see it twice, because once you know the secret, it's pointless.''

''That's what I heard, too.''

I gape at him. ''You haven't seen it either?''

He shakes his head.

''Then you *have* to go with me!'' I say, clutching his arm. ''I can't believe I've found someone who hasn't seen it. I'm so psyched! We're going. Okay?''

He shrugs. ''Sure. When?''

''Tomorrow,'' I say decisively. ''I've been waiting almost a month to find out what the big twist is, and I'm not going to put it off any longer. This is great.''

Suddenly, the blasting Bob Marley tune goes silent. We turn and find Raphael standing next to the stereo, teetering a little. I wonder how many flaming shots he's ingested.

"Everybody!" He claps his hands together. "It's time for cake. Alexander and Joseph have really out-done themselves this year. So please, gather round and get ready to sing your hearts out!"

"He's a little over the top, huh?" Buckley asks, as we push closer to the cake table.

"He's the greatest guy I know," I say fiercely, wishing that were enough to make Buckley fall madly in love with Raphael. But I can't help noticing that he really doesn't seem that interested in him.

After a rousing chorus of Happy Birthday to You— and three encores, coaxed by Raphael—the cake has been cut and devoured, Buckley drifts back over to Alexander and Joseph, and Raphael sidles up to me.

"You've got frosting smeared in your hair," I say, wiping at it with a napkin.

"That's not the only place I've ever had frosting smeared, Tracey," he tells me with a wink. Only Raphael can wink and not look like somebody's grandfather. "Listen, what's up with my new man? Did you talk me up?"

"Definitely. I told him you're the most amazing person I've ever met."

"What did you find out about him?"

I sip a fresh daiquiri. They're getting less slushy-sweet and more rummy as the night wears on, but at this point, nobody cares. "He said something about how he's just come out of a relationship with a guy who thought he wasn't spontaneous enough."

"Tracey, I'm spontaneous enough for both of us." Raphael casts a lustful glance at Buckley. "What else did he say?"

"Not much. But I'm going to see *Flight of Fancy* with him tomorrow afternoon. I'll try to find out more then."

"You finally found somebody to see it with? Tracey, I'm so happy for you!" Raphael slings an arm across my shoulder. "Will Will be jealous?"

"Why would he be jealous of a gay man? Anyway, Will is never jealous. He trusts me," I tell him.

Silence.

"What?" I demand, catching a dubious look on Raphael's face. "He's never jealous. Really!"

"I believe you. And Tracey, I think you should ask yourself why," Raphael says cryptically.

"What do you mean by that?" I ask, but somebody is already pulling him away to join a conga line.

Suddenly, I'm in no mood to conga.

I find myself wondering what Will is doing. I check my watch and decide he might be home by now. Maybe I can take a cab up to his place and spend the night with him.

But when I try calling his apartment, the machine picks up.

I don't leave a message.

Four

Sunday morning.

Will is cranky.

It's raining.

Will is most likely cranky *because* it's raining and *because* it's Sunday morning, but naturally, being me, I can't help feeling like it's somehow my fault. Ever since we met for breakfast at the coffee shop a few blocks from his apartment a half hour ago, I've been struggling to make conversation with him while he broods.

The thing is, he's moody. I've always known that. Part of me is attracted to the temperamental artist in him. Part of me wants him to just cheer up, goddammit.

As the waitress pours more coffee into his cup and then mine, I ask him again about last night's wedding. It turned out the big top-secret affair was the marriage of two major movie stars who left their spouses for each other in a big tabloid scandal last year. I'm dying to know the details, but so far, Will hasn't been forthcoming.

"So what was the food like?" I ask him, taking three of those little creamers from the shallow white bowl in the middle of the table and peeling back the lids to dump them, one by one, into my coffee. I tear two sugar packets at once and pour them in, then stir.

"Shrimp bisque, grilled salmon, filet mignon, lobster mashed potatoes…nothing spectacular." Will sips his own coffee. He takes it black. No sugar.

"What about the cake?"

"White chocolate raspberry."

"Yum." I swallow a hunk of rubbery western omelet smothered in ketchup and Tabasco and wish that it were white chocolate raspberry wedding cake.

I wish that I were a bride eating my white chocolate raspberry wedding cake.

No, I don't.

I definitely want to be a bride, but when Will and I get married—okay, *if* Will and I get married—I'd love to have a fall wedding with a pumpkin cake and cream cheese frosting. I wonder what he'd think of that, but I don't dare ask him.

"So, Will, do you want me to come back to your place after I go to the movies?"

I already told him—first thing—about Buckley and *Flight of Fancy,* and how I was hoping to play matchmaker for Buckley and Raphael.

I also gave him a blow-by-blow description of the party, right up to and including the part where Raphael lit a tiki torch he'd hidden in his closet—defying my warning—and carried it around the apartment until he accidentally set a drag queen's synthetic teased hair on fire. Jones tried to save the day by throwing the shimmering blue fake water fabric over him to smother it, but it turned out that was even more flammable than the wig, and it, too, went up in flames. Luckily, some quick-thinking bystander doused the fire with water from the spray hose at the sink. I left shortly after that, telling Buckley I'd meet him at one in front of the Cineplex Odeon on Eighth Avenue, a few blocks up from Will's apartment.

I was thinking that after we see the movie, I could walk over to Will's and we could get take-out Chinese or something.

Okay, what I was really thinking is that we can have sex. It's been almost a week since we spent the night together, and the last time—the last few times—have been pretty blah.

But Will dashes my hopes now, shaking his head. "Nah, I've got a lot to do after the gym. I'm packing boxes to ship up to the cast house so I don't have to lug everything on Amtrak."

I could help him pack boxes. But maybe that would be too depressing.

Unless I were going with him…

But I still can't work up the nerve to ask him about it.

I try to think of something else to talk about.

We're in a booth beside the window. Will is wearing a maroon hooded sweatshirt I really like. It's from L.L. Bean, and he's had it as long as I've known him, and it's not the least bit raggy, unlike most of my knock-around wardrobe.

Over his shoulder, through the rain-splattered glass, I can see people hurrying by carrying umbrellas. I notice that it's a purely gray landscape dotted with splashes of bright yellow: slickers and taxicabs. I want to point it out to Will, but he won't appreciate the aesthetic in his mood.

I reach for the salt shaker and dump some on my hash browns before taking a bite.

"You really should watch the salt, Trace," Will says.

"If it's not salty enough, I can't eat it," I tell him with a shrug.

There's nothing worse than bland, under-salted food. My grandparents are supposed to be on a low-salt diet, and you never tasted anything more vile than the no-salt-added tomato sauce they tried to serve everyone one Sunday a few years back. We all agreed that it was disgusting, and my grandmother immediately switched back to making her usual sauce. The doctor keeps scolding them about their blood pressure or whatever it is they're both supposed to be watching, but I don't blame them for cheating. I would, too.

"You'd get used to less after a while," Will points out.

"Maybe, but I don't want to. It's not like my health is in any danger." I'm never comfortable discussing my eating habits with Will. I guess I'm afraid he might bring up my weight. So far he never has, but it's not as though I think he isn't aware that I could stand to lose a few pounds.

Okay, thirty or forty pounds.

Luckily, he's never acknowledged it.

And if my luck continues, he never will.

"There are worse vices than salt," I point out to him, still feeling defensive. "Like…"

"Cigarettes?"

I grin. "Exactly. Okay, salt and cigs. So I have two vices. Look at the bright side. At least I'm not a junkie."

He cracks a smile at that.

"Why don't you have any vices?" I ask, watching him take a bite of his toast. Whole grain. Unbuttered. No jelly.

I half expect him to protest that he does have vices—not that I can think of any.

But he doesn't. He just shrugs, smiling and chewing his boring toast, confidently vice-free.

"Listen…what if I came with you, Will?"

Who said that?

My God, did *I* say that?

Apparently I did, because Will has stopped chewing and is looking at me, confused. "Came with me where?"

What the hell was I thinking?

I wasn't thinking. I just blurted it out somehow, and now I can't take it back.

I frantically try to come up with something else to say. Something to add, something that would make sense...

What if I came with you...
What if I came with you...
What if I came with you...
...to the bathroom the next time you go?

No, there's no way out of this.

Now that I've started, I have to finish.

I put down my fork, take a deep breath, then pick up my fork again, realizing that setting it down seemed too ceremonious, as though I'm about to make a major announcement.

I am, but I don't want it to come across that way to Will.

That would only scare him off before he really has a chance to think about it.

I stab a hunk of green pepper-dotted egg and pop it into my mouth. It's always easier to sound casual when you're munching something. "What if I came with you this summer?"

So much for casual.

I sound like I'm being strangled, and he looks horrified.

"Come with me?" he echoes. "You can't come with me!"

I attempt to swallow the sodden hunk of chewed-up egg and almost gag. "I don't mean *with* you, with you," I say quickly, to reassure him. "I just mean, what if I found a place to live in North Mannfield and got a job waitressing or something for the summer? Then we wouldn't have to be apart for three months."

"Tracey, we can't be together this summer! I'm doing a different show every other week. I won't have time to spend with you even if you're two minutes away."

I feel a lump in my throat, trying to rise past the soggy wad of pepper and egg making its way down. I can't speak.

But that's okay, because Will isn't done yet. He's put down his fork and is shaking his head. "I can't believe you would spring something like this on me now. I mean, I thought we'd agreed that this summer stock thing is great for me. I have to do this for my career. You've known that all along, Tracey. Now you have a problem with it?"

I finally gulp down the egg and the lump. "I didn't say I have a problem with it, Will. I just said I want to come with you."

"But you know you can't do that, right? Look, I know what this is. You're just trying to make me feel guilty so that I'll change my mind and stay here. And I—"

"I am not!"

There's an uncomfortable pause.

"You honestly wanted to come with me?"

"Yes! Not with you, though...I just wanted to be near you."

I feel a pathetic sense of abandonment and panic. I feel like a little girl whose Daddy is trying to dump her off at preschool against her will.

"But, Trace..." He's at a loss for words. To his credit, he doesn't mock me. Nor does he look angry anymore.

He looks...concerned.

I realize, with a sick churning in my stomach, that I've overstepped the line I'm always so careful not to cross with him.

I've gone and smothered Will, the Man Who Needs Space.

"Okay, well, I just thought I'd run it by you," I say, trying to be nonchalant.

I pick up my coffee cup and notice that the cream has separated into clumps on top. Ugh. It must have been sour. I plunk the mug back into its saucer and fumble for some distraction, wishing there was something left on my plate besides the strawberry stem and orange rind from the garnish I already devoured.

I have nothing to eat.

Nothing to do.

Will says nothing.

Does nothing.

This is awful. I should never have brought it up.

Not like this.

I should have planned it more effectively.

I should have rehearsed what I was going to say, so that he wouldn't be caught off guard. So that I wouldn't seem like such a desperate cling-on.

But deep inside, I know that no matter when or how I approached him, he wouldn't have thought my going to North Mannfield was a good idea.

So anyway, there it is.

It's settled.

I'll be spending the summer here in New York, without Will.

Five

"You ready?" Buckley asks, turning to me.

"Wait, the credits," I say, still fixated on the screen.

"You want to see the credits?"

Will and I always stay for the credits. But this isn't Will. And anyway, I'm eager to discuss the film with Buckley, so I say, "Never mind."

"We can stay if you want to."

"Nah, it's no big deal." I stand, clutching my almost-empty jumbo box of Snowcaps.

"Want any more popcorn?" Buckley asks, as we make our way up the aisle. "Or should I throw it away?"

"No, don't throw it," I say, reaching into the bucket and grabbing a handful. I love movie theater popcorn, especially with butter. Will never wants to get butter, because he says it isn't really butter—it's some kind of melted chemical-laden yellow lard. Not that he'd be willing to get butter even if it was butter, because butter is loaded with fat and calories.

Buckley ordered extra. He didn't even consult me. Maybe he just assumed I was an extra-melted-lard kind of gal.

Whatever.

It's a relief to be with someone like him after that disastrous breakfast with Will. When we parted ways in front of his gym, it was awkward. He said he'll call me tonight, but I almost wish he wouldn't. I'm afraid he'll bring up the fact that I wanted to go with him. Or maybe I'm afraid that he won't bring it up, and it will always be this huge, unspoken *thing* lying between us.

Meanwhile, here's Buckley, shoving the popcorn tub at me again, encouraging me to take more.

"So what'd you think?" he asks, helping himself to another handful. "Did the big twist live up to your expectations?"

"I don't know." I mull it over. "I mean, it wasn't *Sixth Sense*-shocking. It wasn't *Crying Game*-shocking. I guess there was too much build-up."

"That's why I wasn't really into seeing this movie."

"You weren't into seeing it?" I ask, stopping in the aisle. "But you came with me. You didn't have to come with me. Oh, God, you kind of did. Look, I didn't mean to drag you here.''

"You didn't."

"Oh, come on, Buckley. I pretty much ordered you to come with me. I guess I just assumed—"

"It's okay," he says quickly. "I didn't mind. Everyone I know has seen it too, so I figured this was my only chance."

"Too bad it didn't live up to all the hype. I mean, I was surprised that the whole thing turned out to be a dream, but wasn't it kind of a letdown?"

"I don't know. It was kind of like that short story 'Occurrence at Owl Creek Bridge.' Ever read that?"

"Are you kidding? The Ambrose Bierce story? I was an English major. I must've read it a dozen times for lit and writing courses."

"Me, too," Buckley says. "I remember really loving that story when I read it the first time back in high school. I thought it was such an amazing twist, you know, that it was all just this stream-of-consciousness escape thing happening in the moment before he died. This was the same kind of thing. I liked it."

"But you didn't love it."

He shrugs. "How about you?"

"I really wanted to love it. It's been so long since I've seen a great movie. The last one I really loved was the one with Gwyneth Paltrow that came out at Christmas."

Naturally, Will hated that movie. He thought it was poorly acted, sappily written and unrealistic.

"Oh, I loved that one too!" Buckley says, pulling on his pullover hooded khaki raincoat as we pause just inside the doors. "Man. It's still pouring out."

"What a crummy day. I'll never get a cab." I sigh, hunting through the pockets of my jeans for a subway token I thought I had.

"Want to go have a beer?"

"A beer? Now?" Surprised, I look up at him. Then I check my watch—as if it matters. As if there's a cutoff time for beer on a rainy Sunday afternoon in Manhattan.

"Or…do you have to be someplace?"

"No!" I say too quickly. Because I really want that beer. It beats the hell out of taking the subway back to my lonely apartment while thinking of Will uptown, packing his boxes.

"Great. So let's get a beer."

I pull on my rain slicker. It's one of those doofy shiny yellow touristy ones, and it makes me look as wide as a big old school bus from behind. I'd worry about that if I were with Will—in fact, I was doing just that earlier, when he and I left the restaurant—but naturally, I don't have to worry with Buckley. That's the nice thing about having gay guys as friends. You get male companionship without the female competitive PMS angle and without the whole messy sexual attraction issue.

"Where should we go?" Buckley asks.

"I know a good pub a block from here," I tell him. "I spend a lot of time in this neighborhood."

"So do I."

"You do?"

"Actually, I live here."

"Really? Where?"

"Fifty-fourth off Broadway."

"No kidding."

"You live here, too?"

"No, I live in the East Village."

"Really? Then why'd you want to meet way up here?"

I don't want to get into the whole Will thing, so I just say, "I had an errand to run up here earlier, so I thought it made sense. So do you have someplace you want to go? Since this is your neighborhood..."

"No, let's try your place. I'm always up for something new. Hey, I'm spontaneous, remember?"

I grin at him, and note that he's wearing another crewneck sweater with his jeans. "I see you went with the beige today."

"What can I say? It was a beige kind of day. Apparently, you beg to differ. Do you always wear black?" he asks, eyeing my outfit.

Black jeans. A black long-sleeved tunic-jersey-type shirt that camouflages my thighs—or so I like to think.

"Always," I tell him.

"Any particular reason?"

"It's slimming," I say promptly, and he grins.

"And here I thought you were trying to make some kind of political or artistic or spiritual statement."

"Me? Nope, I'm just a full-figured gal trying to pass for a waif."

We splash out into the rain and cross the street against the light. Two minutes later, we're sitting on barstools at Frieda's, this semi-cool dive Will and I come to sometimes. They have awesome potato skins with cheddar and bacon, a fact I mention to Buckley pretty much the moment we sit down.

"You want to order some?" he asks.

"After all that popcorn?"

"You're too full?"

"See, Buckley, that's the thing. I'm never full. I could eat all day long. I'm always up for some potato skins. Hence the flab."

"Don't be so hard on yourself, Tracey. It's not like you're obese."

"You're sweet." Too bad he's gay. "So tell me about your failed relationship."

"Do I have to?"

"Nah. Not if you don't want to. We can talk about something more upbeat. Like…where are you from?"

"Long Island."

"*You're* from Long Island?"

He nods. "Why do you look so surprised?"

"You just don't have that Lo-awn Guyland thing going on. You know…the accent. You don't have one."

"You do," he says with a grin. "Upstate, right?"

"How'd you know?"

"The flat *a* gives you away. You said *ay-ack-sent*. So where are you from?"

"You never heard of it. Brookside."

"I've heard of it. There's a state college there, right?"

"Right."

"I thought about going there."

"You're kidding. Why?"

"Because it was as far away from Long Island as I could go and still be at a state school. My parents couldn't afford private college tuition and I didn't get any scholarships."

"Really?"

"Why are you surprised?"

"Because…I don't know. You just seem like the studious type."

He grins. "Trust me, I wasn't. With my grades, I barely made it into a state school."

That really is surprising, for some reason. He just seems like the type of person who would do everything well. I like knowing he was just an average student, like I was. It doesn't mean he isn't smart, because I can tell that he is.

"So where'd you end up going to college?" I ask him.

"SUNY Stony Brook. I wound up staying on the island and living at home."

"Why?"

I catch a fleeting glimpse of unexpected emotion in his expression. When he speaks, I understand why, but his face is carefully neutral. "My dad died the summer after I graduated from high school. I couldn't go away and leave my mom and my sister and brother on their own. So I stayed home." He says it like it's no big deal, but I can tell that it is. Or was.

"I'm really sorry about your dad."

"It was a long time ago." He bends over and ties his shoe, his foot propped on the bottom rung of his barstool. I wonder if the lace was untied, or if he just needed a distraction.

"Yeah," I say, "but that's not something that goes away, is it?"

He straightens and looks me in the eye. "Not really. Sometimes it's still hard when I let myself dwell on it. Which I usually don't do."

"I didn't mean to bring it up."

"You didn't know. And anyway, it's okay. I don't mind talking about it."

I don't know what else to say, so I ask, "What happened? To your dad, I mean."

"He had been having stomach pains, and when he finally went to the doctor, they found out it was pancreatic cancer. By the time they found it, it was too late—it had spread everywhere. They gave him six weeks. He died five weeks and five days later."

"God." I see tears in his eyes and feel a lump rising in my throat. Here I am, wanting to burst into tears for the loss of somebody I never even met—the father of this guy I barely know.

"I know. It was horrible," Buckley says. He takes

a deep breath, then sighs. "But like I said, it was a long time ago. My mom is finally getting over it. She even went out on a date a few weeks ago."

"Her first date?"

"Yeah."

I try to imagine my mother going on a date, and it's all I can do not to shudder. But then, maybe Buckley's mother isn't a four-eleven, overweight, overly pious, stubborn Italian woman in doubleknit pants who doesn't bleach her mustache as often as she should.

"Did that bother you?" I ask Buckley. "Your mother dating?"

"Nah. I hate that she's alone. My sister just got married and my brother's in the service now, so it would be good if she met someone else. I wouldn't worry about her so much."

What a guy. I find myself thinking that maybe he's too nice for Raphael. Not that Raphael isn't wonderful, but when it comes to romance, he can be sort of fickle. He's broken more than a few hearts, and I can't stand the thought of nice, sweet, noble Buckley getting his heart broken.

Which reminds me—Buckley's ex. I wonder what happened there, but I couldn't ask for details when he'd already shown a reluctance to talk about it. Just then, the waiter appears. He's flamboyant and effeminate, and he's practically drooling over Buckley as we order a couple of beers and the potato skins. The thing is, Buckley isn't movie-star handsome. He's nice looking enough, but something about him is even more appealing than his looks. Maybe it's the warm expression in his crinkly Irish eyes, or his quick smile or his genuine Mr. Nice Guy attitude. Whatever it is, it's not lost on the blatantly gay waiter, and it's not lost on me.

Too bad he's not straight.

It's becoming my new mantra, I realize. If Buckley weren't gay, and I didn't have Will...

But if Buckley weren't gay and I didn't have Will, we probably wouldn't be here together, and I sure as hell wouldn't be ordering potato-cheddar-bacon skins or blabbing about my excess flab, which is what I do when I'm with Raphael or Kate.

Anyway, I doubt I'd be Buckley's type.

Then again, it still amazes me, three years later, that I'm Will's type. After all, he *is* movie-star handsome, and I'm no goddess. Luckily, relationships go deeper than looks. At least, ours does. Physical attraction was a huge part of why I was drawn to Will, but I think he was drawn to me because I was one of the few people who ever understood his dream of breaking out of a small midwestern town and making it in New York. That burning ambition to escape the mundane lives to which we were born was the thing we had in common, the thing that ultimately brought us together.

Now it seems to be driving us apart. Christ, Will is leaving me behind. Maybe not for good, but for now, and it hurts. It hurts enough that when the waiter leaves and Buckley looks at me again, he immediately asks, ''What's wrong, Tracey?''

I try to look cheerful. "Nothing. Why?"

"You're down about something. I can tell."

"I'm not surprised. I can never hide anything from you, Buckley. You always have known me better than I know myself," I say in mock seriousness.

He laughs.

Then he says, "You know, it really does seem like we've known each other awhile." I realize he's not kidding around.

I also realize he's right. It does seem like we're old pals. And it would be great, having a friend like Buckley. A woman living alone in New York can never have too many guy friends.

"Yeah, we should do this again," I say to Buckley as the waiter brings our beers. "I love seeing movies on rainy weekend afternoons."

"So do I. Almost as much as I love beer and cheddar-and-bacon potato skins."

"I'll drink to that."

"Cheers." He lifts his bottle and clinks it against mine.

We smile at each other.

Can you see it coming?

Well, I sure as hell didn't.

He leans over and kisses me.

Yup.

Buckley—nice, sweet, noble, *gay* Buckley, leans toward me and puts his mouth on mine in a completely heterosexual way.

I'm too stunned to do anything other than what comes naturally.

Meaning, I kiss him back.

It only lasts a few seconds, but that's slo mo for what could have been a friendly kiss topping off a friendly toast to transform into a romantic kiss. The kind of kiss that's tender and passionate but not sloppy or wet. The kind of kiss that you feel in the pit of your stomach, in that quivering place where the first hint of arousal always flickers.

Yes, I am aroused by this kiss. Aroused, and stunned, and confused.

Buckley stops kissing me—not because he senses anything wrong, though. He merely stops because he's done. He pulls back and looks at me, wearing a little smile.

"But…" I just stare at him.

The smile fades. "I'm sorry." He looks around.

We're the only people in the place, aside from the bartender, who's watching a Yankee game on the television over the bar, and the waiter, who's retreated to the kitchen.

"Was that not all right?" Buckley wants to know. "Because I didn't think. I just felt like doing it, so I did it." He looks a little concerned, but not freaked out.

I'm freaked out. "But…"

"I'm sorry," he says again, looking a shade less self-assured. "I didn't mean to—"

"But you're gay!" I tell him, plucking the right words from a maelstrom of thoughts.

He looks shocked. "I'm gay?"

At least, I thought they were the right words.

"Yes, you're gay," I say in the strident, high-pitched tone you'd use if you were arguing with a brunette who was trying to convince you she was blond.

"That's news to me," he says, clearly amused.

There he goes with that deadpan thing again. But this time it's not funny.

"Cut it out, Buckley," I say. "This is serious."

"This *is* serious. Because I always thought I was straight. Maybe that's why it didn't work out with my girlfriend."

He's kidding again. At least about that last part. But maybe not about the rest.

Confused, I say, "I thought he was a boyfriend."

"He was a girlfriend. *She* was a girlfriend." He twirls his stool a little and leans his elbows back on the bar behind him. He looks relaxed. And definitely still amused.

I need to relax. I need a drink. I sip my beer.

"Tracey, I promise you I'm not gay."

I gulp my beer.

"Why would I be on a date with you if I were gay?" he wants to know.

I sputter beer and some dribbles on my chin. I wipe it on my sleeve and echo, "A *date?*"

"Wait, you didn't think this was a date?" he asks, brows furrowed. "I thought you asked me out."

"Who am I, Sadie Hawkins? I asked you to go to the movies with me. Not as my date. I wanted you to date Raphael."

"Who?" He looks around, then says, "Oh, Raphael. The guy from the party. You wanted me to date *him?*"

"Yes! You're perfect for each other," I say in true yenta fashion, though I suspect it's a bit late for that now.

"Perfect for each other." Buckley nods. "Except for the part about me not being gay."

"Right." I'm just aghast at this news, now that I'm positive he's not teasing me.

I take another huge gulp of my beer, trying to digest the bombshell.

Physically, I'm still reeling from the kiss. I mean, he's a great kisser. *Great.* And I realize how long it's been since I've been kissed like that. Will and I never really kiss anymore. We just have sex—and like I said, even that doesn't happen very often these days, and when it does, there's no kissing involved and it's blah.

Oh, hell. Will.

"I have a boyfriend," I tell Buckley, plunking my beer bottle on the round paper coaster with a thud.

"You do? Why didn't you tell me?"

"Because I didn't think to. It didn't occur to me that you thought we were on a date."

A date.

It's just so incredible how the whole situation could've blown right by me. I guess I was so distracted by what's going on with Will that I wasn't paying enough attention to what was going on with Buckley. Rather, to what Buckley thought was going on.

I've cheated on Will. Completely by accident, but still, it's cheating. And right here in his own neighborhood, in a bar that we sometimes come to together. What if someone had seen me here with Buckley? Kissing Buckley?

Again, I scan the bar to make sure nobody's here besides the bartender, who isn't paying the least bit of attention to us. The place is definitely deserted.

So I wasn't caught cheating.

Will never has to know.

Still, I'm mortified.

I look at Buckley. He doesn't look mortified. He looks amused. And maybe a little disappointed.

"So you have a boyfriend?" he says. "For how long?"

For a second, I don't get the question. For a second, I think that what he's asking me is how much longer do I expect to have a boyfriend. I bristle, thinking he just assumes Will and I are going to break up after being separated this summer.

Then I remember that he doesn't know about that. His true meaning sinks in, and I inform him, "I've been with Will for three years."

"That long? So it's serious, then."

Naturally, I'm all, "Yeah. Absolutely. *Very* serious."

Well, it *is*.

"You know what?" I hop off my stool. "I just remembered something I have to do."

"Really?"

No. But I'm too humiliated to stay here with him any longer. Besides, that kiss really threw me.

Basically, what it did was turn me on, and I can't go around being turned on by other men. I'm supposed to be with Will, and only Will.

I pull on my raincoat and fumble in my pocket for money. I throw a twenty on the bar.

"You're really leaving? Just like that?"

"I just…I have to run. I can't believe I forgot all about this thing…."

The thing being Will.

"Well, at least give me your number. We can still get together. I can always use another female pal." He grabs a napkin and takes a pen out of his pocket.

Yes, he has a *pen* in his pocket. Dammit. How convenient for him.

"What's the number?" he asks.

I rattle it off.

"Got it," he says, scribbling it on the napkin.

No, he doesn't. I just gave him my grandparents' number with a Manhattan area code.

"Take this back," he says, shoving the twenty at me. "This is on me. You're not even going to get to eat any of the skins."

"That's okay. I'm not that hungry after all."

He's still holding the twenty in his outstretched hand, and I'm looking down at it like it's some kind of bug.

"Take it," he says.

"No, that's okay. I can't let you pay."

"Why not? Really, I won't think it's a date if I pay," he says with a grin.

That does it. I'm getting out of here.

He shoves the twenty into my pocket and I take off for the door, rushing out into the rain with my slicker open and my hood down.

I'm drenched before I get to the corner.

My first instinct is to rush right over to Will's.

If I were in my right mind, I would stop, reconsider and go with my second instinct, which is to slink home on the subway, take a hot shower and crawl into bed— rather, futon.

Instead, I go with my first instinct.

In the lobby of Will's building, I buzz his apartment.

Nerissa's hollow voice comes over the intercom.

"It's me," I say. "Tracey."

"Hi, Tracey," says Miss Brit in her polished accent. "Will's not here."

He's *not?*

But he's supposed to be here. Packing.

Well, maybe she's lying.

No, that doesn't make sense.

Maybe he had to run out for more strapping tape or a new marker.

"Do you know where he is?" I ask her.

"No, I don't. I just got back from rehearsal. I'll tell him you stopped by."

No offer to let me come up and wait for him, I notice. Well, the apartment is pretty minuscule, and she probably doesn't feel like hanging out with me until Will comes back from wherever he is.

But still, I have a right to be there if I feel like waiting for him. More right than she does, since Will's name is on the lease, I think irrationally.

"See you later, Tracey," she says breezily. Her *later* comes out "light-ah," heavy on the "t." Tracey is "trice-ee."

"Yeah. Cheerio."

I stalk back out into the pouring rain.

Six

"You coming to lunch, Tracey?" Brenda asks in her thick Jersey accent, poking her long, curly, helmet-sprayed hair over the top of my cubicle.

"If you guys can wait two seconds for me to fax something to the client for Jake," I tell her, not looking up from the fax cover sheet I'm filling out. "Otherwise go ahead without me and I'll order take-out."

"We'll wait for you, hon," Yvonne's smoker's rasp announces from the other side of my cube, just before I hear a telltale aerosol spurt as she sprays Binaca. She and my grandmother are the only two people I've ever seen use the stuff.

Then again, they're probably about the same age, although Yvonne looks a lot younger. She's tall and super-skinny with a raspberry-colored bouffant and matching lipstick, which she re-applies religiously after every post-cigarette Binaca burst. Yvonne's claim to fame, other than being secretary to the big cheese, our Group Director Adrian Smedly, is that she was once a Rockette at Radio City Music Hall. She likes to tell stories about the old days, dropping names of celebrities I've mostly never heard of—people who were famous back in the fifties and sixties.

She's what my father would call a real character, and she would take that as a compliment.

What should have been a quick fax job turns into a dragged-out ordeal. All I have to do is send Jake's memo over to the client, McMurray-White, the famous packaged goods company that makes Blossom deodorant and Abate laxatives, among other indispensable products. But for some reason, the fax machine keeps beeping an irritating error code.

I hate office equipment. Whenever I go near the fax machine, the copier, or the laser printer, the damn things apparently sense my uneasiness and jam.

This is not a good day. Earlier, I scalded my hand using the coffeemaker in the kitchenette adjacent to the secretaries' bay. And just now, on my way out of the ladies' room, I slipped on a patch of wet tile and went down hard on my butt. You'd think the extra padding there would have cushioned my fall, but now it's killing me.

Jake comes up behind me as I try to force-feed the memo into the slot for the fiftieth time.

"Having trouble, Tracey?"

I turn around to see him wearing a smirk. By now I know that it's nothing personal. That's Jake's usual expression, unless the client is around. Really. No matter what the circumstances, Jake finds something to smirk about. If I tell him his wife is on the phone, he smirks. If I tell him the NBC rep canceled tomorrow's presentation, he smirks. If I tell him a document is being messengered over from his broker, he smirks.

Let's face it: he's the kind of guy I'd consider an asshole if he weren't my boss. He leers at women behind their backs, laughs whenever somebody does something clumsy and—I'm starting to think—cheats on his wife, Laurie. That really gets me. They've been married a little over a year, and I've never actually met her, but she's really sweet whenever I talk to her on the phone. Sometimes when she calls, Jake makes a face, rolls his eyes, and tells me to say he's in a meeting. I always feel guilty when I do that, because Laurie is so disappointed, and it's like she doesn't even suspect I'm lying.

Meanwhile, lately, no matter how busy he is, he always takes calls from a woman named Monique. Supposedly she's a friend of his. If you ask me, married men shouldn't have friends named Monique. And something tells me Laurie doesn't know Monique exists.

"Can you see me when you're done with that?" Jake says, as the fax machine starts beeping an error code again and latches on to the first sheet of the memo in a death grip.

"Can it wait until after lunch?" I ask, tugging the paper in a futile effort to free it from the machine.

"It'll only take a second," Jake replies. He adds, "Whoa, careful—don't rip that or you'll have to re-print it," before he goes back down the corridor to his spacious office. A moment later, I hear the telltale thump of a small Nerf basketball hitting the wall behind the hoop above his desk. I can picture him sitting there, his polished black wingtip shoes propped on his desk, idly making shots.

Don't get me wrong. He's a busy guy with an important job, and he's really good at what he does. But when he's not in a high-powered meeting or working on a pitch or a presentation, Jake likes to kick back and have fun. He eats in the best restaurants in town. He orders stuff from the most expensive catalogues. He's really into golf and tennis—gentlemen's sports. I heard him on the phone the other day, ordering fishing equipment from Orvis that cost more than I make in a month. Lately, he's been looking at property up in Westchester for a country house, and he says it has to have a private pond or stream so that he can fish.

"Hey, you need a hand with that?" Latisha asks, behind me.

I turn around, exasperated. "Thanks. And you guys should probably go to lunch without me, because Jake needs to see me after this. He says it'll only take a second, but…"

"It's okay, we'll wait," Latisha says, pressing a couple of buttons on the machine. The paper slides right out. Moments later, the machine is humming and my fax is going through without a problem.

"How'd you do that?" I ask her.

She shrugs. "I've been a secretary a lot longer than you have, Tracey."

Secretary. I hate that.

Okay, it's what I am. But it's not what I meant to be, and it's not what I plan to be for long. Though there's a part of me that's convinced that it's better to be a secretary in Manhattan than an *anything* back in Brookside, I keep telling myself that it's only a matter of time before I find something better to do. But for now, I'm stuck here at Blaire Barnett Advertising, working for Jake.

I smile at Latisha. "Thanks for helping me."

"No problem." She wags a finger at me in her sassy, don't-give-me-any-crap way. "Now get into Jake's office and see what that ol' pain in the butt wants so you can come to lunch with us. We're going for Mexican. Chips. Guac. Margaritas."

I brighten. "Margaritas? At lunch?"

"Hell, it's Friday."

Yeah, it's Friday. Will's leaving in less than forty-eight hours. Sunday at this time, he'll be on a train somewhere north of Albany.

"I definitely need a drink," I tell Latisha. "A strong one."

"Tell me about it. In case you haven't been paying attention, my boys are in a major slump."

Her boys would be the New York Yankees. She's an obsessed fan. Has team memorabilia displayed all over her cube. The highlight of her life, according to Latisha and everyone who knows her, was a few years ago when her boss, Rita Sellers, gave her a couple of box seats for a World Series Game at the last minute. I know Rita, who is second in command in our account group, and there's no way she did that out of the goodness of her heart. According to Brenda, there was practically a typhoon that night, the seats were out in the open, and Rita came down with some kind of stomach bug. Otherwise, Latisha would never have gotten those tickets.

As it was, she got to share the box with the mayor and with two of the Backstreet Boys. She got their autographs for her daughter, Keera, who was ten at the time. The Backstreet Boys' autographs—not the mayor's.

"Are you going to the game tonight?" I ask Latisha. "Maybe you can bring the team some luck."

"I wish I was going. They're playing in Seattle."

"Oh." Damn! I just got a paper cut on the edge of Jake's memo. I stick my finger in my mouth and taste blood. Terrific.

Oblivious to my latest work-related injury, Latisha is saying, "But me and Anton will be in the bleachers on Sunday afternoon when they're back home."

Anton is Latisha's boyfriend. I've only met him

once and he seemed nice, but from what I've heard from Brenda and Yvonne, he's got *skank* written all over him. It's obviously a dead-end relationship, but Latisha doesn't seem to mind that it's not going anywhere. She says she'll get out when something better comes along, and that so far, nothing has.

"I know where I'll be on Sunday afternoon," I tell her. "Crying in my bed."

"'Cause Will's leaving?" She shakes her head. "He'll be back in a few months, right?"

"Yeah." I straighten the sheets of memo that have been faxed and pick up the confirmation sheet the machine has just spit out. "But a lot can happen in a few months, Latisha."

"If you're that worried, girl, you'd better get your ass on that train with him."

I never told her that I attempted to bring up that very subject with Will a few weeks ago, and that he was so thrown by it that he avoided me for a few days afterward. He claimed he was just busy packing, but how complicated can it be to throw some shorts and T-shirts into a few boxes and ship them upstate?

"I can't go with him, Latisha," I say now, as though that's the most absurd thing I've ever heard. "I mean, what am I supposed to do? Pick up and leave my life for the entire summer?"

"That's what I'd do if Anton ever tried to leave town without me."

"What about Keera?"

"I'd bring her," Latisha says. "It would do her

good to get away from her friends on the block. I don't like what I'm hearing out of their mouths lately. I don't trust any of them, and I don't want her goin' the way of my sister Je'Naye.''

Okay, so my troubles pale next to Latisha's. She's a single mother trying to raise an adolescent daughter in a rundown neighborhood where her teenaged sister was shot in a drug-related drive-by shooting a few years ago.

I sigh. ''We both need a margarita, Latisha. Maybe a couple of margaritas. Let me go find out what's up with Jake and I'll meet you guys downstairs.''

''You got it.'' She heads off down the hall, shaking her butt in her distinct walk. The way she dresses, you'd think she was built like Jennifer Lopez. She's shorter and heavier than I am, but you don't see her wearing black tunics. Today she's got on a low-cut red V-neck shirt tucked into a beige skirt that hugs her hips and thighs.

I catch Myron, the mail-room guy, checking her out as she passes by him.

''Mmm-mmm,'' he says, shaking his head. He stops pushing his package-laden cart and turns his head to keep watching her. ''Damn!''

''Cool it, Myron,'' she calls over her shoulder, but I know she's loving it.

''Girl, you are lookin' fine.''

''Mmm-hmm, and don't I know it,'' Latisha says smugly.

I wish I had half her confidence. But somehow, I

think that if I wore that clingy outfit Latisha has on, Myron would take one look and run screaming for cover.

I round the corner into Jake's office. Sure enough, there he is, sprawled behind the desk taking aim at the basket overhead. The place is big enough for a couch, a couple of chairs, and four wide windows looking out over Forty-second street. My cube barely has room for my desk, my chair, my computer, and a framed eight-by-ten head shot of Will.

"What's up, Tracey? Yesssss!!!!" Jake pumps his arms triumphantly as the ball sails through the hoop.

"You wanted to see me before lunch," I remind him.

"Right. Two things."

"Do you need me to write them down?"

"Nah." He straightens in his seat and gestures for me to take the chair opposite.

I do, glancing at the framed wedding photo of him with Laurie. If you ask me, she's way better-looking than he is. She's a pretty, skinny, sophisticated-looking brunette. He's a round-faced, reddish-haired frat boy type, and his cheeks still bear remnants of what must have been a nasty case of acne a few decades ago. Not that looks are everything, but I can't help wondering why Laurie married him.

Then again, he can be charming when he wants to be. And he's rich. Really rich. Apparently, he got a hot stock tip a few years ago, scraped together every cent he had, and it paid off big-time. Now he and

Laurie live in a big apartment in one of those nice doormen buildings in the east fifties off Sutton Place, and like I said, they're looking for a weekend house up in Westchester.

I wonder if she's happy. Laurie.

I wonder how long their marriage will last.

My stomach rumbles, and I wonder whether I should order the light sour cream and low-fat cheddar with my quesadilla, or go for full fat.

"First, I need you to find out what I do to get out of paying this parking ticket," Jake says, handing it to me across the desk.

"Why?" I ask, glancing at it. "Was it a mistake? You weren't illegally parked there?"

"No, I was," he says. "But there were no legal spots available. And nobody pays these things. Just make some calls, check around and find out what I have to do to plead innocent, or whatever, and let me know."

"Sure." Guess he won't be winning any Good Citizenship awards in the near future.

"The other thing is…" He clears his throat, like this is something big.

Oh, shit, now what am I going to be accomplice to? Next thing you know, I'll be in the witness protection program and Will will never find me.

"How are you with creative thinking, Tracey?"

"Creative thinking?" I study him warily, wondering why he's asking. Does he want an inventive way to dispose of a corpse?

"It depends on what you mean by creative," I say.

"Okay, well, if you're interested, I might have a fun little project for you. McMurray-White has come up with a new product, and it needs a name. So far, nothing they've come up with has clicked, and now they want our creative team to get on it. They've asked us for help brainstorming. But before I go any further, this is confidential."

"Definitely," I say, my mind whirling. This is far more exciting than my usual duties, like wrestling malfunctioning office equipment and scheduling his appointments with his personal trainer. An added bonus: It's perfectly legal.

"What we're dealing with here is a revolutionary roll-on deodorant that lasts all week," Jake says, leaning forward.

"All week? Does it work?"

"Supposedly. See what you can come up with, okay? Remember. Confidential."

"Sure." This almost makes up for the parking ticket thing. Wait till everyone back home hears about this. Okay, maybe naming a new deodorant isn't my dream claim to fame, but it's definitely more glamorous than any opportunity you get back in Brookside.

"That's it," Jake says, picking up his basketball and aiming again.

"I can go?"

"See ya," he tells me, and lets the ball sail into the air. "Yesss!" he hisses when he scores again.

I'm already out the door.

Latisha, Brenda and Yvonne are waiting for me in front of the building, smoking. They aren't the only ones—the entryway is jammed with white-collar cigarette-toting refugees from the smoke-free offices above. Yvonne is forever talking about the good old days when you could have an ashtray on your desk and puff away to your heart's content, before the militant nonsmokers intervened.

"It's about time," Brenda says, throwing down her cigarette butt and grinding it out with the impossibly pointy toe of her impossibly high-heeled white leather pump.

"Sorry. I was in with Jake." I light a Salem and inhale deeply as we head down the street.

"What did he want?" Latisha asks. "Does he need you to pick up his dry cleaning again?"

"Not this time." I debate whether I should tell them about the parking ticket, and decide against it.

Latisha and Yvonne are always telling me I need to stand up to Jake when he oversteps his boss-employee bounds. Brenda, who's pretty much a doormat type, usually doesn't jump on the band wagon.

The thing is, most of the time I don't mind running personal errands for Jake.

Okay, I do mind. But not enough to confront him.

"So Will is leaving this weekend, huh?" Brenda asks in a way that makes it clear the three of them were discussing the situation before I showed up.

"Yeah, he's outta here," I say lightly, careful not

to burn a stroller-pushing nanny with my cigarette as I brush past her on the crowded sidewalk.

Lord, it's sweltering out here—and crowded with sweat-soaked tourists, even though June has barely begun. I think about the long months ahead and decide that I'd rather spend the summer just about anywhere other than here. Even Brookside isn't looking that bad at this point.

"Are you going to see other people while you're apart?" Latisha wants to know.

"God, no!"

But I have to admit, an image of Buckley pops into my head.

"Is Will going to see other people?"

"No!"

"Are you sure?"

"Yes! Geez."

Latisha's silent, but I catch the look she sends the others.

I narrow my eyes at her as we stop on a corner for a Don't Walk sign. "Why? You don't think he's going to be faithful?"

"Show me a faithful man and I'll show you a eunuch," trumpets the thrice-divorced Yvonne.

"That's ridiculous," I tell her. "Not all men cheat. My father doesn't cheat on my mother."

"How do you know, hon?"

"I just know." And believe me, I do.

My father is still head over heels for my mother even after thirty-plus years of marriage. Don't ask me why. Sometimes it seems like all she ever does is nag him. And as I mentioned earlier, she's overweight, mustachioed and fond of stretch pants, yet his pet name for her is *Bella*—Italian for "beautiful." Proving love is blind. Which explains a lot of things—including the fact that Will is still with me.

"She's right," Brenda says. "Paulie doesn't cheat."

Paulie is her boyfriend, whom she's been dating since they were in junior high. They've been engaged since the summer before they went to community college together, and now, three years later, the big event is coming up in July. It's going to be held at a huge wedding hall out in Jersey, and we're all invited, with dates.

When I got the invitation a few weeks ago my first thought was that it was sweet of Brenda to add me to the invite list since we'd only known each other a few months.

My second—and, might I add, completely asinine—thought was that Will would be able to come home to accompany me.

Naturally, he said he couldn't get away from the theater, especially on a weekend.

I'm bringing Raphael in his place. I would just as soon have gone alone, but Latisha is bringing Anton and Yvonne is bringing Thor, her Swedish pen pal. She's been corresponding with him since they were children, and they're finally going to meet in person when he comes to New York on vacation next month.

Anton the skanky homeboy; Thor the foreign pen pal who reportedly speaks five languages, none of them English; and Raphael, homosexuality's answer to the Baywatch babes, only sluttier.

Gotta love that dynamic trio.

"Of course Paulie doesn't cheat," Latisha tells Brenda in an almost-sincere, comforting tone. "Not everybody cheats—not that I'd bet my life on Anton's fidelity. But Yvonne's right—a lot of men can't be trusted. And maybe Tracey shouldn't just sit around twiddling her thumbs while Will's away."

"I'm not going to be twiddling my thumbs," I protest.

"No? Then what are you going to do?" Yvonne asks.

"Improve myself."

I confess, until this second, I hadn't thought much about it. But the moment it pops out of my mouth, I decide it's the best idea I've ever had. I'll spend the summer on a self-improvement regimen.

"Improve yourself?" Yvonne echoes. "In what way, hon?"

"In every way. I'm going to lose weight. A lot of weight. I need to get into shape. And save money— maybe I can get a part-time job. I'll have more time on my hands with Will gone."

"A part-time job? Like what?"

"I don't know…walking dogs. Or baby-sitting. And I'm finally going to get organized. And…and read classic literature…" I'm on a roll. Instant conviction.

"Good for you, girl," Latisha says, high-fiving my hand that isn't holding a cigarette.

"Yeah. I'm going to do everything I always say I should do. Except quit smoking," I add hastily. If I quit smoking, I'd double my weight the first week. But the other stuff...

I can do it.

I know I can.

For the first time in weeks, I find myself almost looking forward to the upcoming months. I'm going to reinvent myself. When Will comes back, he won't even recognize the new me. I'll be skinnier than a female *Friend*. Skinnier than Lara Flynn Boyle.

Okay, maybe not that skinny. But I'll look good. Damn good. I'll even have a flattering new wardrobe and a chic haircut.

Will, of course, will be totally into the dazzling new Tracey. Next thing you know, we'll be living together. Then getting married...

But I'm not doing this only for Will, I remind myself as we walk into the air-conditioned, dimly lit Mexican restaurant.

I'm doing it for me. So that I'll feel good about myself for a change.

If it makes me irresistible to Will, I point out to my Will-obsessed side, that's just an added bonus.

After all, you should never change yourself just because of a guy—that advice courtesy of Dear Abby, countless magazine articles I've read over the years and Andrea Antonowski, my best friend back home—

whose word I still tend to consider gospel since she's never been without a boyfriend since we were in the sixth grade, and is now engaged to be married.

In a healthy relationship, you will love and accept each other just as you are.

Which is what Will and I have, I remind myself.

Otherwise, we wouldn't still be together. Of course he accepts me just as I am. I guess I just don't accept myself. I want to be better in every way.

Okay, mainly I want to *look* better. If I can get a savings account, organize my closet and read a few classics along the way, great. But my main goal for the summer is to finally lose weight.

So what's wrong with that?

"You should try that cabbage-soup diet," Brenda tells me. "One of my bridesmaids is going to make a copy for me so that I can lose five pounds before the wedding."

"I need to lose ten times that," I tell her, wedging myself between the hostess podium and a group of Japanese businessmen waiting for a table.

Brenda says nothing to that, but I find myself wishing she would. You know, that she—or Latisha or Yvonne—would say, "Oh, don't be ridiculous, you're not that overweight, Tracey."

Even if it's not true.

I try not to feel wounded. After all, do I really want my friends to lie to make me feel better?

Maybe.

"You should do the protein diet," Latisha says. "You like bacon and steak, right?"

"Who doesn't?"

"Those diets don't work," Yvonne puts in, waving her manicured talons in dismissal. "You have to exercise. That's the key. Start working out every day. Join a gym. Get a personal trainer."

"Or join Weight Watchers," Latisha recommends.

"Personal trainer? Weight Watchers? Who am I, the Duchess of York? I'm broke, guys, remember? I can't afford to pay to lose weight."

"Weight Watchers is cheap."

"Not free cheap. I need free cheap."

"Well, it doesn't cost anything to starve yourself," Brenda says. "Until you wind up in the anorexic ward of some hospital."

I think of Sofia, my college friend—the one who taught me how to smoke to lose weight. Obviously, it worked for her, since she was in and out of the Cleveland Clinic a few times. Meanwhile, here I am three years later, with a pack-a-day habit and more inches to pinch than ever before.

"Don't laugh. I know someone who ended up there," Latisha tells her. "One of Je'Naye's old friends, from before she fell in with the bad crowd. I can't believe I used to worry *she'd* be a bad influence on my sister with all that dieting. That was nothing, compared to… Anyway, last I heard, Charmaine was in the hospital again." She shakes her head, but her expression has that faraway look she gets when she thinks about her dead sister.

None of us know what to say, and there's a long moment of silence.

Then Brenda goes on, "Anyway, Tracey, cabbage is cheap. I'll get you a copy of that diet. When are you going to start?"

"The second Will gets on the train," I say. "By the time you guys see me on Monday, I'll be on my way to becoming the new me."

"How many?" the hostess cuts in, materializing in front of us after seating the group of businessmen.

"Four," we say in unison.

As she leads us to our table, I make up my mind to go for full fat on the sour cream and cheddar. Sort of a last hurrah before I set out to release my inner Calista Flockhart.

I know what you're thinking.

And I'll admit, this isn't the first time I've made big plans to lose weight. But this time, it's going to work. I'm going to succeed if it kills me.

And not just on the diet. It's everything. A whole life makeover. Starting on Sunday.

The only thing I have to do between now and then is psych myself up for it.

Oh, yeah.

And say goodbye to Will.

Seven

It might be easier if our last twenty-four hours together are really lousy.

You know, if we spend the time arguing or getting on each other's nerves or bored stiff.

But it doesn't happen that way.

Things with Will have been better this weekend than they've ever been before—or at least in a long time. Since the beginning.

It's a big plus that Nerissa happens to be out of town with Broderick, because the weather is hot and sticky and I don't have air-conditioning at my apartment. We've been able to have Will's place to ourselves.

Not that we've spent all of our time hanging out there.

Friday night, he surprised me with tickets to see *Rent* on Broadway. He's seen it a few times, but I never have. I know all the music because Will has the CD, and I've always wanted to go…probably because I can relate to the lyrics and the main characters, a bunch of down-and-out New Yorkers trying to make a living and pay rent on dumpy lower Manhattan apartments.

At least I'm not HIV positive, like most of the characters are. Too bad I can relate to their plight in pretty much every other way, although I'm not prone to outbursts of angst-ridden song when the going gets tough.

After the show, Will took me to dinner at a cabaret club where some of his friends perform. Nobody he knew was at the mike that night, but it didn't matter. We were only half listening to the music. Mostly, we were talking.

I'm not sure what we were talking about, but we laughed a lot and we drank a lot of wine.

Then we went back to his place, where we had great sex for the first time in months. Maybe it was all the wine, or maybe it was the knowledge that we won't be alone together again for weeks.

This morning when we woke up, we went out for bagels, then spent the day poking around in Soho, where Will bought me a cool pair of earrings and I bought him a carved wooden photo frame. I jokingly told him he could put a picture of me into it and pack it to bring it with him on the train, but when we got back to his place, that was exactly what he did. He found this snapshot that wasn't too horrible—one that I approved—and he stuck the frame into his shoulder bag.

Now, as we sit drinking pinot grigio after eating take-out Chinese, I find myself wondering why I was so worried about him leaving. He actually looks as though he wishes he weren't going, and he's told me more than once that he's going to miss me.

"So it'll probably fly by," I say hopefully, leaning back against his bed. We're sitting on the floor, the white cardboard take-out containers still spread out around us. A jazz CD is playing in the background.

"It's three months," he says, and I can't tell if he's agreeing or disagreeing with me.

"Think about how short a time three months really is," I say. "I mean, three months ago, I was still temping. Now I'm working at Blaire Barnett.... Wait, I guess that doesn't prove my point, because it feels like I've worked there forever."

Will smiles. "Okay, how about this? Three months ago was when I got that horrible stomach bug thing and you came over with seltzer and soda crackers. That doesn't seem like it was so long ago, does it?"

Actually, it seems like ages ago. And I never should have gone over to play Clara Barton, because I came down with the stomach bug, too, and threw up while I was on the subway—an experience I wouldn't recommend to anyone. Nobody helped me, and a group of teenage girls actually made fun of me.

"I have a better one," I say, pushing away the unpleasant memory. "It was around three months ago that we had that really warm day and neither of us had to work and we went to the Central Park Zoo on the spur of the moment. Remember?"

"That was three months ago?" he asks, leaning back so that his shoulder is against my shoulder and his legs are sprawled alongside mine. "I thought that was in May."

"No, it was March. Remember?" I sling one of my legs across both of his, confidently stubble-free. I shaved this morning, now that it's shorts season again. I'm wearing a pair of black denim cutoffs that are long enough to conceal the most jiggly, dimply part of my upper thighs. My skin is pure white and you can see faint dots on my lower legs where the hair follicles are, even though I'm clean-shaven. I've got a few black-and-blues on my shins, too. Lovely.

I vow that by the time Will comes back, I'll not only have lost thirty or forty pounds, but I'll have a tan—don't ask me how. Maybe I can lie out on the roof of my building or something. And maybe I'll even have my legs waxed so they'll be smoother looking.

Will is pondering that day at the zoo. "Maybe it was April...."

"Trust me, it was March. That's what was so cool about it—that it was the week before Saint Patrick's Day and it was almost eighty degrees out and sunny. And we both had to buy sunglasses from that guy who was selling them on the street, and he swore they were real Ray-Bans.''

''Yeah, right. Mine fell apart an hour later,'' Will says, shaking his head.

''That day was really fun, Will.''

''Mmm-hmm.''

His voice is faraway and I wonder whether he's thinking back to that day, or ahead to the immediate future without me.

I'm right back to feeling really down about him leaving.

Because, no matter how you look at it, three months is a long time.

It's an entire season.

A quarter of a year.

A lot can happen in three months…not necessarily for the better.

''I wish you didn't have to go,'' I say, looking into his eyes. His face is really close to mine, and I can smell his cologne.

''But I do have to go.'' He brushes a few strands of hair back from my cheek. ''And I'll be back right after Labor Day.''

''Yeah. And I'll visit you up there.''

''Yeah.''

Only he doesn't look that enthusiastic.

I feel a flicker of panic. My visiting him is something we've talked about in passing, but no definite plans have been made. Now I realize that I might be the one who's always brought it up. I think back, trying to remember if he's ever once told me he's looking forward to me coming, and I can't recall a single time.

"I won't come until you get settled," I say, wondering if he thinks I'll be up there next weekend or something.

"Yeah."

"Will, it's okay if I visit you, isn't it?" I say, watching him. "Because I really want to come see some of your performances…"

And I really have to check up on you and make sure you still love me.

"It's fine," he says. "Just so you know…I mean, I got the rules for the cast house in a package from the theater this week, and no overnight guests are allowed."

"No overnight guests are allowed?" I repeat incredulously, thinking that it sounds like a circa 1940s sorority house. "But I thought the cast house was co-ed."

"It is. It's also really crowded. There's no room for guests. Plus, I think they want us to focus on performing, and overnight guests would be a distraction."

"Oh."

"So you can come to visit for a weekend, but… Look, there are a lot of nice places up there. Motels and bed-and-breakfasts…"

"That would be nice." I brighten, imagining Will and me spending a cozy weekend at a romantic country inn together. "Maybe when you have some spare time you can scout out a place for us to stay when I come up.''

''Actually...''

Oh, geez, there's that hesitant look again. Now what?

''I have to stay in the cast house, Trace. That's another one of the rules. During the season performers aren't allowed to be away overnight unless there's some kind of emergency.''

''Wow. So do they read you bedtime stories and tuck you in, or what?''

He cracks a smile.

I'm barely kidding. ''It sounds more like some kind of prison camp than a summer job, Will.''

''It's important to be self-disciplined to make it in this business, Tracey. This experience is going to teach me a lot and help me make sure I have what it takes. I'm serious about this. I always have been. I want to make it. I want it more than I've ever wanted anything in my life.''

What he doesn't say—what he doesn't have to say—is that he wants it more than he wants me.

That unspoken revelation shouldn't be a surprise to me, but somehow it is. Somehow, I guess I thought that if he had to choose, he'd choose me.

The thing is, he shouldn't have to choose. And he doesn't have to choose.

But I think he has.

''Will, it's fine,'' I say, trying to push aside my hurt so that our last night isn't ruined. ''I'll come up and

I'll find a cute place to stay. Maybe they'll even allow conjugal visits,'' I joke.

He leans over and kisses me. ''As far as I remember, there was nothing against that in the rules.''

It's a quick, sweet kiss. Not a passionate one. Not the kind of kiss that's meant to lead somewhere.

Not like the notorious Buckley kiss.

The very thought of that sends guilt churning through me. It's been a few weeks now, but I still keep remembering exactly what it felt like to be kissed so unexpectedly—and so thoroughly—by a virtual stranger.

I didn't tell anyone about that—not even Raphael. Especially not Raphael.

All I said to him, when he called me that Sunday night with an expectant ''Well?'' was that we were both mistaken, and that Buckley is heterosexual.

Naturally, Raphael doesn't believe it. He thinks every decent-looking, well-dressed, remotely creatively employed man in New York is gay.

''Buckley might think he's hetero,'' he said, ''but one of these mornings, Tracey, he's going to wake up to find that closet claustrophobic and he'll decide to come out of it at last. When he does, I'll be waiting with open arms.''

That's Raphael—ever optimistic.

Meanwhile, I'm currently consumed by pessimism—which happens to be a prominent Spadolini family trait—wishing Will would throw me down on the bed and ravish me.

He seems content to just sling an affectionate arm over my shoulder and say, "By the way, before I forget, I told Milos to call you if he finds himself short-handed this summer. I'm not the only one on the wait staff who's abandoning him for summer stock."

"You did? Thanks. I was thinking I might need to find a part-time job. I need to make some extra cash."

"You're in luck. He pays well and the tips are great. And I told him you have waitressing experience."

"Yeah, if you can compare a high-school summer spent waiting tables at Applebee's suitable experience for a Manhattan catering company serving the rich and famous."

"Don't be intimidated. Not all of Milos's clients are rich and famous, Trace."

"Oh, come on, Will. They might not be famous, but they're not exactly middle-class. He charges more for a few dozen mini-quiche appetizers than I used to make in an entire day of temping."

"True. Which is why you should help him out if he calls."

"I will."

It'll be good to make some money on top of my measly salary. I haven't yet told Will about the self-improvement plan I'm launching. I've decided to surprise him with the new me when he comes back in September.

Will yawns. "What time is it?"

I check my watch. "Almost eleven."

"We should go to bed. I have to be up at five-thirty."

I'm dreading that—saying goodbye to him in the cold, cruel light of dawn. We have less than eight hours left together, and he apparently intends to spend the bulk of it sleeping.

"Listen, I hate to make you get up that early," he says. "You can stay in bed after I leave. Just lock up and leave my extra key downstairs with James."

This catches me off guard.

He wants me to leave the key with the doorman... for the entire summer?

"Is that a good idea?" I ask. "I mean, shouldn't I hang on to the key? That seems safer..."

"Nah, James will give it to Nerissa when she gets back tomorrow," he says, extracting his legs from mine and getting up off the floor.

I've gone all shrill inside—*He's not leaving me his extra key?*—yet my voice comes out deceptively calm. "But Nerissa doesn't really need two keys, does she? I mean, if she ever locked herself out, she could just have James let her in..."

Will has stopped brushing invisible dust from the floor off his khaki shorts, and he just looks at me. "What's wrong, Trace?"

"Nothing." I shrug. "I just thought maybe you'd leave me your key. I mean, I can water your plants for you—"

"Nerissa's going to take care of that."

"Oh. Well, the other thing is, I don't have air-conditioning and summers in the city are so hot...I thought that if it got to be too sweltering, I could come over here to cool off.''

He doesn't flinch or look away, which I take as a good sign until he says, ''See, I thought about doing that, but I don't think it's such a good idea. It wouldn't really be fair to Nerissa to have you showing up unexpectedly. I mean, she's counting on having the place to herself for the summer...''

''Oh. I mean, that's okay, Will, I just— I understand. It's fine.''

But it isn't. He's not leaving me his key, and it sucks. I feel like I'm going to cry.

I need a distraction—something to show him that I'm okay. I glance around, and my gaze falls on the pad of paper and pen he keeps handy by the phone.

I walk over and grab it, saying, ''Before I forget, can you give me your phone number at the cast house? Just in case I can't get you on your cell. I'll put the number in my Palm Pilot when I get home, because I forgot to bring it with me....''

I notice that a shadow has crossed his face and he is shifting his weight from one foot to the other and back again.

Not a good sign.

''Trace, the thing is...''

I don't believe this.

''What? You're not allowed to talk on the phone there, either?''

"There is no phone. I mean, there's a pay phone for making outgoing calls…"

"And it doesn't take incoming calls?"

"Maybe it does. I don't know. I'll find out when I get there, but I don't have the number now. The thing is, there are going to be more than two dozen of us living there, with one phone, and we'll be in rehearsals or performing most of the time…so I guess what I'm trying to tell you is, the phone isn't going to be the best way for us to keep in touch."

"What about your cell phone?"

"I don't know. I mean, you can try me on it, but I don't know how often I'll have it turned on. I wouldn't want it ringing during rehearsals…."

Okay, I'm getting pissed off. I can't help it. "I guess e-mail is out, too."

"If I had a laptop that would be good…but I don't."

"So we'll write letters the old-fashioned way?" It's all I can do to feign nonchalance and mask the sarcasm that wants to infiltrate my tone. "Great. We can be pen pals like Yvonne and Thor. That'll be romantic."

"Who?"

"Never mind," I tell him, heading for the bathroom. "Mind if I go in first?"

"No, it's fine. I want to recheck my bag to make sure I'm not forgetting anything. I'll be in a rush in the morning."

Yeah. In a rush to get out of here, away from me…

Maybe that's not fair.

I know it's not as though he's leaving New York to get away from me. But right now, what's the difference?

I barely get the bathroom door closed before the tears start. I turn on the water and flush the toilet a few times to muffle the huge gasping sobs I can't hold back any longer.

When I come out, he's zipping his bag, looking chipper. "Everything's set," he informs me.

I keep my face turned away so he won't see that my eyes are swollen. "Good."

"I'll be right out."

While he's in the bathroom, I turn out the lights and climb into his bed.

I wish I could say that he comes out, takes me into his arms and tenderly makes love to me—and that it makes everything all right between us.

But it doesn't happen like that.

We make love, but I make the first move…almost out of desperation, needing to prove that everything's okay.

He goes along with it. But it's awkward, mechanical, and…I don't know. Maybe *cold* is too strong a word.

Maybe it isn't.

All I know is that Will falls asleep immediately afterward, curled up on his side of the bed.

And I lie awake, listening to his even breathing and the hum of the air-conditioner and the faint sounds of the street below.

Eight

The alarm goes off at dawn.

Will bolts out of bed.

I roll over, pretending to drift back to sleep…as if I've actually *been* asleep.

Pretending I'm not on the verge of falling apart, crying…or even worse, begging him to stay.

Through narrow slits in my eyes, I watch him scurry around in the milky-gray light, listening to the rush of the water while he's in the shower and his bustling in the kitchen as he pours a glass of orange juice and a bowl of cereal.

He thinks I'm sleeping, so he tiptoes around, quietly opening and closing drawers, cupboards, the fridge.

I hear him crunching his cereal, gulping his juice.

Zipping his jeans, spritzing cologne.

Running water in the bathroom, brushing his teeth for the second time.

Lifting his bag, jingling his keys.

He bends over me, his cologne wafting to my nostrils, his breath warm on my cheek. "I have to leave now, Trace."

"Hmm?" I pretend to come awake slowly.

"I have to go. To catch my train. The spare key is on the kitchen counter."

Right.

I'm supposed to give it to James the doorman.

"Help yourself to whatever you want for breakfast. Just don't leave dishes in the sink, okay?"

I bristle at that.

Does he really think I'd be that much of a clod, leaving dishes in the sink for Nerissa to do when she gets back?

I open my mouth to snap at him when he bends over and kisses me.

I quickly close my mouth against his lips, conscious of his minty-fresh breath and my dragon breath.

"I'll miss you, Trace," he says, and then he's on his way out the door, calling softly over his shoulder, "I'll call you when I get settled."

Yeah.

I cry into my pillow after he's gone, until my eyes are boiling and sore and my hairline is wet and sticky and my nasal passages ache.

Then I get up, make the soggy bed and take a long shower.

After I'm dressed, I smoke a few cigarettes, flushing the butts down the toilet. But I don't bother to spray the potpourri-scented air freshener that I know Will keeps under the sink. Why should I? He's gone until September.

And who cares if Nerissa comes back and smells stale smoke?

In the kitchen, I make myself half a pot of coffee, then scramble a couple of eggs in butter while it brews, thinking the coffee might wake me up and that the eggs will settle my churning stomach.

Nothing helps.

After eating and sipping, I still feel exhausted and nauseous. So nauseous that I do a less than perfect job of cleaning up my dirty dishes. So let Nerissa sue me.

After packing my clothes from the last two days into my shoulder bag—and purposely leaving my toothbrush in the holder above the sink where I always keep it, though Will's is now gone—I walk out the door, locking it behind me.

James is in the lobby, gorgeous and broadshouldered in his navy uniform. "How are you today?" he asks. He doesn't know my name. That's never bothered me until now. Now I want more than anything to belong here, in Will's building. In Will's life.

"I've been better," I say as I hand him the key. "This is for Will's roommate."

"Nerissa," he says, nodding.

Well, of course he knows *her* name. She lives here.

And right now, I loathe her more than ever.

Maybe that doesn't make sense. She's just his room-mate, but I'm his girlfriend.

Stepping out onto the sidewalk is like stepping into a dryer that's just stopped spinning. A wall of hot air hits me head-on.

There's no sun, just an overcast gray sky beyond the towering buildings. But the heat is oppressive already, and it's not even nine o'clock yet.

It's not even July yet.

July is weeks away.

And after the whole month of July, I have to get through all of August, too, before Will is home and my life is back to normal.

I light a cigarette and take a deep drag.

For some reason, despite my roiling gut and throbbing head, that makes me feel better.

Being jostled and jolted on the downtown N train doesn't.

When I emerge onto Broadway in the East Village, I check my watch and realize that Will's long been on his train. Right now, he's probably already an hour or more north of New York City.

I picture him sitting there, looking out the window at the passing scenery, and I wonder if he's thinking about me.

Somehow I sense that he isn't.

No, he's undoubtedly thinking about what lies ahead.

And so should I.

With that, I remember that this was supposed to be the first day on the path toward a new me—a slimmer new me.

Scrambled eggs in butter—what a way to kick off the diet.

Then again…

Isn't that what you're supposed to eat on those high-protein diets?

That's what I'll do, I decide, quickening my pace when I spot the Food Emporium on the next corner. I'll go stock up on protein, and I'll be on a low-carb diet.

In the supermarket, I grab a basket.

Here is what I buy:

Hot dogs.

Eggs.

Bacon.

Beef jerky—teriyaki and hickory flavored.

Cheese—Muenster and Monterey Jack, although the only difference, as far as I can tell, is the orange stuff. What *is* the orange stuff, anyway?

In my protein-snatching frenzy I almost add a package of frozen fried chicken, until I realize that the breading makes it off-limits. Damn.

Well, no diet is perfect.

I charge the groceries on my Visa since I've got fifteen dollars to last me the three days till payday.

My apartment, when I reach it, is stifling and has taken on an unfamiliar smell in my absence. Actually, it's familiar in the sense that this is what the place smelled like the first time I entered it. A blend of Ajax cleanser and cat pee and a faint hint of curry. Now there's also stale cigarette smoke in the mix.

Ick.

Needing fresh air, I open the one window, which overlooks the street. Now I can breathe, but my ears are assaulted by the sounds of a teenaged girl arguing with her boyfriend four stories below. She keeps shouting rapid-fire accusations at him, interrupted by his unintelligible protests, mostly punctuated by frequent *Yo's*. Sometimes there are double Yo's, as in "Yo, Yo, I never said that!" and "Yo, Yo, back off, dude."

I assume she's the one he's calling Dude, but at that point, I look down to make sure nobody else is involved. All I need is for a brawl to erupt under my window.

Finally, all is silent below. Well, not silent. There's still the usual city commotion, but the argument seems to have come to an end.

I look down and see the happy couple entwined in each other's arms, more or less having sex on somebody's stoop. Lovely.

Now what?

The apartment is cluttered with books and magazines and last weekend's newspaper, and I realize that it's been a while since I've had a chance to read anything.

Recalling my vow to read the classics this summer, I make a stack of all the paperbacks lying around waiting to be read. Then I shove the Mary Higgins Clark and the James Patterson under the futon, and I put the latest Joyce Carol Oates on my pillow. It might not be a classic, but it's the most literary thing in my current library.

Then I unpack my purchases in the tiny kitchen area, realizing that I'm hungry already. So I throw a couple—okay, four—hot dogs in a frying pan with a small amount of butter.

While they cook, I check my answering machine.

There are three messages.

Maybe Will called from the train, I think, as I press the button and hear the tape rewind.

A beep, and then the first message:

"Hi, Tracey, it's me," Raphael's voice announces. "Kate and I want to take you to lunch on Sunday. We know Will's leaving. Call me to make plans."

Another beep, and then the second message:

"Hey, Trace, Raphael and I want to take you to lunch on Sunday so you won't be too depressed about Will leaving. Call me."

Another beep. Message number three:

"Tracey, are you all right? Mom says you haven't called her in more than a week. She's worried. Call me or her and let us know you're okay. Love you."

I sigh.

You'd think my mother would pick up the phone and call me herself, instead of expecting Mary Beth to do it. But—and this is the God's honest truth—she has this thing about calling long distance. The expense might be a part of it, but I tend to think she's trying to make a point, in her usual stubborn way, about my moving so far away. It's almost like she thinks that if she doesn't call me, I'll realize how much I miss her and move back home again.

I usually call home a few times a week just to check in, but this past week I was busy at work, and I spent every spare moment with Will.

I pick up the phone and dial my sister's number instead of my parents'. They're at mass right now anyway.

Mary Beth answers on the second ring. "You're alive!" she says.

"How did you know it was me?"

"Caller ID. I just got it, so I can tell when it's Vinnie and avoid his calls."

"Good for you." I'm surprised. I thought she was still pining away for her ex-husband, jumping for the phone every time it rings, hoping he'll call to reconcile.

"My therapist is making me do this. He says I have to stop talking to Vinnie, unless it's about the kids, because it's only hurting me and making me think there's hope when there isn't."

"What, Vinnie's been calling you and telling you there's hope?" Now there's a startling turn of events.

"He's been calling me, yeah," Mary Beth says heavily. "But he talks about these women he's dating, and about stuff he's buying for his new place, and it pisses me off because he's being such a Scrooge about the divorce settlement. I think he's just trying to get to me, rub it all in my face. And George says—"

"Who's George?"

"My therapist. He says I have to stop listening to him and talking to him—"

"To Vinnie?"

"Who else?"

"I don't know—George."

"No," she says, frustrated, "*George* says I have to stop talking to *Vinnie* because it makes me think there's hope."

Why she'd get hope for their relationship out of that situation is beyond me. But the thing about Mary Beth is, she'll probably always be in love with Vinnie, and grateful for any connection between them. That's how it's been from the moment they started dating back in middle school.

"Hey, Mary Beth, do you still belong to that fitness club?" I ask, pacing restlessly across my tiny apartment. I fill a glass of water at the sink, realizing I'm basically dehydrated from all the wine and soy sauce last night and coffee this morning.

"Yeah, I still belong. But I haven't had much time to go lately. Why?"

"Have you lost weight?" I take a sip of water. Ugh, it's warm. I turn on the faucet again to let it run and cool off, then dump what's left in the glass into my philodendron, wondering when I last watered it.

"I've lost some weight," Mary Beth is saying. "But muscles weigh more than fat, you know."

Which is a dead giveaway that she's making excuses for why she hasn't lost weight.

Who knows? Maybe we're both doomed by our family gene pool.

No.

I can't accept that I'll look this way forever, I decide, filling the glass again at the sink and walking across the room with it.

I come to a halt in front of my mirrored bathroom door.

Yikes!

My full-length reflection is hideous. I'm wearing the same black denim shorts from yesterday, with a sloppy-looking white T-shirt that hangs down to the tops of my thighs. Even though the shorts cover the most wobbly, dimply cellulite zone, the fabric can't conceal the fact that they're thick and lumpy.

I picture Nerissa's lean dancer's body.

I feel renewed enthusiasm for my diet plan.

I'll exercise, too. Every day.

And I'll drink eight glasses of water.

I sip from the glass I'm holding. Okay, good start.

"So what's new with you?" my sister is asking.

I'm tempted to tell her about my self-improvement plan, but before I can decide whether to bring it up, she says, as though she's just remembered, "Oh, Will is leaving soon, isn't he?"

"He left this morning."

"You must be devastated."

That's the thing about my sister. She's like my mother—i.e., pessimistic. I constantly have to fight my own tendencies to be the same way.

See, with Mom and Mary Beth, the glass is always half-empty.

Not that there's anything half-full about this particular glass—meaning, Will's leaving me.

But there are plenty of instances where my sister has reacted negatively to something in my life instead of trying to be encouraging.

Like, when I found this apartment and told Mary Beth about it, her reaction wasn't that it was cool that I'd found my own affordable place, it was that I had agreed to pay a ridiculous amount of rent for a place that doesn't even have a separate bedroom.

You'd think I'd be used to her by now, but she's getting on my nerves. "You know what? I have to go now. I'm meeting my friends for lunch."

"Which friends?"

"Kate and Raphael." As if it makes a difference. She's never met any of my New York friends.

"Raphael...isn't he the homosexual?"

It's all I can do not to burst out laughing, not just at the word, but at the painstaking, Brookside way she says it, and the way she puts a "you" in the final two syllables. As in "ho-mo-sex-you-al," instead of "ho-mo-sek-shoe-al."

Or "gay."

"Yep," I tell Mary Beth, "he's the one."

I can tell she's struggling to be open-minded. "Well, have fun, Tracey. Oh, and maybe you should think about coming home for Mom and Dad's anniversary next month. We're thinking of having a party for them. It's their thirty-fifth."

"I don't know…it's hard for me to get time off from work." I haven't earned any vacation days yet— I won't be able to take one until after I've been there for six months, but Latisha says sometimes you can squeak through with one day, depending on your boss.

Hopefully Jake will let me take a long weekend at some point—which I intend to use to visit Will, not to go back home to Brookside.

"See what you can do, Tracey. Even if you just come for a weekend. You haven't been home since Easter. The boys miss you."

"I'll try," I say, caught off guard by a wave of homesickness. It's because she mentioned the boys, my nephews. Her son Vince—Vincent Carmine Rizzo, Junior, but thank God nobody ever calls him that—is four. Nino is almost three. They both have curly black hair and big dark flashing eyes and chubby little bodies, and I adore them. They're always jumping all over me, wanting me to carry them around, smothering me with kisses and hugs.

If they were around today, I wouldn't be feeling so bereft about Will's leaving.

"See what you can do about getting here. We all miss you," my sister says.

"I'll try," I say again.

But this time I actually mean it.

We hang up. I take another sip of water...still luke-warm...and make a face.

Then I call Raphael.

He and Kate have already made plans. He informs me that we're all going to brunch at a new place at Fourteenth Street and Avenue A, not far from my apartment. He'll see me there at twelve-thirty.

Just as we hang up, I hear a male voice in the background. Apparently, Raphael didn't spend the night alone. As I replace the receiver and go over to the stove to check my hot dogs, I wonder if he'll bring his new man to brunch.

Thinking of Raphael's love life brings to mind an image of Buckley O'Hanlon.

Along with it comes the crazy notion that if Will dumps me over the summer, I can always go out with Buckley.

I stop short, my hand poised in midair over the frying pan handle.

What am I thinking?

Will isn't going to dump me!

My God, that's not even an option.

Besides, if Will ever did dump me, I wouldn't replace him. I couldn't. He and I have this whole history....

This whole future, if all goes the way I assume it will.

Yes, Buckley O'Hanlon is a cute, available guy who happens to have kissed me.

Yes, I could be attracted to someone like that if it weren't for Will.

But Will is in my life, and he's going to stay in my life.

My heart hurts just thinking of the alternative.

I grab the handle and jiggle the frying pan a little, tossing the hot dogs around to make sure they're evenly browned in the butter. Then I dump them on a plate, smother them with ketchup and mustard and gobble them down.

It doesn't occur to me until I'm washing the plate and pan ten minutes later that condiments might be off-limits on this diet. That I probably should have checked into it before I indulged.

And that I probably shouldn't have eaten so soon after breakfast and so close to the time I'm meeting Raphael and Kate for lunch.

But, I argue with my disapproving self, I was already heating the hot dogs, and they wouldn't be good later.

Besides, I was hungry. As usual.

I promise myself that I'll just have coffee while Kate and Raphael eat.

But as I round the corner from Avenue B onto East

Fourteenth Street a little over an hour later, I realize I'm hungry again. Okay, what's up with that? I thought eating a lot of protein was supposed to keep you fuller longer, but apparently that's not the case.

Maybe the protein diet isn't such a good idea.

Kate is already at the small restaurant when I get there. She's lingering just inside the door, reading the reviews posted on the wall.

She's wearing a pale yellow sleeveless linen shift and matching flats, and her blond hair is pulled back in a clip. She looks like she should be at a garden party in Connecticut instead of in this dimly lit dive that features typically East Village eccentric decor.

The walls are painted deep red, the floor in black and white zebra stripes dotted with the occasional neon-purple splotch. Dozens of mobiles are suspended from the ceiling, made up of bent cutlery dangling from yellow yarn tied to ordinary wire hangers. They twirl slowly in the warm breeze from the low-hanging ceiling fans.

A bar runs the length of the place, and the rest of the room is occupied by sturdy-looking round plastic tables and chairs painted in psychedelic colors.

The Rob Lowe clone behind the bar motions for us to sit anywhere.

We choose a table closest to the propped-open door. The place isn't air-conditioned, and the fans don't cool things off in the least.

Two other tables are occupied; otherwise, the place is empty.

"So…are you okay?" Kate asks in her sultry Southern accent the moment we're seated. Her perfectly made-up features are concerned.

"Why? Don't I look okay?"

"You look kind of…sad."

Is it that obvious? I thought I was coming across as breezy and contented. At least, that's what I was aiming for.

"Well, of course I'm *sad*." I reach for a menu from the laminated pile of them propped between the salt and pepper shakers. "Will's only been gone for a few hours. But I'll get used to it."

"Maybe it'll even be good for you, being away from him. It'll give you a chance to…to…"

I wait patiently for her to come up with something, though I know she wants me to rescue her.

"It'll give you a chance to find out who you are without him," she finally says. "To explore the inner you."

"Thank you, Oprah."

"I'm trying to be supportive. You know, to find the silver lining."

"That's better than my sister did when I spoke to her a little while ago. She said I must be devastated."

"Are you?"

Of course.

"Of course not!" I stare at the menu. "*Devastated* is such a strong word. People are *devastated* when their husband leaves them for another woman. They're devastated when they lose a child. Or a job. Or maybe even when they break up. Will and I aren't breaking up—we're only apart for a few months.''

I'm talking too much.

She nods.

"Look at military wives,'' I say, gaining momentum. Help! Let me stop talking!

But I can't.

I rattle on, "Military husbands take off for months at a time on a regular basis. They go overseas, and they go on dangerous missions…I mean, I would be devastated if Will were overseas on a dangerous mission, but for God's sake, he's doing summer theater two hundred miles away from here…if that.''

Kate nods again.

I can tell by her expression that she sees right through me. The fact is, the Valley Playhouse might as well be behind enemy lines.

I tell Kate, "There are no land mines up in North Mannfield, last I heard.''

No, but there are actresses.

Actresses who will be sharing a house with actors, most of whom—if the statistics of the theater department back at Brookside University hold true in the grand scheme of things—will be homosexual. Even if Will has every intention of being faithful and celibate—which I'm sure he does—it's not going to be easy.

I picture him, the only hetero male in the house, surrounded by bold, nubile nymphets—his own personal Temptation Island. Then I realize Kate is talking to me.

I blink. "What?"

"I said, why don't you come out to the beach house with me next Saturday? It's my first weekend there."

"Maybe I will."

Yeah, sure.

I don't mean it. The beach isn't my favorite place. The last time I wore a bathing suit was three summers ago. I brought it with me to New York because I brought everything I own with me to New York, but I never really expected to wear it here. Or anywhere.

Ever again.

Kate is saying, "I'm probably going to take Friday off and make it a long weekend, but you can come out first thing Saturday. It'll be fun."

And I'm thinking, no way in hell am I going to a beach with someone who looks like she just stepped out of an ad for a Carribbean vacation. Kate is the slim, bikini-clad honey blonde walking the beach with her sandals dangling from her hand. Put me next to her, and it's goodbye, Carribbean vacation ad, hello Before and After weight loss ad—from the neck down. You know, where the svelte, smiling beauty claims that just six weeks ago, she was an unsightly, porcine slob. Then she started taking Extra Strength Nutrisvelte before every meal, and *voilà!*

Raphael breezes in as I study the menu and listen to Kate chatter about the other people who are doing a half share on her weekends.

Raphael's wearing designer sunglasses, a sleeveless orange shirt tucked into tight cut-offs and espadrilles, and he's carrying a black shoulder bag not unlike mine and Kate's. He couldn't look more flaming fashionista if his toenails were painted. In fact, I check under the table to make sure they aren't.

He hugs us both, plops himself down and says, behind a cupped hand, "Is that bartender a hot tamale or what?"

"There are three things that are certain in this life," Kate drawls, "death, taxes and Raphael's libido."

"If it gets any hotter in here, he'll have to take off his shirt," Raphael decides, wiping a trickle of sweat from his glistening forehead and throwing a lusty gaze at the unwitting bartender.

"If it gets any hotter in here, I'll have to take off my shirt," I inform him. "And trust me, it won't be a pretty sight."

"Speaking of pretty, did Will get off okay, Tracey?" Raphael asks.

Kate snorts at that.

I ignore her, and tell Raphael that yes, he's gone. "And don't ask me if I'm devastated, okay? Because I'm not."

"Of course you're not. You look fabulous."

"There are four things in life that are certain," I announce. "Death, taxes, Raphael's libido and Raphael's bullshit."

"Tracey! That's not nice. I was offering you a compliment, and I meant it," he says in a tone that isn't the least bit wounded. "So what are we having? Bloodies? Mimosas? Or should we go right for the hard stuff? In which case I'll take the bartender."

"I'll have a Bloody Mary," I say.

"Mimosa for me," Kate decides.

"I'll go with your choice, Tracey. I'm in the mood for something spicy. Like a Bloody Mary. Or—"

"The bartender," Kate and I say in unison.

I touch Raphael's arm, dragging his attention away from the current object of his fickle affections. "Raphael, who was that man I heard in the background when I called you this morning? I thought you were still pining away over Buckley O'Hanlon."

"Who's Buckley O'Hanlon?" Kate wants to know.

"Remember him from my birthday party, Kate? Oh, that's right, you had that mustache problem and had to leave early."

"It was not a mustache problem!" Kate injects indignantly, checking over her shoulder to make sure the two men at the neighboring table haven't overheard. One is wearing a turban, the other has a tattoo and they seem deeply engrossed in their own conversation, which isn't in English.

Raphael has gone on without missing a beat. "Buckley was the cute guy in the sweater—the one who came with Joseph and Alexander. He's writing the copy for their new brochure. Kate, Tracey was supposed to fix me up with him, but she seduced him instead."

"I did not!" I shriek. In a moment of weakness, I

recently told him what really happened on our "date." Dumb move.

"Yes, you did, but I don't blame you. You couldn't help yourself."

"You slept with this guy?" Kate asks me incredulously.

"No! We just went out on a date, which I didn't realize was a date until—"

"They kissed!" Raphael is gleeful.

"Until *he* kissed *me*. But that was when I still thought he was gay."

"So he's not?"

Raphael and I say, "Yes" and "Nope" simultaneously.

"Raphael can't accept the fact that he's straight," I explain to Kate, throwing a pointed glance at Raphael. "He's still trying to get over John Timmerman's wife and kids."

John Timmerman being one of the brokers who worked at the firm where the three of us temped last winter.

Raphael says, "Are you still bringing that up? I keep telling you, Tracey, my friend Thomas saw—"

"Never mind," I cut him off, not wanting to hear that whole sordid tale again. "The point is, Raphael thinks everyone is gay until proven otherwise. And I, for one, can vouch for Buckley's otherwise."

"So you kissed another guy, Tracey?" Kate says. "Wow, I can't believe y'all didn't tell me."

"That's because it was so not a big deal."

"Was he a good kisser?"

"Absolutely, Kate," Raphael says. "Just wet enough, not too much tongue."

"How do you know?" I demand.

"You told me, Tracey."

"Raphael, I never said that."

"Are you sure? Then I must've dreamed it," he says airily, waving his menu at us. "What are we having besides alcohol? A Bloody Mary will go right to my head. I haven't eaten since lunch yesterday—aside from a little midnight snack."

"So who was he?" I ask Raphael, because I can tell by his salacious tone that he's not talking about milk and cookies.

"His name was Phillip. He's a sailor in town for Fleet Week."

"Fleet Week is over, Raphael," Kate points out.

"Maybe he lied about being a sailor." Raphael shrugs. "He had a dotcom look about him. Whatever, the avocado omelet looks good." He snaps his menu closed, clasps his hands, and looks at us.

"I'm having the same thing," Kate says. "How about you, Tracey?"

"I already ate breakfast." And lunch. "I'll have the spinach salad with low-fat ranch dressing."

So much for the low-carb diet. I've had my fill of eggs and meat. It's too late to cancel out the butter-drenched eggs and hot dogs, but woman cannot live by protein alone. Cutting fat grams is the way to go.

Mental note: Stop to stock up on fat-free Enten-mann's goodies on the way home.

The salad is delicious, and the two Bloody Marys go down easily. So easily I'd love to order another one and settle in for a while to drown my sorrows in Absolut, but Kate and Raphael—who've had only one drink each—tell me I shouldn't get drunk so soon after Will left.

"Save it for when you're really desperate, and then indulge in a happy hour, Tracey," Raphael advises.

"You want to go out for drinks tonight?" I ask, my spirits lifting a little. Anything would be better than sitting home in my apartment.

"I've got a date."

"With Phillip?"

"With Charles. My new personal trainer. He's going to help me work on my Pilates moves."

I turn to Kate. "How about you? Do you have plans tonight, too?"

"I've got my salsa lesson."

Oh, that's right. For some reason, Kate has decided her life won't be complete unless she can cha-cha or lambada, or whatever it is they're teaching her at Enrique's School of Latin Motion.

"You want to come with me?" she asks.

"No, thanks," I say hurriedly. She's tried to talk me into that before. I exhausted my Latin dancing repertoire back when the Macarena was all the rage, thank you very much.

"How about you, Raphael?" she offers.

"Kate, I'm Puerto Rican, remember? I don't need lessons. I was born to mambo." He raises his arms and does a little exaggerated hip-swaying for the oblivious bartender's benefit as we make our way to the door.

The sun has poked out from behind a cloud. It turns out both Kate and Raphael are free for the next few hours. We decide to walk over to Broadway and browse in and out of a few stores.

By midafternoon, Raphael has a new outfit for his date tonight, and Kate has spent an hour trying to decide whether she prefers a red bikini or a blue one, before deciding on the pink.

Mental note: Never, ever join Kate at her beach house under any circumstances.

P.S.: throw away lone bathing suit the minute you get home, lest you ever find yourself the least bit tempted to put it on.

In the Strand, I buy a used copy of *The Grapes of Wrath.* Somehow, I never read it during my English Major days, and I always thought that I should have. I tell myself it'll be good for me—like the diet and the budget and the exercise.

Kate, Raphael and I part ways after stopping for ice cream. Rather, they both get ice cream, and I get raspberry sorbet. I expect to find myself lusting after their dripping double scoop chocolate cones, but it's so hot that it doesn't matter—anything sweet and icy tastes good.

Back at my apartment, I check the answering machine to see if Will has called—he hasn't—and then I put my ugly box fan into the window. I lie down in front of it to start reading *The Grapes of Wrath*. Joyce Carol Oates can wait.

At first I'm psyched.

But gradually, I realize that there's something depressing about this.

Not the book. Sure, it's not the most upbeat piece of fiction I've ever read, and I've never particularly liked Steinbeck's descriptive style of writing and the hick dialogue is already getting on my nerves.

But beyond my aversion for Steinbeck, there's something depressing about being inside on a sunny summer Sunday, four stories up with only one window, a drooping philodendron and a boring book for company.

By now, Will is someplace green and woodsy. I picture a big, tree-dappled country house with whitewashed rooms and hardwood floors and rag rugs. Maybe he's unpacking his bags by now. Maybe he's gone to explore North Mannfield with his castmates. Maybe it's like my earlier nightmarish vision, and the men are all gay, except for Will, and the women are all oversexed and built like Nerissa.

I stub out my cigarette, snap my book closed and stand up, striding restlessly over to the window.

The tall buildings cast semi-shadows on the street, and there isn't a patch of green to be seen.

Suddenly, I feel trapped.

I can feel my heart racing.

Dizzy, I take a step back from the window.

I need air—that's what's wrong with me.

I need trees. Or grass. Or water—the East River, even. I just need to feel that this city, with its towering concrete and throngs of strangers and stagnant heat, isn't such a foreign place to be on a glorious summer afternoon.

I put on my sneakers, grab my keys and rush out the door.

I feel better the moment I get outside. I don't know what happened to me back upstairs, but my heart rate slows a bit as I walk down the street, and I'm no longer feeling dizzy or lightheaded.

I hesitate momentarily when I reach the avenue before instinctively turning toward downtown and striding off in that direction.

I'm uncertain where I'm going, but I do know that I want to be anyplace but in my apartment right now.

I arrive at the South Street Seaport nearly half an hour later.

This is tourist central, the kind of place any true New Yorker would avoid at all costs on a sunny weekend afternoon in June.

Much as I want to consider myself a true New Yorker after a year in the city, I can't help but find comfort in the blatant commercialism and in-your-face quaint atmosphere of this area. It's as though I've stepped out of Manhattan and into a theme park without the rides.

I hate to admit that I feel at home here among the

clusters of camera-and-shopping-bag-toting people in bright colors and comfortable shoes; people who look like they popped out of Brookside, or, say, Nebraska.

I savor the almost New England feel of the moored historic ships and the weathered deck planks beneath my feet.

And for once, I'm not repelled by the suburban mall aura of the Seaport's enclosed shopping pavilion, with its chain stores and food court and escalators.

This—all of this—reminds me of the world I left behind, a world where I once assumed I would always belong.

Way back when, before I outgrew Brookside and set my sights on Manhattan, summers meant swimming in lakes and backyard pools, and eating burgers off the grill and driving around aimlessly in cars with my friends, listening to top forty stations.

I might not want to go back to that life, but it suddenly seems to me that I'm not entirely comfortable with the one I have, either.

What's so appealing about living alone in a gloomy one-room apartment in the heart of an on-the-fringe neighborhood?

And why haven't I noticed until now that it's lacking?

I guess it wasn't so bad, my new life—not when Will was here.

Now that he's gone…

The heavenly scent of deep-frying grease lures me to a fast-food place that sells fried chicken and onion rings, among other high-fat faves of mine. I'm about to order the three-piece meal with a shake when I catch a glimpse of my double chin in the chrome countertop.

"I'll have…uh…"

The guy behind the register is poised with classic New York impatience, his expression basically hostile as he waits for my decision.

"A Diet Coke," I announce triumphantly.

I can do this.

I can lose weight.

Sipping my Diet Coke—which is flat and has too much ice—I emerge from the food court onto an outside patio. People mill about, licking ice cream cones and munching french fries with careless abandon.

After draining my soda in a few thirsty gulps and tossing it into an overflowing trash container, I walk over to the railing to look out over the water.

The river is dotted with sailboats, and if you ignore the shadow of the Brooklyn Bridge and the jammed urban landscape beyond, you can almost forget you're in the heart of this massive city.

What the hell am I doing here?

Will is gone, and I have a dead-end job and a crummy apartment. Is this the kind of life I envisioned when I moved to New York? I could have a better life than this anywhere.

Including Brookside.

Brookside, where I'd have family watching my

every move, wondering when I'm going to settle down and get married.

Where there are no interesting jobs and no creative people, where I know everyone and I've done everything there is to do at least a few thousand times, and I've seen everything there is to see....

No.

Maybe I'm not convinced, at this particular moment, that I want to stay here, but I definitely don't want to go back there.

So.

Until I figure out what to do with my life, this is it.

My life is here, in New York, and I'd better start making the best of it.

I turn away from the railing and head for the escalators with renewed determination, even though my mouth waters as I pass the pizza place with its pungent sausage-and-oregano aroma.

I walk swiftly back uptown, sweat dripping off my forehead in the humid air.

By the time I'm striding past a vacant bench at the edge of Thompkins Square Park, and my aching legs are begging me to plop down for a rest, the bombshell has hit me.

Hey, this is exercise!

Look at me...

I'm getting a workout by default.

I marvel at the fact that this extended jaunt of mine was exercise, and it was interesting and it was free— except for the Diet Coke.

I allow myself a little window shopping as a cool-down period. There are Grand Opening streamers in front of a cavernous furniture store. I examine the display windows, admiring in particular an enormous oak sleigh bed. It's the kind of bed you could spend an entire day in; the kind of bed that calls for piles of pillows and a big down comforter.

When I get back up to my apartment, I look around, trying to figure out how I can make it more bearable.

Maybe it would help if I had a real bed, like the one in the window, instead of just an ugly futon *sans* colorful mattress cover.

But this is only temporary, I remind myself. All of it. The futon *and* the apartment. I'm not going to live here forever, even if I do stay in New York.

For now, I'm going to keep exercising and stay on my low-fat diet. I'm going to lose weight, and I'm going to save money.

And when Will comes back in September, we're going to move in together.

I notice that the light is blinking on my answering machine.

My heart leaps….

There's one message.

Splat goes my acrobatic heart.

It's not from Will.

It's from Brenda, telling me she's got the cabbage soup recipe and that she'll bring it to work tomorrow.

"Call me if you're lonely and feel like talking," she says before hanging up.

I *am* lonely.

But I don't feel like talking.

Not to Brenda, who's about to marry the man of her dreams.

The only person I want to talk to is Will, and I have absolutely no way of getting a hold of him. The very thought makes me panicky. He's completely out of touch, a world away, and there's nothing I can do to bring him back into my life, even temporarily.

Now the ball is in his court. He'll decide when we speak to each other again.

But I'm getting carried away.

Of course it won't be long before he calls. He promised he would. And he's bound to miss me, too.

Yeah, but not as much as I miss him.

He's been gone less than twenty-four hours and already I've arrived at the philosophical conclusion that it's infinitely harder to be the one left behind in the usual place than the one who goes someplace new. That's because the usual place is full of reminders—full of holes that the other person used to fill. The new place is ostensibly full of fresh experiences to explore, unique details to notice, people to meet.

I try to imagine what it would be like if Will were the one who stayed behind and I were the one who left.

Somehow, I don't think he would be in my shoes.

The thing is, I can't see him pining away for me here in New York.

Nor can I envision me sailing glibly off for a new

solo adventure without constantly looking over my shoulder.

This is an unsettling realization.

I choose not to dwell on the significance of this insight. Instead, I grab a few dollars and head down to the Food Emporium to pick up some delicious cabbage. An as-yet-untried diet is as much of a new solo adventure as I can handle right now.

Nine

Will has been gone almost one week.

I have lost almost five pounds.

No, I'm serious.

Five pounds.

After bouncing from the protein diet to the fat-free diet to the cabbage-soup diet, I decided to do it the old-fashioned way: by simply eating smaller portions, cutting calories and exercising.

I limit myself to about a thousand calories a day. The strange thing is, I'm not starving. I mean, I occasionally get hungry, but I drink a lot of water. Plus, I guess I've been keeping myself too busy to obsess about what I'll be having for my next meal, the way I usually do.

Twice this week after work, I walked down to the Seaport and back. The other nights I had to stay late at the office to help Jake prepare for a new business presentation. On those nights, I walked the fortysomething blocks home. Not only did I burn calories, but walking saved me subway fare.

Okay, three bucks.

Still, I put the money into an empty Prego jar over the sink. I'm planning to open a savings account as soon as I get enough money that the teller won't laugh in my face. Three bucks a week isn't going to add up fast, but I'm hoping Milos will call me to fill in on a catering job at some point. If he doesn't, maybe I can find weekend work baby-sitting or dog walking or something.

Now it's Saturday morning, and I'm on a bus to Long Island. Not just any bus—the Hampton Jitney, which I boarded on East Fortieth Street off Lex. It's billed as a late-model wide-body coach, complete with complimentary beverages, reclining seats and reading lights. For all this, I've paid almost fifty bucks round trip.

So much for the savings account.

So much for my vow never to put on a bathing suit.

Kate has been begging me all week to come out to her beach house, and it's not like I've got anything better to do. I'm not anxious to put on the ancient bathing suit I dredged up from the recesses of my sock drawer. But the thought of another weekend day alone in my apartment with *The Grapes of Wrath* and the silent phone is more than enough incentive to pack the damned one-piece into my overnight bag and splurge on the Jitney.

Will finally called me on Tuesday night and left a message while I was out walking to the Seaport. I was upset when I came home and found that I'd missed his call, even though he said he'd try me again later.

I guess I didn't believe that he would, but he did. He called at about midnight, when I was nodding off on my futon in front of *Late Night with David Letterman.*

I muted the volume on the television. But as we talked, I could hear voices in the background on Will's end. Loud voices. But it didn't seem to bother Will. In fact, a few times, he interrupted himself to talk to whoever was there—a crowd of his castmates, by the sounds of it.

I tried hard not to let myself be jealous, especially when he covered the mouthpiece at one point to carry on a muffled conversation. As I stared at the television, watching David Letterman silently hand a canned ham to an exuberant balding audience member wearing a turquoise windbreaker, I heard some girl laughing hysterically before Will came back on the line.

"Who was that?" I asked, trying to sound casual.

"It was Esme. She's a real trip."

He said it admiringly.

I know it sounds insane, but at that moment I wanted more than anything for him to consider me a real trip, too. I found myself wondering what he had told his castmates about me, his girlfriend back home. I tried to imagine him saying, "Her name is Tracey and she's a real trip," but somehow it didn't seem as flattering as it did when he said it about the enigmatic Esme.

Furthermore, I wanted my name to be mysterious, rare, exotic: Esme. Instead, I'm Tracey because my mother was reportedly a big Partridge Family fan and her favorite character was the youngest daughter, Tracy—the one who played the tambourine and had no lines. What an inspiration, huh? Mom daringly added an "e" to the spelling.

Anyway, as Will and I talked about other things, I found myself mentally conjuring the fun-loving Esme, undoubtedly a confident, willowy brunette with a bawdy sense of humor and a penchant for practical jokes. I wanted to ask him more about her, yet he had mentioned her only in passing, and only because I asked. I didn't want to come across as a cliché: the jealous, prying, long-distance girlfriend.

Yet that was exactly who I had become.

Will told me that the first show had been cast. It was *West Side Story,* and he was a Shark.

I could tell he was disappointed he hadn't gotten a lead, even though he quickly said, "My voice isn't right for Tony, anyway."

"Yes, it is!" I protested loyally.

He sounded irritated with me when he pointed out that they would be doing a new show every other week, and theater management had promised that everyone would get a shot at a lead sooner or later.

"Well, when you get your lead, I'll be in the front row, Will."

Somehow, I knew from his muttered response that hadn't been the right thing to say, either.

He seemed distracted, and we didn't talk for long—he said other people were waiting to use the phone, and that he'd try me back again after the weekend. Opening night is Saturday—tonight—and afterward, there's a cast party. Sunday there's a matinee and an evening performance. Monday, the theater is dark, just like Broadway, so I'm assuming he'll call me then.

So here I am on a bright Saturday morning, riding on a glorified bus with other pasty, beach-house-bound Manhattanites. There are plenty of good-looking Wall Street types onboard, and hordes of linen-clad Upper East Side girls in groups and gay men toting shopping bags: bottles of French wine and fresh basil and goat cheese.

I had a grapefruit for breakfast before I left my apartment, but I'm already famished. A stick of sugarless gum doesn't help in the least. A cigarette would, but I can't smoke on the bus, so I'll have to be content with Trident until we reach our destination.

I brought along *The Grapes of Wrath, The Great Gatsby* and the latest issue of *She* magazine, courtesy of Raphael. I used to have a subscription, but now that Raphael works there, he gives me every issue for free, so I let my subscription expire.

I find myself opting for *She* and an interview with Kate Hudson over the tribulations of the Joads. I'll save their westward journey for my own when I return to Manhattan tomorrow night.

I've never been out to Long Island, and as far as I can tell from my occasional glances out the window, it's one big concrete highway dotted with strip malls and split levels.

But gradually, the view becomes a little more rustic as we pass through the pine barrens, and is downright seafaring by the time the bus pulls into West Hampton at ten-thirty.

Kate is there to meet me, wearing shorts and a cropped T-shirt, the telltale pink straps of her new bikini visible at the wide neckline. She's accompanied by this guy I've never seen before.

She gives me a big hug as though we haven't seen each other in lo, so many months. But I've known Kate long enough by now to know that it's not fake affection; that's just her warm, Southern way.

She releases me and motions at the guy. "Tracey, this is Billy. Billy, Tracey."

Apparently, we're gong to be on a first-name-only basis, as though we're new arrivals being introduced on one of those reality TV shows.

Billy smiles at me and says hello, but not in an overly friendly way.

Or maybe it's just my own insecurity. What do I expect, another big ol' Kate-style hug?

I wonder who he is, but Kate offers no explanation as we walk through a parking lot.

I light a cigarette, and assume Billy's a nonsmoker when he looks at me as though I've just injected crack cocaine into my vein.

He has on Timberlands without socks, khaki shorts and a rumpled pink Ralph Lauren button-down with the sleeves rolled up and the tail hanging out. Somehow the color doesn't look the least bit effeminate on him. Even his name manages to be masculine on him. Funny, isn't it, how "William" would be decidedly faggy, but Billy is somehow rugged.

He obviously works out, and he's strong, considering the way he effortlessly hoists my bulging, leaden overnight bag over his shoulder.

He's got sun-streaked blond hair—yes, sun-streaked, in New York, in June—and a healthy-looking tan. Both look natural, but then, so do Kate's hair and her tan—and her blue eyes. So you never know. As I said before, Kate's hair is bleached blond and her eyes are tinted blue with contact lenses, and I happen to know that her honey-toned tan came out of an outrageously expensive cosmetic-counter bottle over the past week. She doesn't believe in exposing her delicate Delacroix skin to the sun.

It turns out Billy has driven Kate to town to meet me, and that he's one of her roommates. They only met last night, but they seem pretty friendly already.

I learn that Billy lives on the Upper East Side and works on Wall Street. Surprise, surprise.

Leave it to Kate to rent a beach house with a guy who looks like this.

Again, with the TV reality thing, I look at him and imagine a caption superimposed over his onscreen-image: *Billy, 24, Commodities Trader, New York.*

His car is even more impressive than he is—a black BMW convertible.

As we walk up to it, Billy gives me a look from behind his Ray-Bans. Catching his drift, I hurriedly stub out the cigarette before he can ask me to. As if I'd consider smoking in somebody's car—even a convertible. I mean, I'm not that gauche.

I feed my food-and-nicotine-deprived self another stick of Trident as Kate offers me the front seat. Of course, I decline.

So here I am, perched in the middle of the back seat, leaning forward like a four-year-old trying to eavesdrop on her parents as we drive through the quaint, traffic-clogged, tree-lined streets of the decidedly upscale old-fashioned town. We head out along a highway past weathered-looking shingled houses perched on stilts in the grassy dunes.

The sky is a deep, clear blue today. So is the water in the distance. And so, I'd be willing to bet, are Billy's eyes behind those movie-star sunglasses of his.

The radio is blasting and Kate and Billy are chattering away in the front seat, and the warm wind is whipping so that every time I open my mouth to make a comment, my hair flies into my gum. I want to chuck the gum overboard, but somehow I know Billy wouldn't approve if he caught me.

Finally, we're turning down a narrow, sandy lane and pulling up in front of a boxy, modern, shingled two-story house set high off the ground. Rather, we're pulling up in *back* of the house; Kate quickly points out that the front of it faces the water. That explains the no-frills look of things from this angle. Knowing what she's paying for a half share in this place, I expected something far more extravagant.

Billy politely carries my bag up the flight of steps and deposits it just inside the door, then turns and informs us that he'll see us later.

"Where's he going?" I ask Kate, hearing his car start up outside momentarily.

"I have no idea." She sounds disappointed, and I realize she's into him.

This shouldn't be news to me. He's just Kate's type—a rich, good-looking WASP.

Kate admits freely that she's not living in Manhattan to launch a serious career or even to soak up culture—even though she majored in art at the University of Alabama. She's hoping to land a certain kind of husband. A Billy kind of husband.

That's why she continues to work as an office temp—the better to meet a Wall Street guy. She sure doesn't need the piddling salary, since her parents pay her rent and all her expenses, and deposit "pocket money" into her account weekly.

I've seen pictures of their house back in Mobile,

and it looks like Tara in *Gone With The Wind*. Swear-to-God, it's one of those big old Southern plantations with white pillars and a circular drive and towering moss-draped trees.

Kate has two older sisters, both of whom apparently live in Mobile plantation houses of their own with their wealthy fellow-Alabaman husbands.

But Kate says she's never been attracted to Southern men. Her college boyfriend was a New Yorker, and he apparently gave her a taste of the Manhattan society life she craves.

Knowing Kate, I guess I was expecting more of this house in the Hamptons—maybe china and crystal and chandeliers.

Now I look around the big combination kitchen-living room we're standing in, taken aback by the lack of elegance.

The furniture is strictly functional, all of it as beige and rectangular as the house itself. The place seems to be empty, but there is evidence of its inhabitants.

Snapple bottles and today's *Times* litter the coffee table.

A fragrant half-full pot of coffee sits on the countertop.

Several pairs of shoes are scattered on a mat by the door.

A stereo is playing in the background…hip-hop music—not my favorite.

At the far end of the room there are sliding glass

doors leading out to a wide wooden deck. Beyond that are the dunes and, presumably, the beach.

"So what do you think?" Kate asks expectantly.

"It's nice."

"Not the house," she says, as though I should've known. *"Billy."*

"Oh, *Billy*. He's nice."

Her disappointed, expectant expression says, *Is that all?* So I try to come up with a new adjective. Something other than *arrogant*.

"Cute, too." I am nothing if not articulate. "Very cute."

"Yeah, he is cute," Kate agrees readily.

"What's up with you and him?"

"How did you know something is up with us?"

"Because I'm psychic, why else?"

She smirks.

"So what's happening with you guys, Kate?"

"We hooked up last night. We all went out to this club, and…well, you know. Not that there was any privacy when we got back here. We're all three to a bedroom, and there are twelve people staying here— thirteen, including you. So, you know, things didn't really…advance," she says demurely.

"Meaning, you didn't have sex."

"Of course not! I just met him, Tracey." Her Southern accent is more pronounced than usual, which is what always happens when she's doing her best to act offended and ladylike.

I happen to know she bedded her last fling—a Boston blueblood visiting New York en route to grad school on the West Coast—the night she met him at a happy hour at some wine bar in the East Forties.

But hey, if she's in the mood to reclaim her virtue, who am I to burst her bubble?

"How do you like it out here?" I ask her as she shows me the way up a flight of stairs and down a hall to the room we'll be sharing with two other women. I'm dragging my bag up step by step. *Thump, thump, thump.* It weighs a ton.

"I love it out here. It's great," Kate says, and stops to look down over her shoulder at me. "What do you have in there? Bricks?"

"Just some shorts and a bathing suit," I tell her innocently.

Actually, I also brought several potential outfits for tonight, not knowing what people wear to clubs in the Hamptons and hoping skimpy isn't in. I don't do skimpy.

Plus—just in case I somehow finish *The Grapes of Wrath*—there's that hardcover edition of *The Great Gatsby*. Yeah, it's set on the North Shore rather than in the Hamptons, but it seemed a logical literary choice for a Long Island weekend.

Makeup, sunscreen, shampoo, conditioner and a hair dryer.

Sneakers, sandals and two pairs of black flats, one dressy, one not.

Oh, and a six-pack of Diet Raspberry Snapple Iced

Tea, just in case there's none at hand and I'm tempted to indulge in something more caloric.

"Next summer I want to do a full share," Kate says as we head down the hall past several closed doors. "I can't believe I can't come out here every weekend. But we're all trying to work it out so that some of us can come out on our off-weekends if we don't mind sleeping on the floor in the living room."

"You? Sleep on a floor?"

"I know, it doesn't sound very comfy, does it?" She bobs a perfectly arched eyebrow at me. "But Billy has a full share, which means he gets a bed every weekend, so you never know, Tracey."

"But Kate, y'all just met!" I do a perfect imitation of her drawl.

"Yeah, but we've got the whole summer ahead of us, if you know what I mean." She grins and opens the door to our room.

The two twin beds are unmade. The queen-size one is neatly made up, and I recognize the pink-and-green flower-sprigged Laura Ashley comforter on it.

"That has to be yours, Kate," I say, going over and sitting on the edge. "I didn't realize you had to bring your own bedding."

"You don't, but I can't sleep without my comforter."

"So you're dragging it back and forth every weekend?"

"Every other weekend," she amends, "but no, I'm not. I bought a new one for my apartment."

This strikes me as incredibly indulgent. So typical of Kate. "So what are you going to do with identical comforters after the summer?" I ask her.

"I'll give one of them to you," she offers.

"That's okay. My futon isn't queen-size."

"By then maybe you'll have a big-girl bed," she says in a mock-Mommy tone.

"Mmm-hmm."

What she doesn't know is that by then, I'll be moving into a new place with Will.

Okay, it's not as though my heart is set on it, but let's face it, that's the logical next step. I mean, how long can a level-headed, committed couple live in two separate studio apartments, me in a borderline dangerous neighborhood and he with a borderline dangerous—if only in the *temptress* sense—roommate?

"The bathroom is in there," Kate says, nodding toward an adjoining door. "Why don't you get changed, and we'll go down to the beach?"

The moment of truth.

I knew it was coming, yet now that it's here, I feel as caught off guard as I would if she'd just told me I'm going to be driving the getaway car while she knocks over a bank.

But the sun is shining and the ocean is yards away, and all I can say is, "Sure, I'll be right back."

After all, I've lost five pounds. Maybe it won't be so bad—me in a bathing suit, I mean.

Kate goes over to stand in front of the mirror on

the back of the closet door, unfastens her ponytail, and starts brushing her hair.

I start lugging my boulder-filled bag toward the bathroom door.

"Why don't you just grab your suit out of there?" Kate asks around the bobby pins sticking out of her mouth.

"Oh, I need to dig for it—it's buried. Plus I need to find my cover-up."

Cover-up.

Only a painter's drop cloth will do, and unfortunately, I've brought along everything but.

The closest I can come is an oversize T-shirt in a weathered khaki green that looked flattering when I bought it at Eddie Bauer last summer, but now—at least in the yellowish light above the sink in the windowless bathroom—makes me look even more washed-out and pale than I really am.

But at least it hides my bathing suit, a hideous black getup designed for "full figures," with a bold purple vee down the stomach, supposedly an optical illusion to slim the waist. The high-cut legs are supposed to do the same thing for my thighs. How, I have no idea, since common logic says that if you want to camouflage something, you show less of it, not more. My thighs are fully bared in all their dimpled glory, sagging below my gut that seems to defy confinement in this delightfully girdle-like memory fabric, or whatever the salesgirl called it way back when I bought it.

There's no full-length mirror in the bathroom,

which I'm not sure whether to consider a blessing or a curse. I have no idea how I look in this thing.

Actually, I have an idea. Hence, the tent-like green T-shirt. I throw on a pair of shorts for good measure, along with the only pair of sandals I own: black Teyvas that seem like they'd be more at home on a desert trek than in this chi-chi beach community.

I emerge from the bathroom to find Kate standing there waiting for me in a cute little terry-cloth cover-up. Her bare legs and feet are evenly "tanned," and her toenails are polished in a pink that perfectly matches her new bikini. She's Southern California perfect: blond and toned and pretty, from the tousled, sun-streaked hair she's casually pinned on top of her head to the gold ankle bracelet she's fastened around one slender ankle.

It's the ankle bracelet that gets me.

It's so slinky/sexy—so right on Kate. And Kate is so right in that outfit, in this place.

My first thought is that I would give anything to be her.

My second thought is, *Thank God Will isn't here.*

I wouldn't want him to see me looking like this.

Nor would I want him to see Kate looking like that.

The funny thing is, Kate doesn't even find him attractive, and Lord knows she would never do anything about it if she did.

But there's no question in my mind that Will would find this scantily clad, beach bunny Kate attractive.

Any red-blooded man would. Next to her, I'm woefully inadequate.

The last bit of lingering pride over my five-pound weight loss trickles out of me, replaced by utter despair.

"All set?" Kate asks sunnily, picking up a straw beach bag that's as right as her outfit and her—well, her *self.*

It's hard not to hate her right now; it really is.

It's harder still not to hate myself.

We grab a couple of folding sand chairs from the deck. As we make our way down the sandy path toward the wide expanse of beach, I remind myself that I'm already making progress toward my goal. That by this time next year, I, too, will be a goddess.

But it doesn't help.

For one thing, I'm not convinced I can successfully diet and exercise my way down to true goddess status.

For another, I want to look good *now*...not next year, or even next fall, or next month.

"There's everyone," Kate says, pointing to a cluster of people straight ahead.

"Everyone?"

"My housemates. Come on, I'll introduce you."

There's nothing for me to do but walk over to the half-dozen or so people who are just as attractive as Kate. Well, not all of them. There's one weasly-looking guy, Kenny, with glasses, kinky black hair and a knobby body. But he's sharing a blanket with

Shelby, a gorgeous redhead who turns out to be his girlfriend—and Kenny turns out to be filthy rich.

He's not staying in the beach house; he's staying at his parents' place in South Hampton. So is Shelby. But they're here for the day visiting Lucy and Amelia, friends of Shelby's. Lucy lives in Kate's building, which is how Kate hooked up with this crowd in the first place.

Lucy is as pretty and skinny as Kate and Shelby, but I'm relieved to see that Amelia looks like she's consumed her share of chips and beer—both of which are in her hands as she lounges in a sand chair, not looking the least bit uncomfortable to have her cellulite on full display in front of these bathing beauties and Chad and Ray, the two hottie guy roommates who are basically drooling over everyone but me and Amelia.

I sit on my sand chair facing the water, keeping my knees bent because my upper thighs don't seem to look quite as flabby that way. I refuse to take off my T-shirt, telling everyone that I forgot my sunscreen and I don't want to risk a burn.

"You can use mine," Kate offers graciously, tossing me a bottle of Clinique SPF 30.

"I'm actually allergic to this," I tell her.

"Nobody's allergic to Clinique, Tracey."

Uh-oh. Really?

"I am," I lie. "I have to use special sunscreen. My dermatologist prescribes it. I have ultra-sensitive skin."

"So do I," Kate says, frowning. "I never heard of—"

"Really, Kate, I'm fine," I say, shooting her a look. Maybe she gets it then, because she shuts up.

For a while, we all sit there and talk and drink beer, and I'm much more relaxed. But the sun is directly overhead now, and I'm sweating profusely in my T-shirt.

Billy shows up with a cooler, and a couple of other guys, Randy and Wade. Once he's there, Kate pretty much abandons me. I'd be irritated if it weren't for Amelia, who turns out to be friendly and not the least bit snobby, unlike Lucy and the others.

I marvel at how she can sit there in her bright yellow one-piece, a good forty pounds overweight, and not seem the least bit self-conscious about how she looks or what she eats. She downs half a can of Pringles—the full-fat kind—and at least three beers.

She also admits that she can't swim, for which I'm grateful, because I don't have to sit here by myself when everybody else goes into the water.

"Can't you swim, either?" she asks me, rubbing coconut-scented lotion on her chubby, freckled arms.

"Not very well," I lie. "Besides, the water's too cold at this time of year." I wipe a trickle of sweat from my hairline.

"It doesn't seem to bother them," she says, motioning at the splashing group out in the water. I hear Kate shriek as Billy tries to dunk her under.

I decide I don't like him. He's too cocky.

"He's such an ass," Amelia says, and I think she's talking about Billy until I see her pointing at Wade.

"Really? What's up with him?" I glance at the square-jawed dark-haired guy who's good-looking but shorter than me. He seemed really quiet while he was sitting here.

"He's a user. When he gets drunk, he's all over anything that moves. I stupidly fell for his big act last summer, but I won't do that again. Stay away from him, Tracey. Trust me."

"Oh, I have a boyfriend," I tell her.

"Really?"

I tell her about Will.

"I went out with an actor, once," she says. "Actually, we're still friends."

"How long ago did you break up?"

"Three years ago. We were in college. He realized he was gay. Now he and his lover live two blocks away from me, and we all hang out."

"Oh." I don't know what to say. It sounds awful.

I try to imagine me and Will broken up yet still hanging out. There's no way. Especially not if he had another lover—even a male one.

Not that there's the slightest chance Will is gay, no matter what Kate suspects.

"He's always trying to fix me up," Amelia goes on. "But I keep telling him, I don't want to go out with any more actors. They're all too self-absorbed— I mean, not all of them," she adds hastily, for my benefit, "but the ones I've met have been. I'm sure your boyfriend isn't...."

"No, he's not self-absorbed," I assure her.

But the truth is, he is.

It's not as if I've never noticed before.

But I find myself suddenly angry at Will, noticing how many times it's all had to be about him. How it's never about me.

Whose fault is that? a tiny voice asks in my head.

I'm the one who puts up with Will's ego. I'm the one who never demands anything for myself. Why?

Because everyone has their faults.

And because I love him.

What's wrong with that?

"Are you okay?" Amelia asks, and I turn to see her watching me. "You look like you're suddenly upset about something."

"It's just...my boyfriend. I miss him. That's all."

"Maybe you can visit him."

"I'm definitely planning on it."

But suddenly, I'm not at all anxious to see Will in his new environment. I don't want to see the cast house and meet Esme and see how much fun he's having without me.

I just want him back in New York, where he belongs. I want everything to be back to normal.

It's only been a week since he left.

How am I going to survive eleven more?

Ten

"Tracey, it's nice to see you again," Milos says, meeting me in the reception area of his brownstone apartment that doubles as headquarters for his catering business, Eat Drink Or Be Married.

I've only met him once, when I stopped by with Will, who had to pick up a paycheck. But Milos clasps both my hands in his, as though we're old friends.

He's a tiny man. Basically, I dwarf him. Yet there's a commanding sense about him anyway; a charisma and confidence that manage to impress but not intimidate me.

"I'm sorry I didn't call you back right away. I was out on Long Island all weekend, and I didn't get your message until Sunday night."

"It's all right. I appreciate your coming over to meet with me," he says in his Slavic accent. "I know you're on your lunch hour, so let's get down to business right away. Will says you're an experienced waitress."

I nod, hoping I don't have to go into detail.

"Have you ever French-served?"

Huh?

"No," I tell him.

At least, I don't think I've ever French-served. Who knows what that even means?

He raises one dark eyebrow. "Have you ever worked for a caterer before?"

"No, I actually…I worked in a restaurant."

"Here in the city?"

"Back in my hometown. But I'm a fast learner. I'm sure I can catch on."

He looks reluctant, but he nods. "I'm short-handed. Will said you might be able to fill in. I'm doing a cocktail party Tuesday night on Central Park South…can you make it?"

Tuesday? That's tomorrow. I'm still exhausted from my weekend in the Hamptons—too much drinking and dancing, and only an hour and a half of sleep, not counting my snooze on the Jitney on the way home yesterday afternoon.

But I can go to bed early tonight to catch up, and I can definitely use the money, considering what I spent over the weekend.

I ask Milos, "What time do you need me? I usually don't get out of work until—"

"If you can be there at seven so that I can have somebody show you what to do, it would be good. We'll be there doing setup."

"Seven is fine."

"Good. The party starts at nine."

Nine? That means I won't get home until late, and I have to get up for work Wednesday morning.

"Basically, all you'll be doing for this event is circulating trays of hot and cold hors d'oeuvres," Milos tells me.

Oh, so that's what he meant by French-serve. I can do that.

"You'll learn to French-serve before I need you to do a formal affair, like a wedding," Milos informs me.

Formal affair? Wedding? Clearly, he has big plans for me. Clearly, French serving has nothing to do with passing hors d'oeuvres.

"I'll have you take our three-hour training course at some point in the near future," Milos promises, "but for now, you'll wing it. It won't be hard. We're in the midst of a ragout craze."

I nod.

"Any questions?"

I shake my head no. What the hell is a ragout craze?

"Okay. Good. Now it's back to my croquembouche."

Mental note: Ask Will ASAP what the hell Milos is talking about.

Five minutes later, I'm on my way back to my office with a pale-gray Nehru jacket tucked under my arm. That's the top half of my catering uniform. Milos said I should wear black slacks and flat black shoes with it. At least my lower half will be in slimming black.

The jacket isn't exactly flattering, and it seemed to cling around my hips when I tried it on in Milos's dressing room, but I was too embarrassed to ask him for a bigger size. Anyway, it was a Large. Who knows if there even is a bigger size?

I've got enough time to walk the twenty-some blocks back uptown. I haven't gotten any exercise all weekend, aside from dancing on Saturday night. The good thing is, I haven't eaten much, either. In fact, Saturday night at the beach house, all I had when we barbecued on the deck was a plain hamburger—no bun—and some salad. I didn't want to pork out in front of everyone.

We went out drinking and dancing at some club. I nursed a Bloody Mary the whole time—alcohol can really put on the pounds. As Amelia predicted, Wade drank too much and tried to come on to me. I'd have been totally turned off even if she hadn't warned me about him. He kept trying to grab my butt on the dance floor, and he made a comment about how he's into big-breasted women. I guess he thought I'd find that flattering. What a jerk. He ended up taking off with some girl who had a share in Quogue, and we didn't see him for the rest of the weekend.

For that matter, I barely saw Kate, either. She and

Billy hooked up and left the club together. She checked with me first, though, just to make sure I wouldn't mind catching a ride back to the house with the others. If it hadn't been for Amelia, I would have insisted on third-wheeling it with Kate and Billy, since none of the other housemates had given me the time of day. But Amelia was fun, and she and I hung out on the beach all day Sunday while Kate and Billy and some of the others went waterskiing.

For lunch, Amelia inhaled three hot dogs from the beach snack bar.

I had a small bag of popcorn and a Diet Snapple.

It was late when I got back to my apartment last night, so I didn't eat then, either. I was too exhausted. All I wanted to do was sleep.

This morning, I had half a Kaiser roll and some nonfat cream cheese before I headed for the subway. I'm hungry again now, but not starving. I figure I'll stop and get something before I go back up to my office.

Maybe it's my imagination, but the black linen skirt I'm wearing seems pretty loose around the waistband. I may have lost another pound over the weekend. Maybe two pounds.

It's another steamy summer day, and the midtown sidewalks are jammed. I light a cigarette and smoke as I walk, thinking about the weekend I just had and the catering job ahead of me, and Will, as usual. He's never far from my thoughts.

Heading home on the subway last night after getting

back into town, I convinced myself there might be an answering-machine message from him—even though he'd said he wouldn't call. Naturally, I was disappointed. I shouldn't have set myself up. The only message was from Milos.

But I'm sure Will will call tonight, I remind myself as I walk into the deli adjacent to the lobby of my building. The place is jammed, as usual. I make my way through the crowd, past the deli counter and the big hot and cold buffet tables. Maybe I'll get a salad, I think, glancing at the cold food.

Or some steamed vegetables.

The crowd is two deep around both buffets, so I go to the back to get a beverage first, my thoughts drifting back to Will.

He said he would call, after the weekend. Which means tonight.

I don't know what I'll do if he doesn't—not that—

"Oh, sorry!" I blurt as I crash into someone just as he opens the door to the refrigerated beverage compartment.

"Tracey!"

The guy turns around, and I recognize his face and I know that I know him, but for a split second, I think he's someone from work.

That's because I'd never in a million years expect to find *him* in here.

"Buckley?"

Yup, it's him. Buckley O'Hanlon.

"What are you doing here?" I ask, stunned.

"Getting lunch, actually," he says, grabbing a Pepsi from the compartment and closing the door again. "I'm doing a freelance job for a firm in the building."

"What kind of firm?" I ask, wondering, with a sinking heart, if it's Blaire Barnett.

"Seyville Inc.," he says. "It's a cleaning service with offices on the second floor."

"Oh."

"Do you work around here, too?"

"Upstairs. The thirty-third floor." A whole separate elevator bank, thank God. Not that it isn't the most bizarre coincidence in the world that he ends up working in my building.

He states the obvious. "What a coincidence, huh?"

"Yeah, really." I pretend to be fascinated by the row of diet sodas inside the compartment. Never mind that the glass is almost completely fogged-over.

"You know, Tracey, I tried calling you after—"

"Oh, you did?" I quickly cut in, not wanting him to elaborate, since we both know what he's talking about.

But elaborate he must.

"Yeah, after that date we had…the one that really wasn't a date because you thought—"

"I know. I'm sorry," I say, irritated with him. Does he have to spell everything out? I mean, it's not as though we had more than one encounter.

"Every time I tried to call, I got an answering machine."

"Oh, well, I'm not really home that often," I say,

wondering where he got my number. I thought I gave him a fake one. Maybe Joseph or—

"It was the answering machine of somebody whose outgoing message was in Arabic," he informs me.

"Really?" I feign confusion. "That's odd. You must have had the wrong number."

"Yeah, every time," he says, but in a good-natured way.

I reach into the compartment and grab a Diet Raspberry Snapple Iced Tea. What I want to do is step right into the chilly interior and close the door after me…and not just because my head is sweat-soaked from the long walk in the midday sun.

"Unless you accidentally gave me the wrong number?" Buckley asks when I remove my upper self from the fridge.

"I must have, by accident. Sorry."

"It's okay. The reason I was calling was to tell you it was no big deal—your thinking I was—"

"Oh, good. Thanks. Because I didn't mean to…you know…"

"Insult me?" He grins. "It's okay. There are worse things you could have assumed about me. And I figured you might be embarrassed, so I wanted you to know it was okay."

I notice that he has nice, white teeth—the kind of smile that, if it belonged to a cartoon character, would have a big sparkly glint bouncing off the front tooth. He's wearing a pale blue long-sleeved dress shirt with khaki pants and a yellow tie. The sleeves are rolled up, and I see that his forearms are tanned.

"Are you on your way to the dry cleaner's?" Buckley asks, motioning at my plastic-wrapped Nehru jacket.

"Actually, just coming from a lunch, uh, meeting," I say. Now I feel compelled to elaborate. "I had to, uh, meet with someone downtown. This catering guy I'm going to do a job for," I add, for some reason feeling inclined to give this almost-stranger the intimate details of my life.

Sometimes I do that. Only when I'm nervous.

And Buckley O'Hanlon makes me nervous.

If he hadn't kissed me, everything would be fine. I mean, yes, it would have been a little awkward, my having assumed he was gay and that we were going to the movies platonically when he thought it was a date. But that kiss made everything incredibly uncomfortable.

And the reason for that is…

I liked it.

I thoroughly enjoyed being kissed by Buckley O'Hanlon.

Worse yet, seeing him again makes me wish he would kiss me again. Here. On the lips. In the narrow, crowded aisle of this dingy Third Avenue deli.

Somebody jostles him from behind, and he takes a step closer to me to get out of the way.

Now his face isn't far from mine, and I have to

admit: I desperately want him to put his arms around me and kiss me senseless.

But he doesn't.

He just smiles and says, "They're making me a sandwich."

"What?" I blink, trying to decipher his words, wondering why I feel as though he's speaking a foreign language when they're plain English. He's not making sense. Have I been drinking?

No. Maybe it's all that walking in the hot sun....

"I've got to go get it before they give it away," he adds cryptically.

"What?" I say again.

What's he talking about? Is it just me, or is he speaking in non-sequiturs?

Either he's the one who's been drinking, or I must have missed something while I was fantasizing about kissing him.

"My sandwich," he says, and points to the deli counter on the opposite end of the store.

"Oh!" *Duh.* Now I get it.

"I ordered a roast beef and Swiss and I only came over here to grab a soda," he says, motioning with his can. "So I guess I should..."

"Yeah, go ahead," I say, practically shoving him away.

Because the thing is, as long as his face is only inches from mine, I can't be expected to avoid thinking about kissing him.

"See you," Buckley says with a wave from the deli

line as I march up to the register with my bottle of Snapple.

I wave back, telling myself that it's not him. It could be any reasonably attractive guy, and I'd react the same way. Nine days of celibacy have left me all hot and bothered. I just didn't notice until Buckley came along and I remembered that kiss.

I carry my Snapple back up to my office, remembering only when I get into the elevator that I forgot to get something to eat, too. Well, it's too late now. I can't go back down to the deli knowing I might bump into Buckley in the lobby.

"How'd it go?" Brenda asks, sticking her head out of her cubicle as I walk by.

How'd it go? How does she know?

"Did he like you?"

I must be giving her a blank look, because she prompts, "Milos."

"Oh!"

"What'd you think I meant?"

Buckley.

"I knew what you meant. I just…I think I'm having heatstroke," I say, holding the cold, slippery Snapple bottle up to my burning forehead.

"You look flushed," Brenda agrees. "Did you walk back in this heat?"

I nod. "I need the exercise. I've been trying to walk every day."

"You're crazy. You can't keep that up in this

weather. You're going to collapse on a sidewalk some-where.''

"I'm fine, Brenda," I say, grinning at her worried expression.

"If you want to exercise, do an aerobics video," Brenda suggests.

"Aerobics? Me? I'm the least coordinated person you'll ever meet, Brenda."

"Anyone can do aerobics," she says. "I'll bring you one of my Jane Fonda tapes tomorrow. You've got a VCR at home, right?"

I nod. It was a going-away present from my family last May.

"I'll bring you a tape tomorrow. How's the cabbage soup thing working out?"

"Great," I say, not in the mood to tell her that woman cannot live by cabbage soup alone.

"Really? I went off it the first day," she tells me. "I've gained two pounds since last week."

"You don't look it," I say truthfully. Brenda is one of those people whose figure is hard to gauge. She wears a lot of baggy clothes and blazers, and it's hard to know just what's under them. But she doesn't look overweight to me, in her loosely fitted, poppy-colored cotton summer dress. Plus, that big pile of hair of hers tends to call attention away from the rest of her.

"Paulie wanted me to make him a lasagne yester-day," she tells me. "He ate half of it. I ate almost all the rest."

My mouth waters immediately. Lasagne. My God, I haven't had lasagne since...

That reminds me. "Brenda, do you think Jake would let me leave work early on the Friday before the long Fourth of July weekend?"

"Maybe. Why?"

"Because I want to take a bus back home. It's my parents' anniversary. We're supposed to have a party for them."

"You should go." She lowers her voice and leans toward me. "Just call in sick that Friday."

"I don't think I should do that. What if Jake found out I wasn't really sick?"

"How would he?"

"What if he calls me at home?"

She shrugs. "You're too sick to answer the phone."

"I think I'd better just ask him if I can leave early. I think there's a three o'clock bus from the Port Authority."

"Can you take a later one?"

I shake my head. "It's a nine-hour trip, Brenda."

"I thought you were from upstate!"

"I am. It's a big state."

"Wow. That big?"

"Nine hours' worth," I say solemnly.

It never ceases to amaze me how oblivious some people are to the rest of New York State. To them, upstate means Westchester county.

"Tracey? Is that you?" Jake calls from down the hall.

"Sounds like you're being summoned," Brenda says, rolling her eyes. "Love the way he expects to sit at his desk and yell for you instead of coming to get you like a normal human being."

"It's okay," I say, heading for Jake's office.

But maybe she's right. I never noticed how demeaning it was until she pointed it out.

I find Jake lounging in his chair, feet on the desk as usual. "I need you to run an errand for me," he says. "It's my mother's birthday, and I forgot to have Laurie get her something over the weekend. Go down to the chocolatier on the corner of Forty-third and buy her a few pounds of Belgian truffles. Here's some cash."

He reaches into his pocket and hands me a fistful of tens and twenties. I take the money. What else can I do? Refuse to do a personal errand for him?

Maybe Brenda would.

I know Latisha and Yvonne would. They're always telling me not to put up with Jake's crap. But I can't figure out how to say no.

Besides, is it so bad? He's just asking me for a favor. And I get to get out of the office for a little while, too.

I can have a cigarette.

And get more exercise...

Although I can just imagine how tempted I'll be in a chocolate shop on an empty stomach.

"How much should I spend?" I ask him.

"See if you can keep it under a hundred. Oh, and

when you walk by Hallmark on your way back up, pick up a card for her, too, okay?'' he adds. ''One that says Happy Birthday, Mother, from your Loving Son, or some bullshit like that.''

''Okay.'' I clear my throat as he picks up his phone, poised to dial. ''Listen, Jake, I've got a list of possible product names for you.''

He obviously doesn't know what I'm talking about, because he looks vaguely up from the phone and says, ''What?''

''For the all-week deodorant?'' I remind him.

''Oh! Right. Great.'' He starts dialing.

''Do you, uh, want to discuss them?''

''Sure. Get me the list.''

''Now?''

''No, just put it in my in-box, and I'll check it out later.''

''Sure.'' There's nothing for me to do but go back to my desk and put the list in his in-box before grabbing my cigarettes and sunglasses.

''Where are you going?'' Yvonne asks as I pass her in the corridor on the way to the elevators.

''I have to run an errand for Jake.''

''Really?'' She rolls her eyes. ''Where is he sending you this time?''

I pretend not to hear her as I press the button for the elevator.

Why do I care if my friends think Jake takes advantage of me? He's my boss. I'm supposed to do whatever he asks me to do, right?

Right.

Even if it's personal business on company time?

I guess.

As I walk across the lobby, I find myself scanning the place for Buckley O'Hanlon. No sign of him.

That's a relief, I tell myself. The last thing I need is to run into him again.

Which is exactly what I tell Kate when I meet her after work for a drink. I'd really rather just go straight home, but she called this afternoon and begged me to have a glass of wine with her at a sidewalk café not far from my apartment. She said she needs advice.

But we've been sitting here almost fifteen minutes, and so far, she just wants to talk about me. Which is how Buckley came up in the first place.

Because Kate asked me how my day went, and after I told her about the upcoming job for Milos and the chocolate errand for Jake's mother's birthday, I couldn't very well leave out the whole Buckley part.

Okay, maybe I could have.

Maybe I wanted to talk about him.

About how reluctant I was to see him, and how I hope I don't see him again.

"Are you sure about that?" Kate asks slyly.

"Of course I'm sure. Why?"

"You kissed him—"

"He kissed me—"

"And Raphael says he's a hottie."

"Raphael says everyone's a hottie. Buckley's no big deal."

And really, he isn't. Not by Kate's standards. Not by most standards. He just happens to be a very nice, friendly, middle-class, guy-next-door type. Everything about him is middle-class ordinary. Maybe that's what's so appealing about him. There aren't many guys like him in New York.

But I left a generic town full of middle-class ordinary people. I never wanted to be one of them, or date one of them.

Not that I want to date Buckley, I hastily remind myself.

"Well, if you're not interested in him romantically, can't you just be friends with Buckley?" Kate asks. "The guy works in your building. It's like some kind of sign."

Kate is a big believer in signs. She claims that the way she decided to break up with her college boy-friend was when they were walking in the park one day, having an argument, and a bird flew overhead and pooped on his shoulder.

"I have enough friends," I assure Kate, and take a sip of my merlot before asking her, "What was it you wanted to talk to me about?"

"My mother called me last night when I got home from the beach. She said Daddy took a hit the last time the stock market fell, and they want me to move into a cheaper place, or find a roommate."

"Wow, really?"

I'm surprised.

For one thing, I was sure she had asked me to meet

her so that she could ask my advice about her new relationship with Billy.

For another, I've never heard Kate speak so candidly about the fact that her parents support her. I mean, it's no secret, but she doesn't usually come right out and admit it.

"What are you going to do?" I ask her.

"I don't know. I love my apartment. And I do have two bedrooms. I thought maybe..." She trails off, spinning the stem of her wineglass between the palms of her hands.

"Maybe what?"

"Maybe you might want to move in with me. Not for July first," she adds hastily. "That would be too soon. I know you'd have to give notice for your own place. But maybe on August first..."

My mind is whirling. Move in with Kate?

Her apartment is beautiful. It has a fireplace, and crown moldings, and a tiny terrace. It's on one of the nicest blocks in the village.

But what about Will?

If I move in with Kate in August, I can't talk to Will in September about us moving in together.

"How much is the rent?" I ask Kate.

"I couldn't charge you half. That wouldn't be fair, since I'd want to keep my bedroom, and it's bigger than the other one."

She's hedging. I can tell.

"How much, Kate?"

"Fifteen hundred," she offers.

So there's no decision to be made.

"I can't afford it," I tell her.

Case closed.

"Fourteen hundred?" she amends. "I can kick in the extra hundred from my temping money."

"Kate, that wouldn't be fair. And actually, I think you can get more than fifteen hundred for the place. It's a beautiful apartment."

"I know, but I wanted you to live there with me."

"I can't," I say, even though it's tempting.

"You said you were going to be doing some catering jobs over the summer. You'll make a fortune, Tracey. Enough to make up the difference in rent between your place and mine."

Maybe.

But it's not the money.

It's Will.

I can't tell Kate that I'm counting on us moving in together when he gets back in the fall. Either she'll think it's just a big fantasy on my part, or she'll think it's not a good idea.

"I really don't want to ask a stranger to move in with me," Kate says desolately. "Not after what you went through with Mercedes."

"That was fine," I tell her.

She raises an eyebrow at me. "Honey, the girl was a crack ho."

"Okay, it wasn't fine. But who says you're going to end up with someone like her?"

"A stranger is a stranger, whether they're like her or not."

"Look, why don't you ask Raphael? He's making more money now that he's working for *She*. Maybe he'll want to move in with you."

"I could never live with Raphael," Kate says in a how-can-you-even-suggest-such-a-thing tone. "His lifestyle and mine would just never mesh. I mean, strange men—*sailors*—coming and going at all hours... Think about it, Tracey."

I grin. "You're right. Well then, maybe you should move into a smaller place."

"But I love my place," she wails. "What am I going to do?"

I shrug.

"Just think about it, will you, Tracey? Just give it some thought. Don't say no right away. Okay?"

"But, Kate—"

"Wait and see how the catering job goes," she insists. "You're going to make a bundle. Why stay in your apartment when you can live in mine? We'd have so much fun."

I nod.

We would have fun.

And if it doesn't work out with Will and me moving in together...

Not that I think it won't, but if it didn't, I wouldn't mind living with Kate. In fact, I would like that. Then I wouldn't have to be lonely.

But I won't be lonely when Will gets back and he and I move in together.

No, I can't jeopardize my future with him.

"Will you think about it, Tracey?" Kate asks.

I say yes, to humor her, even though I have no intention of thinking about it.

I pick up take-out Chinese on the way home, and eat it in front of a rerun of *Ally McBeal*.

And surprise, surprise, the phone never rings.

Eleven

"You're Tracey, right?"

I nod at the pleasant-looking African-American guy who greets me as I step off the elevator and find myself in the entryway of a penthouse apartment on Central Park South.

"I'm John Wilson with Eat Drink Or Be Married," he says. "Milos asked me to train you."

The security guard who escorted me up in the elevator—*after* my name was checked off a list in the lobby and telephoned ahead to the penthouse—heads back down to his post.

It's all I can do not to look around with my jaw hanging open as John leads me through a vast sitting area to a room he calls the "atrium." Three walls are made of glass, and there's an incredible view of Central Park sprawled twenty stories below. But if you don't look at that, you can almost convince yourself that you're on some tropical terrace. Terra cotta, plants galore, antique-looking wrought-iron furniture, a trickling fountain. Several men are moving a grand piano through the wide double doorway from the living room.

The entire apartment is filled with bustling people, all of them more attractive than I am, and all of them wearing gray Nehru jackets and black slacks like mine. At least I'm getting some use out of this boring pair of gabardine dress pants I bought more than a year ago for my great-aunt's funeral. And at least they still fit—although they might not have, at this time last week. The waistband is snug, proving that I probably gained at least ten pounds since college—and that it's a good thing I lost five or more of it this past week.

I get a quick tour of the spectacular apartment as John tells me about the event. It's a cocktail party in honor of some guy's fortieth birthday, thrown by his wife. I glimpse a prominently framed portrait of an attractive couple over the mantel, and assume they must be the birthday boy and spouse.

I wonder what they do to be able to live in a place like this. We're talking Trump meets Vanderbilt. I want to ask John if they're celebrities or foreign royalty or something, but that's so…Brookside. So I try not to gape as he shows me around, pretending I'm totally accustomed to the trappings of vast wealth.

Priceless paintings? Private gym off the bedroom? Walk-in dressing room twice as big as my apartment?

No big deal.

Right.

John shows me how to carry trays and offer appetizers to the guests. How hard can it be? I wonder, until I practice with an empty silver tray and realize that it's heavier than it looks.

I'm told to be polite and personable.

"Remember," John says, "the guests aren't here to talk to the wait staff."

"Are you sure?" I ask gravely. "Because I was practicing some new knock-knock jokes earlier and—"

He looks horrified.

"Relax, I'm kidding!" I say, laughing.

"Oh!" He's obviously relieved. "I thought you were—"

"Some kind of nut?"

"Well, we've gotten some nuts, believe me. People who don't know how it works. A lot of catering people are in show business. Once, when we were doing a party for a record producer, I had a new waitress break into song while she was serving him his sorbet."

"Are you serious?"

He nods. "She was hoping to be discovered."

"Well, I'm not. And trust me, I know how this works," I tell him. "Will's told me enough about it. I'm strictly background, right? Quietly efficient."

"Will?"

"Will McCraw. My boyfriend. He works for Milos."

"Oh, I know Will. We work together all the time." But he looks and sounds surprised. "He has a girlfriend?"

"What? Wait, I know. You thought he was gay?"

"No! It's not that...."

So if he wasn't surprised because he assumed Will was gay...

Then he was surprised because he didn't think Will was in a relationship.

"Then what is it?" I ask pointedly.

"Nothing! I just never knew he had a girlfriend." John isn't making eye contact with me. "Come on, let's go back to the butler's pantry to help with the food."

Why isn't he making eye contact with me?

All sorts of paranoid thoughts enter my head.

All of them involve Will having cheated on me, and John being aware of it. Maybe everyone here is aware of it. Maybe people are whispering behind my back, pointing at me and saying, "Look, there's Will McCraw's girlfriend. She's so oblivious. She thinks he's actually been faithful."

I pretty much convince myself that that's the case as I help load silver trays with feta and artichoke crostini and smoked salmon and dill tartlets with creme fraiche.

I keep checking out the other waitresses, wondering which of them would be most likely to seduce Will.

They're all potential femme fatales: Sheila with her glorious long red hair, Kelly with the model's cheekbones, Zoe with the boobs that are even bigger than mine and the body that's tiny everywhere else.

I rule out Sue, even though she's adorable, with an outgoing personality. For one thing, she's a fellow newcomer—not just to Milos's catering place, but to New York; she's just moved here from Pittsburgh. For another, she's super-friendly to me, unlike Sheila, Kelly and Zoe. I've known her twenty minutes, and she keeps saying we should hang out sometime. Either she's super lonely or she's hitting on me. Maybe both.

Every time John introduces me to someone, he says, "This is Tracey. Will McCraw's girlfriend."

Everyone is surprised.

Everyone reacts with a *Will has a girlfriend?* expression even if they don't come right out and say that. Which some of them actually do.

Luckily, once the guests start arriving and we start working, the evening flies by.

My stomach was rumbling as I put the canapés on the trays before the party. But by the time everyone is gone and we're engaged in clean-up, my appetite has passed. John tells us to help ourselves to what's left— and there's a lot. But even the marinated grilled Gulf shrimp wrapped in basil does nothing for me.

Finally, I'm on my way home in a cab, more than a hundred dollars richer, wondering how I'm going to get up for work in six hours, and alternately rubbing my aching feet and shoulders all the way downtown.

The message light is blinking when I get upstairs to my apartment.

I press the button and start getting undressed as the tape unwinds.

I'm too lazy to unfasten all the buttons on the Nehru jacket, so I just undo the top one and start pulling it over my head. It's caught around my ears when I could swear I hear Will's muffled voice saying, "Tracey? Tracey?"

For a split second, I stupidly think he's here, in the room.

I know. Crazy. What can I say? It's late, and I've got low blood sugar.

Of course, I realize a moment later that it's a recorded message from him—that he must have thought I was screening my calls.

That he must have thought I couldn't possibly be out at...

"It's midnight. Where are you? Okay, I'll try you back another night. Hope everything is okay."

There's a click, and then the machine beeps twice and a disembodied mechanical voice says "End of messages."

I try to pull off the damned jacket so that I can look at the clock and see if it's too late to call back.

But the jacket is hopelessly wrapped around my head, rendering me not only half deaf, but completely blind.

And anyway, I realize as I try to work it back down

to my neckline, I can't call Will back. I don't have his phone number.

This sucks.

It really sucks.

I try telling myself that at least he called, but that doesn't help.

He didn't say "I miss you," much less anything else that would help to erase the bad feeling I got when I discovered that nobody he works with at Eat Drink Or Be Married seemed to realize I existed.

Obviously, Will doesn't discuss his love life at work.

And okay, maybe that doesn't mean anything other than that he's a typically close-mouthed guy.

I mean, my brothers never like to discuss their relationships with anyone. Back when everyone lived at home, my mother would always ask—make that pry, because there's nothing low-key about my mother— and my brothers would invariably clam up and escape. We never even knew my middle brother Joey had a girlfriend until he asked my oldest brother Danny if he could borrow money to buy an engagement ring for her.

So maybe Will hasn't mentioned me to his co-workers because guys just don't do that.

Or maybe he hasn't mentioned me to his co-workers because he wants them to think he's single so that he can screw around behind my back.

You're probably thinking this is my imagination getting carried away with me.

And yes, it very well could be.

But I can't help wondering whether there's a part of me that's been blind by choice, and for too long.

Now that there's some distance between me and Will, I can see our relationship more clearly.

I've always known there were problems. For one thing, I've been scrounging for a commitment for ages, while Will seems content to coast along without regard for our future as a couple.

But suddenly, the problems that were there before seem to be symptoms of something huge and pervasive.

I tug the jacket down past my shoulders and slowly work on the buttons as I ponder this turn of events.

Maybe Will isn't who I thought he was.

Maybe he'll never be who I need him to be.

Maybe the very thing that draws me to him—the fact that he's different from everyone I ever knew in Brookside—is the very thing that makes him unattainable.

Like me, he's done his best to shed that small-town, middle-class background. But I can't imagine him ever looking back and feeling homesick, the way I did last week. He wants none of the trappings that go along with that kind of life.

Maybe that includes marriage.

And I…

Well, I want marriage. Someday. And I can't pretend that I don't. I want to know that I belong to someone and he belongs to me. That he's never going to leave me.

Granted, marriage doesn't always give that guarantee.

Look at Mary Beth and Vinnie.

But I wouldn't marry a creep like Vinnie. I would only marry someone who loved me as much as I loved him—someone I trusted as much as he could trust me.

Like I said, I don't know if Will can ever be that person.

"But I can't let you go, Will," I whisper. "I can't."

Not yet.

Maybe not ever.

And maybe…

Just maybe…

I'm wrong.

But that possibility doesn't help me to get much sleep. I watch the clock hit three, then four, then five. The next thing I know, the alarm is bleating and I'm tempted to call in sick and roll over and go back to sleep…until I remember that I might have to use a sick day to visit Will at some point.

I manage to go through the motions of getting ready, and I drag myself to work.

I'm on my way into the deli in my building when I hear somebody calling my name.

Naturally, it's Buckley. I look up to see him looking freshly pressed, well-scrubbed and neatly combed, carrying a steaming paper deli cup and a brown paper bag. Today I'm too exhausted to be flustered, much less turned on.

"Fancy meeting you here," he says.

I manage a polite chuckle.

"How's it going?" he asks.

I yawn in response.

"Late night?"

"Yeah." I don't elaborate. Let him think whatever.

"Listen, I've been wondering about something ever since I saw you yesterday."

Uh-oh.

"Really? What have you been wondering?"

"Whether you deliberately gave me a wrong phone number."

"Why would I do that?"

"Because you never wanted to hear from me again."

"That's crazy. I was actually hoping you'd call because I had fun hanging out with you," I hear myself say.

"You're kidding."

It's dangerous, being this numb with exhaustion.

The next thing I know…

"Then why don't we hang out?"

…I'll be saying something really stupid.

Like…

"Sure. When?"

Did I just say that? Or am I still in bed, dreaming?

Unfortunately, it's not the latter, because Buckley hands me his very real business card with his very real home phone number on it, and says, "Great. Why don't you call me?"

"I will," I lie.

I shove the card into my bag, give him a fake-friendly wave and head back out to the street. This calls for something stronger than deli coffee.

I cross the avenue and walk down a block to Starbucks, where I order a double espresso. I need to wake up before I do something really scary.

As I wait by the counter for my beverage, I pull Buckley's card out of my bag again and look at it.

It just says his name, address, phone number, and e-mail. No job title, but there's a small, tasteful drawing of an old-fashioned quill pen and inkpot in one corner. Suitable for a copywriter.

My espresso comes up, and I carry it over to the counter to add skim milk and sweetener. As I toss the empty blue Equal packet into the trash, I realize I'm still holding Buckley's card in my other hand.

I should just throw this away too, I think, holding it poised over the garbage. After all, I'll never call him. And I'm supposed to be reducing clutter in my life.

Getting organized.

Which is why, the moment I get back to my office, I enter his name and number in alphabetical order in my Palm Pilot before I throw the card away.

After all, you just never know when you might need a copywriter.

Twelve

Three weeks and seven pounds—give or take on both—later, I find myself stepping off a bus in Buffalo just before midnight. This is no state-of-the-art Hampton Jitney with reclining seats and fresh herbs wafting in the air.

In fact, you don't want to know what's been wafting in the air on this bus, which is filled with men, most of whom look, smell and act like they just got out of prison. You would be surprised how many ex-cons take the bus to Buffalo to kick off Fourth of July weekend. It appears to be a tradition that's somehow escaped me until now.

Three different men, all of them missing at least one tooth, offer to carry my bag as I walk toward the terminal. I thank them all politely—thanks, but no thanks. Two of them scuttle off into the night, but a third calls me a bitch and follows me all the way into the terminal.

My brother Joey and his wife Sara are waiting there for me, just as they promised.

After we've hugged and kissed and talked about whether my trip was as awful as they imagine—it was—we head to the car.

"Why do you keep looking over your shoulder, Trace?" Joey asks.

"No reason." Actually, I'm making sure the hostile would-be-bag-carrier isn't still shadowing us. Hope I don't run into him on the return trip Monday.

"Have you lost weight, Tracey?" Sara asks, behind me holding the door open as I climb into the back seat of their two-door Blazer.

"You can actually tell from that angle?"

"Definitely!"

She's so sweet, Sara. It's almost enough to make me stop resenting her for being able to eat absolutely anything she wants and still be built like a lollypop with hair. My mother and Mary Beth are always saying she's too skinny. But they're the ones who told me I looked beautiful in that red dress with the gathered skirt and shoulder pads for the junior prom, so what do they know?

"Have you been dieting, or exercising, or both?" Sara asks.

"Both, actually." I tell her how I've been walking

all over Manhattan every chance I get, and how I've been doing the Jane Fonda workout tape Brenda loaned me. At first I felt like a clod and I wanted to give up, but Brenda urged me to stick with it. It took me a few times to figure out the moves, but now I actually kind of enjoy it.

As we drive the forty-some miles back to Brook-side, Sara and I do most of the talking. Like I said, Joey is the silent type, especially now that he has a wife around who can converse on his behalf. Sara tells me about their new house and their Memorial Day camping trip and how they're trying to get pregnant.

She also tells me that she's worried about Mary Beth.

"Why?" I've talked to my sister a few times over the past week or two, and she always sounds fine.

"Did she tell you she had dinner with Vinnie?"

"No!" I can't believe it.

"She didn't tell us, either, did she, Joey?"

"Nope."

"We found out through Joey's friend Frank's brother Al. He saw the two of them at Applebee's with the kids."

"With the kids?" I echo. "Then maybe it wasn't—"

"It was," Sara assures me. "Al said Mary Beth had this hopeful look on her face. And his wife, Amy, said that Vinnie kept flirting with the waitress."

"In front of his kids?" But I wouldn't put it past him, the slime.

"That's what I mean. He hasn't changed a bit, has he, Joey?"

"Nope."

I glance at my brother, whose gaze is fixed straight ahead on the sporadic Thruway traffic, and I wonder whether he even knows what we're talking about.

"Somebody should talk to Mary Beth," Sara tells me. "I keep telling your brother to do it...."

Joey snorts at that. Obviously, he's been following the conversation.

"She's your sister, Joe," Sara points out. "I can't do it—I'm just an in-law. Maybe while you're home, Tracey, you can find out what she's doing with Vinnie. I just hate to see her make a mistake and go back to him."

"He'd never take her back even if she wanted him," I say.

"You never know, Tracey. He had it pretty good when he was living with her. Home-cooked meals, a house, someone to watch the kids—now when he takes them for visitation he tries to dump them off on his mother."

"Really? How do you know that?"

"Vince Junior told me."

"Vince Junior told you that his dad tries to dump him and Nino off on their grandmother?"

"In so many words," Sara says, and Joey snorts again.

"Cut that out, Joey," she tells him, then turns back to me. "Your brother thinks I'm making this stuff up, but I'm not. And anyway, he heard what Al and Amy said about Mary Beth and Vinnie in Applebee's. Amy said Mary Beth was all glowing, like they were out on a date or something.''

I can just picture my sister's face wearing her Vinnie look. She's always been starry-eyed around him. Even after they were married a few years. Even after she knew for sure he was cheating on her.

With that thought, an image of Will slams into my mind.

It's not the same thing, me and Will.

It's not.

I know I almost convinced myself that he was cheating on me a few weeks ago. But I've done a few more jobs for Milos since then, and I've decided it might have been my imagination. Everyone's been nice to me, even Zoe. Nobody seems to be acting suspiciously or trying to hide anything, the way they would if Will had been fooling around with someone at Eat Drink Or Be Married.

Will has called me every week since he's been gone, and we even made tentative plans for me to go up and visit him later in July. He said there's a rumor that he might get the lead in *Sunday in the Park with George,* and that I should come for that if it happens.

Every time we talk, there's a big commotion in the background. But I'm getting used to it now. It's kind of like talking to someone who's living in a dorm. There are always people around, and somebody always needs to use the phone. No opportunity for intimate conversation. We pretty much just tell each other what we've been doing.

Will has been immersed in musical theater from morning till night. He's had minor roles in two more shows—one of Herod's henchmen in *Jesus Christ, Superstar,* and Laza Wolf, the wealthy guy who loses Tzeitel to the lowly tailor she loves, in *Fiddler on the Roof.* I was surprised, since he seems more like romantic hero material than character parts. But maybe that's just my perception.

"How are Mom and Dad?" I ask Sara and Joey, needing to think about something other than Will or my sister's troubled relationship with her ex.

"They're fine," is Joey's typically vague reply.

"Your mother had to get a stronger prescription for her glasses, and your father thought he was going to be laid off at the plant last week but nothing's happened yet," Sara tells me. "Oh, and they ordered a new couch for the living room."

"It's about time!" I picture the low-backed brown-and-tan plaid couch that's been there so long I can remember throwing up on it one day when my kindergarten teacher sent me home early from school.

"Yeah, your father didn't want to get it because of the layoff that might be happening, but little Danny drew all over it in colored markers—not the washable kind—and they really have no choice."

Little Danny is my other nephew—my brother Danny and sister-in-law Michaela's little boy. He's only eighteen months old, and I can't wait to see how he's grown since Easter.

"Your parents are going to be so happy when they see you tomorrow at the party," Sara tells me. "I'm glad you decided to surprise them."

"Yeah, it'll be fun." I'm thinking that it's too bad my friend Andrea isn't going to be around this weekend. She's at her cousin's wedding in Rochester. When I called her the other night to try and make plans to see her while I'm here, we talked about how she should come to New York to visit me. But I can tell it's not going to happen. People from Brookside have the same attitude toward New York City as people from the city have toward the nether regions of the state. East is east, west is west, home is best.

We're in Brookside now, pulling off the exit and paying the toll. Everything looks exactly the same, I notice, as we pass the strip with its fast food joints and the infamous Applebee's. We've left the skimpy business district behind before you can say K-mart, and now we're heading toward my sister's house. I'll be spending the night there so that my parents will be surprised tomorrow when I show up at their party.

"I wish you could stay with me and Joey," Sara says. She and my brother are living above her parents' garage, where they've been ever since they got married three years ago.

She promises, "When we move into our new place, you can stay in the guest room any time you want, Tracey."

"That would be great," I say, trying to imagine what it would feel like to be happily married with a house with a real live guest room. I wonder if I'll ever know. "When do you move in?"

"We close in August, but it needs a lot of work."

"Should be livable by Christmas," Joey says.

"Oh, Joey, come on." She swats his arm.

"What? I'm serious, Sara."

"We're not waiting till Christmas to be in our own place."

I half listen as they argue about it.

I'm staring out the window as we drive through the quiet, streetlight-illuminated streets of my hometown. We pass the gray stone library and the redbrick elementary school and the rough patch of sidewalk where I once fell off my bike and needed stitches in my knee. I wonder if they've fixed the concrete there. Last time I walked down that block, when I was home last Thanksgiving, it was still pothole ridden. They get so much snow up here in winter that the sidewalk plows wreak havoc from late October till March.

Brookside isn't the kind of town where municipal workers give a lot of care to repairs. It's a blue-collar town that's seen one too many of its factories shut down. My father and Danny are both employed by one of the few remaining plants, and there are always rumors that it's going to be swallowed up by some big corporation that will decide to move operations to Mexico or Asia. My mother's claim to fame is that in a layoff situation, she can feed a family of eight for weeks with the staples in her cupboard and, if the layoff is timed right, the contents of the backyard vegetable garden.

I think about some of the parties Milos has catered over the past few weeks—parties in the most elegant homes I've ever seen, with food that costs more than it does for my mother to do a year's worth of grocery shopping at Tops Market in Brookside.

Until recently, I'd never tasted Dom Perignon and Beluga caviar. Now that I've had a sip and a nibble, I can't say that I get what all the fuss is about.

Especially now, being back here in Brookside, where everyone in my family is still living off pasta and white bread and generic-brand soda. I imagine what my parents could do with the money Milos's clients spend on flowers alone for a single event.

But the funny thing is, some of the stuff my mother used to make in a pinch is now considered haute cuisine—Italian gourmet. Sauteed dandelion greens, broccoli rabe with garlic, even pasta fagiolo. Peasant food, she used to call it.

We pull up in front of the small cape where my sister lives. There are lights on, and Vinnie's green SUV is in the driveway.

"He's here!" I say in disbelief.

"No, she's using his car while hers is getting a new muffler," Sara tells me. "It was supposed to be ready today, but there was some problem, so she's getting it back in the morning."

"That's a relief." I'm not in the mood to see my

two-timing ex-brother-in-law. "I'm surprised he's letting her drive the Explorer."

"It's just so that he doesn't have to cart the kids around while her car is in the shop," Sara says. "Vince Junior has T-ball practice, and they both have swimming lessons, and your sister's always carpooling them someplace. And don't worry about Vinnie—he's got his mother's car while Mary Beth's using his."

My sister's face appears in the picture window, and then she's opening the front door.

I climb out of the car, give Sara a quick hug and try to take my bag from Joey, who insists on carrying it to the house for me.

"I tried calling you at work this afternoon," Mary Beth says, escorting me into the familiar, toy-cluttered living room. "But I got your voice mail."

"The company closed at noon because of the holiday weekend," I tell her.

"That's nice."

"Yeah." Especially since I didn't have to waste a sick day or ask Jake for a half day off. "Why did you call me?"

"I couldn't remember if I told you the party tomorrow is going to be dressy. But it's okay if you didn't bring anything—you can borrow something of mine." She gapes at me. "Or maybe you can't. Look at you, Tracey! You've lost a ton of weight!"

"I have not!" I protest, loving it. "Not a ton."

Not yet, at least.

"How much?"

"About thirteen pounds total, last time I checked."

"Don't overdo it," she warns, sounding just like my mother.

I look at my sister, standing there in her sweatpants and sweatshirt that do little to conceal her belly and hips and thighs, and I feel sorry for her.

"Trust me, I'm not overdoing it," I assure Mary Beth. "I have at least twenty more pounds to lose."

"Twenty! You do not!"

"Mary Beth—"

"Five more pounds, maybe," she says. "You want something to drink? I've got pop."

Pop. I'm definitely not in New York anymore.

"Do you have any diet stuff?" I ask her.

"Sure. You want anything to eat?"

"No, thanks."

"Did you eat on the bus?"

"Yep," I lie, because I don't feel like having her force-feed me. She and my mother freak out if they think somebody's missed a meal.

I watch her leave the room, and I feel guilty for wondering if my butt has ever been as big as hers is. I love my sister. She's my favorite person in the world.

But we're so different.

At least, that's what I've always told myself.

I look around the living room, with its Fisher Price meets Sears decor. I smile when I see the boys' latest school pictures framed on a shelf in the entertainment center. I stop smiling when I notice that my sister and

Vinnie's wedding portrait is exactly where it's always been.

"Why haven't you taken that down, Mary Beth?" I ask, pointing at it when she reappears with two Diet Cokes and a bowl of potato chips.

"What? The wedding picture? What would the boys think if I took it down? That's me and their dad."

"The boys already know you're getting divorced." This is a given. I was with her last fall when she told them. Vince Junior seemed to get it, but he wasn't fazed. Nino was oblivious to the news.

"They know we're getting divorced, but I don't want them to think I hate their dad," Mary Beth says, sitting on the couch and crunching a chip.

"That's crazy. For one thing, you do hate him... don't you?" I demand when I catch the fleeting expression on her face.

"He cheated on me when I was pregnant. I found out he was with another woman while I was in labor, Tracey. How do you think I feel about him?" she replies.

"Well, then, get rid of this picture," I insist, crossing the room and taking it off the shelf.

"Now?"

"Here." I hand her the frame. "Throw it away."

"But you gave us the frame for a wedding present."

She's right. It's sterling silver, and it's engraved with their wedding date. I bought it at Things Remembered, and it seemed extravagant back then. When my mother saw it, she said I should have gotten the brass because silver would tarnish.

I realize it hasn't.

And I realize Mary Beth must polish it regularly.

This makes me ill.

"Throw it away," I say again.

"That seems so—"

"I'll do it for you." I march into her kitchen and stomp on the pedal of the plastic garbage can. As the lid swings open, I drop in the frame. It lands with a splat on top of somebody's leftover Spaghetti-Os mixed with coffee grounds.

"There. Don't you feel better?" I ask my sister as I return to the living room.

"I guess."

But she doesn't. I can tell it's killing her.

She wants the picture back where it belongs.

She wants Vinnie back where he belongs.

"Are these *Wow* chips?" I ask, grabbing one and biting into it.

"Nope. Full fat."

"Oh." I eat just that one chip, and then I sit on the chair opposite the couch, taking a sip of my Diet Coke. "So how are the boys?"

"Oh, you'll see them first thing in the morning. And I mean first thing." She smiles. "They're so excited you're going to be staying here, Trace. They wanted to know if you can spend the whole weekend with us, but I told them you'll probably sleep at Nana and Poppi's tomorrow night."

"Yeah, I probably should," I say. My parents would be hurt if I didn't.

But I know my mother's going to be driving me crazy within twenty-four hours. She'll keep trying to make me feel guilty for moving away. She'll act like it's only a temporary thing, the way she always does.

"I heard Mom and Dad are getting a new couch," I tell Mary Beth.

"Yeah. It's god-awful."

"I know. I remember barfing all over it, and I'm not the only one who did over the years."

"No, I mean the new one. It's this brown and beige pattern with nubby fabric and stiff cushions. I went with Mom to pick it out."

"Are you serious?" I have to laugh. "What's with the earth-tone color scheme?"

She laughs, too. We proceed to make fun of our parents' furniture. Then we make fun of our parents in general. It sounds mean, I know, but we do it in a loving way. And I realize how much I miss my sister.

When Mary Beth tells me I can sleep in her queen-size bed with her instead of out here on the couch, I take her up on it. It's peaceful, snuggled beside her, listening to her even breathing, knowing that she loves and accepts me unconditionally.

Thirteen

So do my parents.

Love me unconditionally, that is.

But when I see them at their party the next day, the first thing my mother says to me—after she's screamed and hugged me and cried, and then gotten over the initial shock of seeing me there—is, "Where did you get that dress? You should wear things like that more often. You look beautiful!"

The dress is from the back of Mary Beth's closet— at least a decade old and four sizes smaller than her current wardrobe. I wouldn't be caught dead in this thing east of the Hudson River. It's a totally outdated style. Plus, it's pink. And sleeveless. But look at my mother, in an ill-fitting turquoise number with a gold chain belt. She's not exactly the fashionista of Brookside.

My father tells me, repeatedly, that it's about time I came home for a visit. He says it on the buffet line, he says it during his toast to my mother and he says it as we're dancing to an old Frank Sinatra tune.

He says it so often, and to so many relatives, friends and neighbors, that I'm sure everybody assumes I haven't been back since I moved to New York over a year ago. I'm already the talk of the town because I left. Now I can be the talk of the town because I've not only left, but I've turned my back on my loving parents.

The party is held in the Most Precious Mother church hall—the same place where I went to CCD (i.e., Catechism) classes while I was growing up, where as teens we had our CYO dances and where Mary Beth and Vinnie had their wedding reception. It's funny—I've been here hundreds, maybe thousands, of times in my life, but the place suddenly seems completely unfamiliar.

I can't believe I never noticed that the place reeks of smoke from Saturday-night bingo, or that the linoleum floors are so scratched or that the folding gray metal chairs and the long tables covered with paper tablecloths printed in wedding bells are so…well, tacky.

So is the buffet table, with its tinfoil trays of baked ziti and sausage with peppers and salad made with

whitish-green iceberg lettuce, orangey-yellow tomatoes and Seven Seas Italian dressing.

And the decorations: crepe paper draped from the
rafters and folding honeycomb wedding bells dangling
from the basketball hoops—I never noticed that there
were basketball hoops in here. On the tables are little
white crinkle cups filled with those vile-tasting candy-
coated almonds.

But the pièce de résistance has to be the DJ: Father
Stefan's younger brother, Chaz, who's wearing a tan
polyester leisure suit, and not in a cool retro way, but
in an oblivious, geeky way. He's played "Celebration" at least three times, and every time it comes on,
a big cheer goes up and the dance floor is promptly
jammed.

I compare this scene to the events Milos puts on in
New York, and I find myself feeling sorry for my parents and my siblings. None of them has any idea that
this is woefully inadequate. They're having a blast,
dancing and eating and mingling.

Don't get me wrong—I'm having fun, too.

But I can't help feeling like I don't belong here.

No...

Like I don't *want* to belong here.

I try to imagine what will happen when Will and I
get engaged and my family tries to plan our wedding.
They would be crushed if I told them that we wanted
to get married in New York City. They would point
out that the wedding is always in the bride's home-

town, and that if they're going to pay for a wedding, it better take place right here in Brookside.

All the more reason for me to keep socking away money in that Prego jar, which I have to take to the bank now that I've got a respectable amount—almost five hundred dollars—from working for Milos these past few weeks.

Will and I will have to save money and pay for our own wedding if we want to have it in the city.

Otherwise, we'll find ourselves here, in Most Precious Mother hall, boogeying to Kool and the Gang and doing the chicken dance, which Chaz has now forced on everyone not once, but twice.

I sit on a folding chair sipping warm white zinfandel from a foam cup. I watch Vince Junior and Nino out on the dance floor, waggling their elbows like poultry before they collapse on the floor in hopeless giggles. And I find myself thinking that maybe the chicken dance isn't so bad.

But then I try to picture Will doing it, and I can't.

He just wouldn't fit here.

And that isn't a bad thing.

I would kill for a cigarette. Lord knows I could bum one from somebody, since there are smokers galore, but I never light up in front of my parents. Somehow, I know that if I'm still smoking when I'm in my fifties and they're in their eighties, I will continue to sneak cigs behind their backs.

The chicken dance gives way to the Tarantella, which is a big hit with this crowd. It's a traditional

Italian folk dance that involves much clapping and bouncing and linking of arms.

Someone sits down beside me. "Hi, Tracey."

I look up to see Bruce Cardolino. His parents and my parents have been friends for years. In fact, Bruce's father was friends with my dad, and his mother was friends with my mom, and they set my parents up on a blind date. That's how they met.

Bruce is wearing gray slacks—not pants, but *slacks*—and a black silky-looking shirt with an open collar that reveals chest hair and a gold cross. In other words, he'd be right at home on the set of *The Sopranos*.

"Hey, Bruce, how's it going?" I've always liked him. In fact, I brought him to a couple of CYO dances when we were teenagers and I couldn't get a real date. We never kissed, or anything—we were strictly friends. But I always thought he was cute, and if he hadn't always had a girlfriend—or if he had ever been willing—I would have been totally into him.

He's still good-looking, in a strictly Guido sense. Black hair combed straight back, tall, nice build. I haven't seen him in a few years—he went away to St. John Fisher college up in Rochester, but I heard that now he's back in town working for his dad's business.

Mr. Cardolino is a plumbing and heating contractor. My father's always talking about how he makes a fortune, and I guess he does, by Brookside standards. He's always driven a new Buick, and Mrs. Cardolino has a fur coat and the whole family is always decked out in gold jewelry, right down to Bruce's sister Tanya's one year-old daughter, who has pierced ears and who is currently chicken-dancing with my nephews.

"You still living in New York?" Bruce asks. When I nod, he says, "Yeah? What's that like?"

"It's great," I say, not wanting to elaborate. Anything I say is going to get back to my parents, so I have to tread carefully here.

"Ever see Donald Trump around?"

"No, I've never seen him."

"How about those people on the *Today Show*. You ever seen them?"

"No, I never have."

"So you never went over there when they're taping the show and waved a sign at the camera?"

"No."

"Huh. My girlfriend keeps saying she wants to do that. She says that if we ever get married, she wants me to take her to New York on our honeymoon so she can hold up a sign that says we just got married." He snorts in a *go figure* kind of way.

"Who's your girlfriend, Bruce? Anyone I know?"

"Angie Nardone. You know her?"

"Angie Nardone! Yeah, she's a few years younger than I am, but we were in Key Club together."

"Yeah, she's only nineteen," Bruce confides. "I figure she's too young to be talking about getting married."

"Yeah, nineteen is young."

"I keep telling her that if we're still going out next year, when she's older, then we'll see."

"Yeah," I say, deadpan. "Then she'll be twenty."

"Yeah. That's better than nineteen. My parents got married when they were nineteen, but things were different back then."

"Exactly. But then, Tanya got married right out of high school, and she and Joey seem really happy," I point out. Obviously, she's not married to my brother, Joey—there are countless Joeys in Brookside. In fact, most of them are right here at my parents' anniversary party.

Bruce's sister Tanya and her Joey have at least five kids and she's pregnant again, but the two of them have danced every slow dance Chaz has played.

"Yeah, but that's different, too," Bruce says, leaning closer to me. "They *had* to get married, remember?"

"Oh, yeah." I had completely forgotten about that.

Here in Brookside, if you're single and Roman Catholic and you get pregnant, you *have* to get married. There's simply no alternative.

"So what do you do?" Bruce asks me. "In New York?"

"I work for an advertising agency."

"What do you do there?"

No way am I going to use the "S" word. Not when Bruce is sitting here looking all impressed with the mere fact that I live in Manhattan.

I say vaguely, "I do a lot of different things. Like,

right now, I'm trying to come up with the name for a new product.''

''You're kidding! What kind of new product?''

''A new deodorant. It's formulated to last a week at a time.''

''Cool. What names have you come up with?''

''*Persist* is my favorite,'' I tell him. ''But I don't know if they're going to go with that, so I'm still working on it.''

''Hey, I'll give it some thought and write down a few names for you, okay? I'd love to help out with something like that.''

''Thanks, Bruce…'' I want to tell him not to bother, but I don't know how to do that politely, so I just say, ''That would be great.''

He asks for my address, writes it on the paper tablecloth and tears it off and puts it into his shirt pocket. We chat awhile longer, mostly about the plumbing and heating contracting business and about people we used to know.

Then ''Celebration'' comes on again and Bruce leaps to his feet and shouts, *''Whoo-hoo!* Want to dance, Tracey?''

To this not-so-golden oldie? Not if my life depended on it. But I politely say, ''No, thanks. But you go ahead.''

''Come on! Angie wouldn't mind. She had to work today—did I tell you she's a phlebotomist over at Brookside General?''

''No, I don't think you mentioned it.''

"Come on, let's dance."

"No, that's okay. I'm going to go see if my nephews got a piece of cake yet," I tell him, and I go off in search of Vince Junior and Nino while Bruce joins the bopping crowd on the dance floor.

I find the boys sprawled under a table dumping candied nuts out of the little paper cups and making a big pile of them.

"What are you guys doing?" I ask, peering at them.

"This is the rock quarry," Vince Junior says solemnly.

Nino nods and produces a miniature yellow metal bulldozer from the pocket of his tiny Baby Gap khakis. "We-o pwayin' wock quawwy," he informs me.

"Cool. Can I play?"

Naturally, they're thrilled.

We all pway wock quawwy for a while, and then I get them each a big piece of cake, which they promptly strip of the sugary bakery frosting before telling me they're full.

I'm tempted to eat the remaining cake, but it's looking a little slimed, so I dump their plates.

I'm cleaning the icing off their faces with purple napkins that are printed in silver with my parents' names and their wedding date when Nino shouts, "Hey, wook! They-o's my Daddy!"

I follow his gaze.

Sure enough, there's Vinnie, out on the dance floor, dancing with Mary Beth to "Always and Forever."

"What's Daddy doin' here?" Vince Junior asks.

"I was just wondering that myself," I mutter.

As the boys rush over to greet their dad, I march over to the table where my brother Joey and Sara are sitting.

"Did you guys see who's here?" I ask.

"Trust me, he wasn't invited," Sara says. "He said he was just here to drop off Mary Beth's car and pick up his Explorer from the parking lot."

"Yeah, that's exactly what he's doing," I say, glaring at Vinnie, who is now balancing a giggling Nino on his shoulders, pretending he's going to drop him on Vince Junior, while Mary Beth looks on, beaming.

"I guess he came in to say hi to Ma and Pop, and somebody asked him to stay and have cake," Joey says.

I'd be willing to bet that that somebody was Mary Beth.

It hurts to see my sister so unwilling to shove him out of her life for good.

Yes, he's the father of her children.

But can't she see how he's using her?

"The thing I don't get," Sara says, "is why he even does this. He supposedly has a new girlfriend—at least one—and he's told Mary Beth he doesn't love her anymore. So why does he keep her on a string?"

"Because his ego needs to be fed by her blatant adoration. He gets off on seeing her so into him, and knowing that no matter what he does, she'll be there." I shudder. "If he so much as looks my way, I'm going to drag him outside and tell him off."

But Vinnie doesn't look my way. He leaves.

And after he's gone, Mary Beth deflates.

I want more than anything to talk some sense into her, but there's just not an opportunity. We have to pose for enough family pictures to fill a dozen albums and package the leftover cake into individual boxes that are printed with my parents' names and wedding date, and we have to hand one box to each guest on his way out the door.

By the time it's just our family left, Nino is having a post-bakery-frosting meltdown, screaming and kicking on the floor, and my brother Frankie is helping Mary Beth wrestle him and Vince Junior into her car.

Then I'm back home with my parents, who are in a panic because nobody told them I was coming and my bed isn't made up.

"Ma, it's no big deal," I say as she bustles around, pulling down blinds and shoving things into the closet. Apparently, they now use my room as a dumping ground for stuff that doesn't fit anyplace else—bulky sweaters and magazine clippings and junk mail and toys the grandkids play with when they're here.

I tell myself it shouldn't bother me—after all, it's their house, and I don't even live here anymore—but I can't help feeling resentful.

Was I expecting them to keep my room an untouched shrine in my absence?

Yes, apparently I was.

"How long are you staying?" my mother asks as she retrieves a set of worn, faded flowered sheets from the top drawer of my dresser, where I used to keep my white cotton panties and my industrial-strength bras and my baby-sitting cash and, way in the back, my cigarettes and a dog-eared copy of *The Sensuous Woman*.

"I'm staying until Monday," I tell my mother.

"Monday!" She pauses in the process of stretching the ancient, shrunken fitted sheet over the sagging, stained twin mattress. "But that's the day after to-morrow."

"I know. I have to work on Tuesday."

"Can't you take a few days off?"

I shake my head and help her stretch the sheet. "I haven't earned any vacation yet."

She looks horrified. "What do you have to do to earn vacation?"

"Nothing, Ma, just work there for six months. Which I haven't done yet." I tug an elasticized corner of sheet beneath the mattress, and the opposite corner pops off.

"Well, do they know your family lives five hundred miles away?" She puts the opposite corner back on.

My corner pops off again. "Ma, it's company pol-icy."

"What kind of company is this?"

"I told you, it's an advertising—"

"No, I mean what kind of company holds a young girl hostage from her family?"

Okay. I've had it.

With her, and with the damned sheet.

But before I can say a word, she goes on to say, "And what kind of man turns his back on a woman for months at a time so that he can go be on the stage, singing and dancing?"

Here we go.

She's never liked Will.

Nobody in my family has ever liked Will.

He has so many strikes against him:

1. He's not from Brookside.
2. He didn't stay in Brookside after he got here.
3. He looks, acts, and sounds different from anyone in Brookside.
4. And he took me away from Brookside...

Or so they assume. They can't fathom that I'd ever have left on my own.

"Ma, Will's an actor. Actors do summer stock. The fact that he's gone for the summer has nothing to do with me or our relationship."

She's silent. She gives up on the fitted sheet and leaves one top corner untucked, turning her attention to the flat sheet. Her chin is set stubbornly. Not a good sign.

I watch her. I notice that everything about her is round. Her pouf of dark, sprayed hair. Her big dark eyes outlined in too much liner and mascara for the special occasion. Her face with its circular application of rouge. Her arms, her body, her butt—everything about her is elliptical. I've seen pictures of her in her youth, and she was always pleasantly plump, but pretty. I wonder if I'll look like her one day.

I try to imagine myself middle-aged. I try to imagine myself middle-aged, looking like my mother and married to Will.

I can't.

Will, at middle age, will undoubtedly be a cross between Harrison Ford and Michael Douglas. And a man who looks like that won't have a wife who looks like this.

I shake the thought, turning my attention back to the matter at hand.

"Ma, how'd you know Will's gone, anyway? I didn't tell you." *Because I knew you'd react just like this.*

"Mary Beth told me. She's worried about you."

"Mary Beth should worry about herself. She's got enough problems with Vinnie still hanging around, leading her on."

"They have two children, and they took marriage vows in the church, Tracey," my mother retorts.

"But that doesn't mean she should take him back!"

My mother says nothing, just takes a fleece blanket out of the closet and starts putting it on the bed.

"Ma, it's July," I say, stopping her. "I'll roast under that thing."

"Nights are chilly."

"Not sub-zero chilly." I start folding the blanket again.

She shrugs, as if to show me that it's my own fault if I freeze to death during the night.

"He's not right for you, Tracey."

"Will?" I sigh. "Ma, how do you know that? You barely know him."

"I know enough. He's wrong. He doesn't make you happy."

"Vinnie doesn't make Mary Beth happy. Why should she stay with him?"

"She has a marriage and children." To my mother, staunch Catholic that she is, that's reason enough. "Don't make the same mistake your sister did, Tracey. Marry somebody who loves you."

"I plan to. Ma—"

She leans closer to me, dropping her voice to a whisper. "Marry somebody who loves you more than you want him to. Marry someone who loves you more than you love him. Because he'll always treat you like a queen. He'll always be there. And you'll learn to love him back."

What kind of advice is that?

Uh-oh.

I realize, looking at her face, that it's advice that stems from experience.

"So you...you didn't love Pop when you married him?" I ask, stunned.

"I loved him. Sure I loved him. But he didn't make my heart crazy, the way I expected. He was crazy about me, though." She shakes her head. "Thought I was the best thing that ever could have happened to him. I could do no wrong.''

''You still can't.''

She smiles and taps me in the chest. ''Now you see.''

I don't, actually.

But I let her think she's given me food for thought.

The rest of my visit flies by. We spend Sunday at church, then having a spaghetti dinner at my grandparent's house at high noon, even though it's ninety-five degrees out and so humid that everyone's face is moist and flushed and everyone's hair is plastered to their head. It's not a pretty sight. The good thing is, it's too hot to eat. Meaning, I'm able to stick to my diet, which I had expected to be a challenge this weekend.

Sunday night we go to see Joey and Sara's new house, then we go to my Aunt Mary's for coffee and homemade pizzelle. All of us. The whole family. I never noticed before that in Brookside, everyone travels in packs.

I don't have a minute to myself until I'm on the bus headed back to the city on Monday afternoon. It's a humid, gray day—the crappiest Independence day weather I can remember in years. That should make it easier to spend the entire day on a crowded bus, but somehow, it doesn't.

I didn't realize, until I was onboard, that this is a local. It's going to take a full twelve hours to get back to Manhattan, with stops in every godforsaken run-down industrial town across the state.

Utica, Rome…they all look the same. Nothing to see, no reason to get off the bus for the five minutes we're stopped—unless it's to smoke. Which I do, until I realize I'd better conserve the few cigarettes I have left.

When we have an extended stop in Albany, I realize that I'm less than an hour away from Will. If I switched buses in this terminal, I would be in North Mannfield before this bus had even covered half the distance between here and the city.

But I can't do that.

I can't just show up on Will's doorstep—does the cast house have a doorstep?—and demand to see him.

So I smoke my third-to-last cigarette and my sec-ond-to-last cigarette and I get back on the bus when the driver announces that it's leaving.

Somewhere around Poughkeepsie, I finish reading Henry Fielding's *Tom Jones,* which I've been working on for two weeks and which was surprisingly enter-taining. I move on to *Moby Dick,* the only other read-ing material I have with me. When I bought it back in New York, I promised myself that if I can get through this one, I can read the new Danielle Steel just to give my brain a rest.

I'm grateful when, after only a few pages, it be-comes too dark for reading and the light over my seat doesn't work. I put the book aside and am perfectly content to stare out the window.

There aren't as many lowlifes on the bus now that we're almost to the city. There are lots of college students, and old ladies, and single mothers with young kids.

Traffic grows heavier as we head down through Jersey.

By the time we've reached the George Washington Bridge, we're in a full-fledged traffic jam. We inch onto the bridge. Inch by inch.

I'm starting to feel trapped.

The bus is getting hot.

The driver announces that there's a problem with the A.C. and he's had to turn it down a notch so we don't stall out on the bridge.

Sweat is trickling down my head.

The old man next to me is snoring.

The little kid in back of me is rhythmically kicking my seat.

The college kids in the back are playing rap music with a grinding beat.

My heart is starting to pound.

If only I could smoke.

But there's no smoking allowed.

I need a distraction, so I try to think about something else.

Will.

But when I think about Will, I realize that he's probably having a fabulous Fourth of July. He's probably under the stars, on a beach by the lake, with all his new friends.

The bus is creeping across the outer lane of the bridge.

There's an explosion.

I shriek.

The old man wakes up sputtering.

The kid behind me is screeching.

"It's just fireworks!" his mother keeps saying.

I look out the window, and she's right.

There are fireworks over the city.

But I find myself wincing at every boom, wondering if it's my imagination or if the bridge is shaking every time there's a brilliant flash in the sky.

For a split second, I thought the first explosion was a bomb. Now that I know it's just fireworks, I find myself wondering what would happen if there really was a bomb. With New York City a prime terrorist target, it isn't far-fetched that some evil mind has considered blowing up the George Washington Bridge on the Fourth of July.

The bus is right up against the railing, and we're not going anywhere.

If a bomb went off at this very moment, we would pitch over the railing into the Hudson River.

We would drown.

We would die.

I'm sweating profusely, but it's a cold, clammy sweat, and I'm having a hard time swallowing. It gets worse when I think about it—the mechanics of swallowing, I mean.

Oh my God.

My throat is closing and I can't breathe and I'm trapped.

And I'm going to die.

I'm careful not to look out the window.

If I look out the window and see the railing and the river, I'm going to lose it.

The bus moves forward another fraction of an inch.

I feel like it's teetering on the edge of the bridge.

I glance at the other passengers to see if anyone else realizes how precarious our predicament really is, but everyone seems to be unfazed.

Then again, I probably look unfazed, too.

It's not as though I've hurtled myself into the aisle in a Nino-style frenzy.

Yet.

We move forward.

Inch by inch.

Hour by hour.

The fireworks finale erupts overhead in a dazzling commotion of flashing lights and smoke and sound.

I clasp my hands in my lap so tightly that my index fingernail on one hand draws blood from the palm of the other hand.

Finally, mercifully, we're off the bridge.

As the bus makes its way through the clogged west side traffic, I find myself calming down gradually.

By the time we make it to the Port Authority, my heart rate is almost back to normal.

I had planned to take the subway back home, but

the thought of being trapped underground is terrifying right now.

I need air.

I need a cigarette.

I step out of the dingy but climate-controlled bus terminal into a putrid steambath of Manhattan night. My hands are shaking as I fish my last cigarette out of the pack and put it into my mouth.

I light it and take a deep drag.

I feel better now.

The streets are jammed. I buy another pack of cigarettes at a newsstand on the street, then shoulder my way through the crowd, lugging my heavy bag.

I'm trying to figure out what the hell happened back there on the bus, and I can't come up with an answer. It was as though every ounce of logic flew right out of my head.

I try to flag a cab, but it's impossible to find one.

No way am I going to get on a city bus or the subway now.

There's nothing for me to do but keep walking, zig-zagging my way across the city, down a block or two and over a block or two, toward my East Village neighborhood. I'm on Twenty-ninth and Park when a couple steps out of a cab on the corner, and I flag the driver.

Five minutes and five bucks later, I'm home.

The message light is blinking on my machine. I press the play button, wondering if it's Will calling.

But it isn't.

It's Buckley.

"Hi, Tracey. Since you haven't called me, I thought I'd call you. Joseph gave me Raphael's number, and he gave me yours. I hope you don't mind. I'm done with that freelance job in your building, which is why we haven't run into each other lately. I was just thinking we should get together for drinks or something. Platonically."

Well, of course platonically, I think, wanting myself to be irritated, but unable to muster much reaction. What else would he expect?

"Call me," is all that's left on Buckley's message.

And his is the only one I've got.

No call from Will.

Well, it's not like the Fourth of July is one of those occasions where you call to give someone holiday greetings. I mean, it's not like Christmas or New Year's or Mother's Day or Valentine's day. But still.

He could have called.

I mean…

Buckley called.

And I'm thinking that maybe I should call him back. Why wouldn't I? He's a nice guy, and it would be fun to get together with him.

Especially now that Kate is so busy with Billy in the Hamptons—they've been an item ever since the weekend I was out there. Which is presumably why she hasn't invited me back again.

Meanwhile, Raphael is hot and heavy with some Czechoslovakian ballet dancer he met in a leather bar in Jersey City. Brenda's wrapped up in wedding plans, and Latisha's in a foul mood over the Yankees' latest losing streak, and Yvonne's showing Thor around town every free moment.

Where does that leave me?

Fresh from a weekend in Brookside and obsessed with the notion that terrorists are going to blow up a bridge with me on it.

Impulsively, I take out my Palm Pilot and look up Buckley's number. I dial it before I can stop myself. As it rings, I think that I should hang up, and then I think that he's probably not home, and if he isn't, I won't leave a message because once I give this some thought I'll realize that it probably wasn't such a good idea to—

"Hello?"

"Buckley?"

"Tracey!"

He sounds psyched.

Now I'm psyched. It's nice to be so welcome, even just over the phone.

"Hey, you called back. I seriously doubted that you would."

"Why wouldn't I? You, uh, said to."

He does a surprisingly dead-on imitation of my mother, whom, of course, he's never met: "If I told you to jump off a bridge, would you do that, too?"

He has no idea of the relevance of that particular comment, and I'm not about to tell him, so I force a laugh, too.

Then he asks me about my holiday weekend, and tells me about his—he went home to Long Island for a family barbecue and spent today at Jones Beach. Apparently it was a gorgeous, sunny day here in the eastern part of the state.

"Lucky you, spending the day on the beach while I was on the bus," I say.

"Nah, the beach was loaded with freaks," he says.

"Freaks? As in circus?"

"As in you never saw such a mass gathering of complete and utter losers." He launches into a hilarious description of fellow beach-goers, doing accents and dialogue. He's got me laughing so hard, I'm straining my newly developing abs.

"I haven't laughed this hard since the first Austin Powers. You should be writing stand-up comedy, Buckley, not cover copy and corporate brochures," I tell him when I finally catch my breath.

"Oh yeah? Don't say that until you've read my corporate brochures. You'll laugh your ass off."

I laugh again.

"So you want to have drinks with me sometime, or what?" he asks out of the blue.

Before I can respond, he adds, once again, "Platonically."

"Damn! And here I wanted to date you, Buckley."

"I *am* a hottie," he says. "But you, my little minx, have a hottie of your own."

"I know." I heave an exaggerated sigh. "I'll try to keep my hands off."

"Aren't *we* saucy!"

We make plans to meet for cold, slushy rum drinks at a restaurant in his neighborhood on Wednesday night after work. He suggests the time and place, and I'm glad that it's nowhere I've ever been with Will.

And it's great that I don't feel the least bit threatened anymore by the fact that he kissed me. The ice has been broken between us.

Or maybe it was just my ice, because the thing about Buckley, I'm starting to see, is that he's always totally relaxed and casual. I don't think it's an act, either. Nothing seems to bother him.

Anyway, things are looking up now.

Especially when I step on the scale before changing into my pajamas, and see that I've lost four more pounds since I last checked.

I'm actually doing it. Everything I said I would do: losing weight. Reading classics. Saving money.

I even organized my apartment one night last week and threw away two big garbage bags full of packrat debris.

I stand in front of the mirror, still dressed in the rumpled black linen shorts and short-sleeved black T-shirt I wore on the bus trip.

I study the new me.

Not bad.

It's funny how much difference that extra almost-twenty pounds makes. But when you consider that it's like carrying four five-pound bags of flour in your hips, butt, thighs and gut, it's almost shocking that it doesn't make a more drastic difference. Don't get me wrong—I like the new me.

She's noticeably slimmer than the old me.

But still recognizable.

I sigh, realizing that no matter how far I've come, I still have my work cut out for me.

Fourteen

On Wednesday night, I'm on my way to the elevators to meet Buckley after work when Jake stops me. He's been in meetings with the client all day, and we've barely seen each other. I hope he doesn't want me to stick around, because I called Buckley five minutes ago and told him I was on my way to meet him.

"Can I talk to you about something, Tracey?" Jake asks.

"Sure." I wait for him to elaborate, wondering what's up.

"Okay, come on back to my office." He starts walking.

I follow him, taken aback. Why can't he talk to me right here?

I notice that he doesn't make conversation when I catch up with him on the way back to his office. It doesn't help that I can't think of anything to say. I wonder if I'm in some kind of trouble, but I can't think of anything I possibly could have done wrong.

Then I realize that since whatever he wants to discuss is obviously discreet, it might be about the product names I gave him a while back.

He never did get back to me about the list.

Maybe he ran them by the client. Maybe they've chosen one of my ideas.

"Close the door," Jake says, walking into his office and sitting behind his desk. "Sit down."

I close the door. Sit.

"So you remember the day a few weeks ago when you got those chocolates for my mother for her birthday?"

My heart sinks. I guess this isn't about naming the deodorant.

"Yeah…"

"Remember how I had you package the gift and bring it down to the mailroom later that afternoon?"

"Yeah…"

"I just found out she never got it."

"She never got it?"

"No. And she's pissed because she thinks I forgot her birthday."

I just look at him, unsure what he wants me to say. "But that's…I mean, I don't know how she could have never gotten it."

"I don't know, either. A hundred dollars' worth of Belgian chocolate seems to have mysteriously disappeared."

Is he accusing me of stealing it?

I can't tell.

But if he is...

"I'm not saying you took it, Tracey...."

He isn't?

"But I'm wondering if maybe you forgot to bring it to the mailroom."

I think back to that day. I definitely remember going to the mailroom with his chocolate. Myron was down there, and he took the package from me. He pretended he was about to drop it, catching it right before it hit the floor. He always likes to give me a hard time, teasing me because I work for Jake.

The thing is, nobody in the mailroom likes Jake. Probably because he treats everyone in the mailroom like they're invisible. Or maybe because I've overheard him telling racist jokes—and chances are, they have, too.

It occurs to me now, as I think back to that day, that Myron might have noticed that the last name on the package label was the same as Jake's.

Meaning, Myron might have figured out that Jake was using the company mailroom to send personal mail to his family.

That wouldn't go over big with Myron. I mean, he makes a fraction of Jake's salary, and I happen to know he pays child support to his ex-girlfriend, too.

But I'm not about to tell Jake that Myron might have sabotaged his package of chocolates. For one thing, I have no proof. For another, I can't really blame the guy...even if I'm the one who's getting blamed in his place.

"I remember taking it to the mailroom," I tell Jake, because he's waiting for a reply.

"Did you hand it to someone there, or did you just leave it?"

"I handed it to someone."

Here comes the inevitable. "Who was it?"

"I have no idea," I lie. "It was a long time ago."

"Then how can you be sure you brought it down? Can the package be lost on your desk or in your cubicle?"

"I doubt it."

"Can you check?"

"Sure." I shrug, and look at my watch. "First thing tomorrow morning, I'll—"

"Check now," Jake says curtly, then adds, in a gentler tone, "Okay?"

What can I say?

"Okay."

I spend the next fifteen minutes going through the piles of stuff in my cube, looking through my desk and even my file cabinet. I do it because I have no choice. Jake keeps poking his head in, asking, "Find anything yet?"

Finally, I go back to his office and tell him there's no sign of the package.

He's pissed.

Maybe not at me—but it sure seems that way. I'm almost tempted to tell him he should talk to Myron about the chocolates, but I don't.

Finally, I'm on my way to meet Buckley.

I walk across town. It's another muggy night, the heat of the day trapped in the concrete, radiating back at me as I trudge along the sidewalk. I'm shoulder-to-shoulder with strangers' sweaty bodies, my hair sticky on my neck and forehead. I'm not really prone to sweating, except on my head. It's embarrassing. The slightest sign of humidity, and I look like somebody turned a fire hose on me from the neck up.

When I get to the restaurant, which is on the same block as mine and Will's favorite sushi place, I see that it's your typical Tex-Mex neighborhood hangout. Happy hour frozen drink specials, complimentary chips and salsa, white votive candles, colored Christmas lights strung above the bar. There's a jukebox, and right now it's playing Steely Dan.

The place is hopping. Half of the people jammed into the bar area look like they've just come from office jobs, the other half like they're on their way to the theater. Buckley's sitting at the far end where it's less crowded, drinking a foamy white drink in a stemmed glass with pineapple chunks and maraschino cherries on a plastic skewer. An ultra-attractive female in a red summer suit with long, curly, *dry* black hair is perched on the stool by his side, sipping a similar drink.

In fact, I think they're together until Buckley has to ask her what her name is again as he's introducing me.

"Sonja, that's right," he says. "And this is my friend Tracey. Who's late."

"Sorry. I got hung up at work when I thought I was on my way out." I wipe a trickle of sweat from my temple and put my big black bag on the floor between their stools, wishing Sonja would take her cue and leave.

She is *so* not taking her cue that she takes off her jacket to reveal the naughty little black top she'd concealed under her suit.

I hate her.

"What do you want to drink, Tracey?" Buckley asks, dragging his gaze away from Sonja reaching to drape her jacket on the back of her seat.

"What are you having?" I shove my damp hair away from my face, wishing they'd turn up the air conditioning. It's cool in here, but I need an arctic blast. Or a blow dryer.

"We're having something the bartender suggested," Buckley tells me, offering me his straw for a taste.

"We don't know what they're called," Sonja says with a giggle, "but they're wicked strong."

"Wicked strong," Buckley agrees, then turns to Sonja and asks, "Where are you from? Boston?"

"How did you know?"

"I have wicked good ESP," he says, and she cracks

up as though that's the most hilarious thing she's ever heard.

"We'd better go easy on these cocktails," she tells Buckley. "I'm getting giddy."

As I take a sip of Buckley's rummy, tropical-tasting drink, I can't help noticing that Sonja's pretty eager to make herself and Buckley, whom she's just met, into a *We*. And even though I happen to be half of another *We*—the Will and Tracey *We*—I feel jealousy bubbling up inside of me.

"So you guys just met now, at the bar?" I ask— mostly to remind them that they're virtual strangers.

"Yeah. Sonja is waiting for someone, too," Buckley tells me, raising a hand to summon the bartender.

"Really?" Presumably, it's her boyfriend. Or at least her date.

She nods and says, lest Buckley assume the same thing I did, "Just my roommate. She's new in town and she's always after me to go out, so I finally gave in. Figures that now she's the one who's late. I knew I could've had time to go to the gym first."

Of course she goes to the gym.

I picture her, skinny and sweaty, working out in a skimpy leotard. I glance at Buckley's face and notice that he seems to be picturing the same thing.

He catches my eye and leaps off his stool, as though he's just realized something. "Here, sit down, Tracey," he offers.

"No, it's okay," I say, hoping he won't believe me and sit down again. I feel like a third wheel, standing.

He doesn't believe me. He's gentleman enough to insist that I take his seat.

Why, I wonder, as I sit, doesn't Sonja feel like a third wheel?

"So how long have you guys been friends?" she asks.

Oh. That's why.

Because Buckley made a point of introducing me as his friend. Obviously, he did that because he wanted her to know that I'm not competition.

Which I'm not.

In fact, if I thought he thought there was any chance of something romantic happening between me and him, I wouldn't even be here in the first place.

Which is why Sonja shouldn't be irritating me every time she flashes that broad, white-toothed smile at Buckley, or touches his sleeve whenever he makes a funny joke—which he does regularly.

Because let's face it, the guy is funny. I'm talking Seinfeld funny, with a super-dry sense of humor and a subtly hilarious way of making wry, dead-on observations about life and human nature.

Laughing at Buckley's jokes puts me into such a good mood that as the night wears on and the liquor goes down easily, I'm starting to find Sonja a tiny bit more tolerable. I mean, basically, she has a right to be into Buckley. He's fair game. And I have Will.

Besides, it occurs to me that she has no way of knowing that Buckley and I have kissed—not that I'm sure what that has to do with anything. But it seems relevant as I start to feel the effects of this fruity, frozen whatever-you-call-it.

I've drained my first drink, and Buckley and Sonja are halfway through their second, when Sonja's roommate, Mae, shows up at last. She turns out to be a stunning Asian investment banker, and I'd be jealous of her, too, if she didn't announce, practically upon meeting me and Buckley, that she has a fiancé back on the West Coast.

"Why are you here if he's there?" Buckley asks her after ordering two more drinks—one for Mae, and one for me.

"Because I landed a job here first," Mae says. "We plan to settle in New York. He's finishing up his doctorate, and then he'll be here."

"But not until after Christmas," Sonja tells us. "I keep telling her she's nuts to be away from him for so many months. Long-distance relationships never work out."

Is it my imagination, or does Buckley glance pointedly at me?

"Of course they work out," I say—almost harshly, I guess, because Sonja blinks and Buckley mocks me, echoing my words with a feral snarl while pretending to wave claws in the air.

"Buckley!" I can't help smiling, though.

"Don't mind Tracey," he tells the others. "Her boyfriend is away for a few months. Summer stock," he adds in a whisper, with a sympathetic shake of his head, as though he's just informed them that Will was a victim of some horrible natural disaster.

"Sorry," Sonja says, pretending to be sheepish. I say *pretending* because I'm not convinced that there's anything about her that isn't fake, from her perfectly manicured long nails to her high, full boobs.

Looks like I'm back to hating her again.

"I didn't mean to bring up a sore subject, Tracey," she says, all but patting me on the shoulder.

"It's not a sore subject."

"I just meant that I've never personally had any luck with a long-distance relationship, and I've never known anyone who has. That doesn't mean that it's impossible, though."

"Of course it's not impossible," Mae says.

Her, I like.

"I totally trust Jay," Mae goes on. "And he totally trusts me. Just because we have to be apart for a while doesn't mean our relationship is at risk."

"But you two are engaged," Sonja points out. "And at least he's not an actor—oh, Tracey, I'm sorry, there I go again. I just meant, from what I hear, it's hard to have a stable relationship with someone who's in show business. After all, actors have to kiss other people, and they tend to travel a lot, don't they?"

"Some do." I don't believe her *oops* act for a second. She's out to make me look like a fool in front of Buckley.

Okay, maybe she's not *that* vicious.

Maybe it's the rum that's making me loathe her.

As I sip my second drink, which is going down very easily, I remember belatedly that I was so busy this afternoon that I never did get a chance to eat lunch. All I've had all day is the Raisin Bran with skim milk and a banana that I gobbled down before I left my apartment this morning.

Somebody orders another round, and before I take a sip of the fresh drink, I realize I'm slurring my words.

But just a little.

And nobody else seems to notice.

Sonja, who's a production editor at some obscure publishing house, is telling Buckley she might be able to get him some copywriting work. And Mae is on her cell phone, talking to her faraway fiancé, who apparently calls her every night at this time.

I think about how I haven't spoken to Will since before I went home last weekend. I got home early Monday night, thinking he'd call, but he didn't. I worked a gallery opening for Milos last night, and there were no messages on my machine when I got home.

Why hasn't he called me, dammit?

Why can't I be confident, like Mae is, about our long-distance relationship lasting?

My head is swimming with boozy thoughts of Will. I check my watch. It's almost ten. I wonder if he's back at the cast house yet after this evening's performance. What would happen if I called him there?

The question is strictly rhetorical, of course, because I don't have a phone number where he can be reached.

But let's just say I call directory information, and I get the main number for the theater, and whoever answers gives me the number for the pay phone in the cast house.

Let's just say that it's not busy for a change—Will has told me it's *always* busy so there's no point in giving me the number—and somebody picks up and I ask for Will.

What will he say when he finds out that it's me?

Will he be surprised?

Hell, yes.

Pleasantly surprised?

Sure.

Or maybe not.

It's hard to say.

As Mae smooches kisses into her cell phone and Buckley writes down Sonja's phone number on a cocktail napkin, I become fixated on my plan.

I have to call Will. I *have* to.

I drink more of my drink. This one is stronger. Less fruity.

I have to talk to him tonight. *Now*.

My heart is pounding.

I realize that I'm starting to have that same sensation I had the other night on the bus, and before that in my apartment.

This time it's not as intense. But I'm afraid. What's happening to me?

The jukebox is blasting an old Eagles song.

I look at Buckley.

He's wrapped up in Sonja and whatever she's saying.

Mae is laughing into her cell phone.

The bartender is pouring rum into a blender.

Did he put something in my drink?

I take another cautious sip.

It doesn't taste toxic.

Just strong.

Everyone else's drink came from the same batch, and nobody else looks like they've been poisoned, so it's just me. It's just that weird thing happening again.

I need to call Will.

"I'll be right back," I tell the others, grabbing my bag.

I start pushing my way blindly toward the far back corner of the restaurant, instinctively going for the rest rooms.

Please let there be a pay phone there. Please.

There is.

Please let me have a quarter. Quarters. I need lots of quarters. Please.

Luckily, I haven't completely eliminated the clutter from my life. The bottom of my bag is filled with loose change. No wonder my shoulder is always aching, I think vaguely as I sort through the fistful of silver and copper, shove a quarter into the slot, and dial.

I fish a pen and a stray Big Red wrapper from the

depths of my bag and scribble down the number for the Valley Playhouse.

Then, after feeding more change, dialing, and feeding additional change, the phone is ringing in my ear.

I lean against the wall, grateful that the small corridor outside the rest rooms is empty for the moment. There's a swinging door separating the area from the blaring jukebox and drunken voices in the bar.

I'm a wreck.

The hand that isn't pressing the receiver against my ear is trembling like crazy, and my heart is still racing. I feel like I can't catch my breath.

It's not just the booze, or the lack of food—although I'm sure that's not helping the situation.

It's something else. I'm terrified.

Am I having a heart attack?

There's a tightness in my chest.

Oh, God.

Was it there before I thought about the heart attack?

I'm not sure.

I'm so focused on analyzing my physical symptoms and the growing intensity of my heart rate that I forget exactly what it is that I'm doing here until there's a click in my ear and a male voice says, ''Valley Playhouse, Edward speaking.''

It's stammer time.

''I...um, I was wondering...is this...uh, is this the Valley Playhouse?'' I finally blurt helplessly. I am a complete idiot, but I can't help it.

''Yes, it is.'' Edward is patient.

Encouraged, I manage to ask for the phone number for the cast house.

Instead of rattling it off, Edward says, "I see. And are you trying to get in touch with one of our cast members?"

Now who's the idiot? Why else would I need the number?

"Yes, I am," I tell him, and ask for Will.

How can my voice sound so calm when I'm frantic inside?

"Is this an emergency?"

Yes, it's an emergency.

I need Will.

I need him desperately.

I'm having a heart attack and I need to speak to him before I die.

"Yes, it is," I say, on the verge of hysteria, praying Edward senses that I'm not faking the urgency in my voice.

"Please hang on," he says promptly.

And I try.

I really do.

I try to hang on.

But I'm falling apart.

A cigarette will help me.

Open the bag.

Find the pack.

Good.

Find the lighter.

No lighter.

Shit.

Find matches.

Light a cigarette.

Inhale deeply.

It doesn't help.

My heart is throbbing, and I've broken out in a cold sweat. It's all I can do not to drop the phone and get the hell out of here.

Get the hell out of this rest room corridor, and this crowded bar, and this Will neighborhood, and this unfamiliar city, and this lonely life.

But no.

I can't go.

Edward is going to get me a telephone number where I can reach Will. And if I can just speak to Will, everything is going to be okay.

I take another drag.

What if smoking is making the heart attack worse?

It doesn't seem to be.

I have the same symptoms, but now I seem to be getting woozier, too. From the drinks. The alcohol is taking a stronger hold.

Is it just that? Maybe I'm just drunk.

No. What about my heart?

What if it's a heart attack?

What if it's *not* a heart attack?

Then what is it? What's wrong with me?

Two women pass by on their way to the ladies' room. One gives me a dirty look and whispers something to the other. At first I don't realize why.

Then I see that I'm standing beneath a No Smoking sign.

Oh. So? So what?

I raise the cigarette to my lips and inhale again.

Drunken defiance.

They can't stop me.

Then there's a clatter in my ear, and Will's breathless voice is on the line. "Hello? Hello? Mom? Is that you?"

Ecstasy.

It's Will.

Confusion.

Mom?

"Will? It's me."

There's a pause on his end, followed by an incredulous, "Tracey?"

"Yes!"

"I thought you must be my— What's wrong?"

"I just wanted the phone number. For the cast house. I mean—that's what I asked Edward to—he didn't have to get you."

"Tracey, what the—? What are you doing?" Another pause.

It's my pause, I guess. Because it's my turn, and I'm afraid to speak.

"Edward said there was an emergency phone call for me," Will says succinctly. "I was backstage, in between songs. In two minutes I have to be back onstage singing 'We Go Together.'"

"'We Go Together,'" I echo, my mind racing

wildly. I'm a momentary contestant on *Millionaire.* And I know this one. "We Go Together."

There! I've got it. "Will, you're doing *Grease!*"

"Yes, I'm doing *Grease.* Tracey, you sound wasted. Are you wasted?"

"No!"

"Tracey, tell me…is this an emergency phone call, or what?"

"Yes!"

"What's wrong?"

This. This is wrong. His attitude is wrong. His tone is impatient, as though he doesn't believe me.

Why the hell wouldn't he believe me? Edward believed me. Edward, a total stranger, believed me, and Will, my boyfriend, doesn't.

"Tracey, for God's sake, I have to be back onstage in a minute. What's going on? What's the emergency?"

He wants me to name my emergency. Is he for real?

"Tracey, speak!"

"Why are you talking to me like this?" I wail.

"Because…is this an emergency, or are you drunk?"

"I'm not drunk!" I bellow, just as the two women from before come out of the ladies' room.

Dammit.

This is a mess.

I'm a mess.

But I'm not drunk.

That is not why I'm calling him.

That is not why I have these symptoms.

"Then what's the emergency?" Will repeats.

He's still impatient. Still not kind, or loving.

Still not the person I need him to be.

"It's my heart," I say, taking a deep breath. Shuddering, because it hurts and I can't seem to take as deep a breath as I need to take and there's something wrong, dammit, and Will won't—

"What about your heart, Tracey?"

What about my heart? I'm trying to focus. To answer the question.

What about my heart?

It aches.

It's breaking. Will is breaking my heart. I lean against the wall, my head tilted back, eyes closed. I feel limp.

He doesn't understand.

He's on the phone, the way I wanted. But this is not helping. This...

This is hostile.

Will is hostile.

"Tracey, I have to go," he says shortly. "I've got to get back onstage."

"But, Will...I need you."

"You called this number and told Edward it was an emergency. This was the emergency? That you need me?"

"Why are you so angry at me?" I'm crying now. "Will, stop talking to me this way. Don't you care?"

"Don't I care about what?"

About me?

No.

Don't say that.

"Don't you care that I'm in pain?"

"Tracey…"

"No, Will, I mean real, physical pain. I'm a mess. I can't breathe and I'm lightheaded and my heart is beating too fast…."

"That's because you've been drinking."

"No, it isn't! Stop saying that!"

"You're drunk, Tracey. I can tell. You're slurring. This is pathetic. I have to go."

"No, Will, don't—"

"Goodbye."

"Please, Will, don't—"

Click.

Dial tone.

Panic.

He's gone!

Where's that gum wrapper?

Search your pockets.

Search your bag.

Please. It's not here. Where is it? I need it. I need the phone number of the Valley Playhouse. I need to call him back.

But by now he's singing "We Go Together."

Ramma lamma ding dong.

So I'll wait until he's finished.

"Excuse me…"

I look up.

A stranger is standing in front of me, framed in the doorway leading to the restaurant. A strange man. A strange, blurry man is talking to me. Why?

He seems angry at me.

Oh, Christ. Him, too?

Why?

Why is everyone so angry at me?

Tears are streaming down my face.

"I need the gum wrapper," I tell the man. "Please...can you help me find it?"

"We don't allow smoking back here," he says, motioning at the sign.

"I know, but my boyfriend just hung up on me, and I can't find the gum wrapper and my heart—"

"Please put that out," he says firmly, motioning at the butt in my hand.

"But I'm trying to explain why—"

"Please. This is not a designated smoking area."

Who is he, this strange, blurry man, coming out of the woodwork to yell at me?

"Did they tell you I was smoking here?" I ask, realizing that those two bitchy women must have reported me. I hate them. And I hate this man.

I think I should tell him.

"I think you should leave," he says.

"But...why? Why do I have to leave?" I cry harder.

"I'm the manager, and I think you've had too much to drink. Are you here alone?"

I can't remember.

I struggle to think back to before the phone call, but my mind is as blurry as his face is, and now things are starting to spin.

"I can put you in a cab," the man says.

Now he's not being mean.

Now I don't hate him.

I sob harder. "Thank you," I say. "Thank you."

"All right, let's just—"

Oh.

I have to throw up.

Right now.

The nausea swoops over me with a sudden violence that sends me fumbling for the ladies' room door. I hurtle myself into a stall and vomit into the toilet.

Oh, God.

"Oh, God," I say, and I wonder where God is when you need him.

I should have gone to church, like my mother said.

I've never been so miserable in my entire life.

I hurt.

I think I'm dying.

I should have gone to church.

Now it's too late.

Because maybe I'm already dead.

Because I could swear I'm in hell.

Fifteen

"Tracey?"

"Tracey…"

"Tracey!"

"Mmm?"

"Tracey, are you okay?"

I come awake slowly, wincing at the sheer pain of being conscious.

My head is killing me.

My throat is killing me.

I open my eyes into a glare of direct sunlight.

My eyes are killing me.

And…

And there is no direct sunlight in my apartment.

I close my eyes quickly, but they still hurt.

Where am I?

"Tracey?"

Who is that?

I force my eyes to open again.

I roll over.

And gasp.

"Hi," Buckley says, looking down at me. "You okay?"

Buckley?!

What's he doing here?

Wait…

This isn't my apartment.

The sunlight.

This must be Buckley's apartment.

What am I doing here?

"I brought you home with me last night," he says, as if he's read my mind.

Oh, Lord. Last night.

The last thing I remember is…

Frozen drinks.

Many frozen drinks.

Many strong frozen drinks.

Did I sleep with Buckley?

I'm utterly mortified.

I close my eyes and turn my head away. The motion makes me seasick. I try to fight back the nausea, but the wave is already gagging me. I sit up, starting to retch.

Buckley shoves a bucket under my face.

I have dry heaves over it.

I see that it's not empty.

Somebody has already thrown up in it.

Why would Buckley—

Oh.

That somebody was probably me.

I sink back on the pillows in shame and exhaustion.

Buckley puts the bucket on the floor again.

"I'd say you're all out of puke, and none too soon."

Oddly, there's nothing nasty about that comment. He says it dryly, yet gently. I venture a glance at him, and his eyes are kind as he looks down at me.

"What happened?" I manage to croak.

"Last night? You don't remember?"

I try to shake my head, but there's blinding pain with the slightest movement.

I take a deep breath, and there's a bad smell.

It's me.

I'm the bad smell.

I want to die.

"You had too much to drink. You got sick in the bathroom. Sonja happened to go back there and she saw the manager trying to help you, and she came and got me."

Sonja? Who the hell is…?

Oh.

Sonja.

"I brought you here because I didn't think you should be alone."

No.

No, I should never be alone.

Never.

There's a lump in my throat, and this time it's not a dry heave.

"Thank you," I manage to tell Buckley. "You're being so nice to me."

"It's okay." His hair is all tousled and he's wearing a T-shirt and boxer shorts. The kind of boxer shorts that are more pajamas than underwear, but still…

I see that I'm lying in a bed, and that there's clearly only one room to this apartment, and that this is the only bed. It's actually a futon. There is no separate bed, or couch. Nowhere for a second person to sleep.

Which means…

"I'm sorry I kicked you out of your bed," I tell Buckley.

"You didn't."

I'm confused.

Then I'm not so confused.

I'm horrified.

He grins.

"I won't tell anyone if you don't," he says in a sly whisper, leaning toward me.

"Oh my God," I say, "did we…?"

He nods. "It wasn't that great the first few times, but we hit our stride."

"Oh…" I feel tears welling up in my eyes. I'm mortified.

"Tracey, relax." His smile has vanished. He sits next to me. Now his face is really close to mine. "I'm just kidding. Do you honestly think I'd take advantage of you in the state you were in last night?''

"Nothing happened?" *Thank you, God.*

"Nothing happened. I only slept in the bed because my other option was the floor, and I've had a roach problem lately—but they just sprayed again," he adds quickly. "And it's not that I'm such a pig—all New York apartments have roaches."

"I know...."

"Anyway, I promised nothing was going to happen when we were on the phone the other night, right? We're strictly platonic. Remember?"

"I remember."

Yeah, and I just remembered something else. Something he said triggered it.

The phone.

"Buckley...do you know if I called anyone last night? Before I got sick in the bar?"

He shrugs.

"Oh, no." It's coming back to me now. "I think I made a huge mistake."

"Let me guess. The drunken, crying phone call to your boyfriend?"

I nod. "How do you—?"

"I've been in a relationship. I've gotten the drunken, crying phone call. I've made a few, too," he admits, and there isn't a trace of humor in his voice. "It sucks."

"Getting the call, or making it?"

"Both." He's so earnest, patting my shoulder. "But you'll get over it, Tracey. And so will he."

"That's easy to say. But he's far away. It's not like we can fix it today. We won't even see each other until…God knows when. So I don't know how we can get over it and move on that easily."

"It's just a phone call, Tracey. Don't beat yourself up."

"I'll try not to," I say, because he expects it.

But it wasn't just a phone call.

There was something wrong with me.

Aside from the drinking.

I was having some kind of—well, if not a heart attack, then it was some kind of attack.

It wasn't the first time. And I'm scared. So scared that I expect it to happen again, right here and now.

I brace myself for my heart to start pounding.

But it doesn't.

"Are you okay?" Buckley asks.

"Yeah." I close my eyes and turn away. "I just can't believe I made such a fool out of myself. Not just with Will. The people at the bar… And Sonja, and Mae—thank God I'll never see them again."

"Don't worry about them. They completely understood," Buckley says. "Actually, they helped me get you back here after we left. It's only two blocks—too close for a cab—so we walked."

"I don't remember."

"No, you wouldn't." He pauses. "We pretty much carried you."

God, every new detail elevates the scenario to disastrous new heights. I bury my head in the pillow. "I'm so humiliated."

"Don't be. Sonja and Mae were really nice about it. And Sonja even used her own hair clip to pull your hair back so you wouldn't get—you know."

Yeah, I know. So I wouldn't get barf in it.

I reach up and feel my head. I'm sporting a big barrette directly over my forehead, which means Sonja clipped all my hair, including my bangs, straight back from my face.

How could she?

Every woman knows that this, hands down, is the most unflattering style in the history of hair. Unless you happen to be a toddler. Or a supermodel.

"That was sweet of her," I tell Buckley, who seems to agree wholeheartedly, oblivious to the fact that Sonja has clearly sabotaged my appearance.

In fact, he tells me he'll give Sonja her hair clip back when he sees her on Sunday. It seems they have a date to go Rollerblading in Central Park.

This bothers me because:

A.) I can't Rollerblade. I will never be able to Rollerblade, due to the notoriously weak Spadolini ankles.

B.) Buckley was apparently scamming a date with Sonja while I was lying in a pool of vomit.

Don't get me wrong. Buckley can date Sonja if he wants. He can date anyone his heart desires—aside, of course, from platonic me. And I'm not interested in dating him. I'm only interested in repairing my relationship with Will.

But that doesn't mean I don't mind the fact that Buckley has now seen me at my absolute, rock-bottom worst—forehead hair clip, dragon breath, vomit and all.

This situation couldn't possibly be any more mortifying.

Oh, yes, it could.

Because it has just occurred to me that I have to go to the bathroom.

Now.

Which means I have to get out of this bed. Which means I have to pull down the navy-blue cotton blanket Will must have covered me with last night.

What if I'm naked under there?

For all I know, he stripped off my disgusting clothing last night. That's what always happens in the movies—the guy tells the hungover girl that he had to help her get undressed while she was out of it. And she realizes he must have seen her naked.

In the movies, this is always a titillating thing.

In the movies, the drunk female is free of flab, cellulite and ancient, unsightly cotton underwear with worn-out elastic.

In the movies, there is no puke.

In the movies, a drunk female is silly and adorable and sweetly vulnerable. Think Julia Roberts in *My Best Friend's Wedding*.

Okay, maybe there aren't *that* many movies in which this type of thing happens, but there are a few.

At least two.

I know I saw one.

Anyway, this, my friends, is *so* not the movies. And it will send me over the edge if I find out that I'm not wearing anything under this blanket.

I lift the blanket and take a peek.

What a relief. I'm still fully dressed.

Still fully dressed in clothes that are caked with dried throw-up. Charming.

"The bathroom?" I inquire of Buckley, who is already standing and leading the way.

As we cross the room, I notice details about his apartment. The overflowing bookshelf. The open bag of Lays Barbecue chips on the counter. The clothes he wore last night, heaped on one of those wood-and-canvas director chairs you can buy dirt cheap at Ikea.

There are no plants. There are no show-tune CDs. There is no exercise equipment.

Buckley's apartment is nothing like Will's apartment.

Buckley is nothing like Will.

I try to imagine Will nursing me through my drunken blitz, but I cringe just imagining what he would have been thinking.

Buckley doesn't seem the least bit fazed.

"Hang on a second," he says, opening the bathroom door for me.

I lean weakly against the door, feeling sick.

A few seconds later, he's handing me a towel, a sloppily folded T-shirt and a pair of lightweight jersey-sweatpant-things.

"Take a shower, then put this stuff on," Buckley advises. "You'll feel better. I'll run down to the deli and get us a couple of bagels and some coffee."

"Coffee," I echo, trying to decide whether the thought of it makes me crave a cup, or feel sicker. I guess it's a little of both.

"And bagels. You need food."

"Yeah...but can you have them do mine with fat-free cream cheese?"

"Fat free." Buckley rolls his eyes. "Why bother? That stuff tastes like someone added water to ground-up chalk."

"Shut up. I'm on a diet."

Buckley looks me up and down in all my vomit-covered glory. "Yeah, I thought you looked like you lost weight. I meant to tell you last night."

"Really? You can see the difference?" The first bright note in a dismal morning.

"Definitely. Take your shower. I don't know how long I'll be. The deli is usually mobbed at this hour on a weekday."

A weekday?

It hits me.

"What time is it, Buckley?"

He checks his watch. "Almost eight-thirty."

"Oh, God. I have to be at work in half an hour."

I lean my aching head against the door frame. "How am I going to do that?"

"Call in sick," Buckley says with a shrug.

"I can't," I say automatically.

"Why not?"

"Because…"

Come to think of it, why not? After what happened last night with Jake and the missing package, I'm in no mood to go into the office this morning.

"If you call in sick, you can hang out here until you feel better," Buckley says. "We can watch morning TV."

Tempting, but…

"Don't you have work to do, Buckley?"

"I have to read a new legal thriller and write the copy for it, but it's not due until tomorrow morning. I can do it later."

Wow.

"Do you know how lucky you are?" I ask him. "Why don't you have to go off to some horrible, boring office job five mornings a week?"

"Because I refuse," he says, as though it's obvious and simple. "Why do you do it?"

"Because I need to make a living."

"And the only way to do that is to go off to a horrible, boring office job five mornings a week? Come on, Tracey. This is New York. Land of opportunity. There must be something else you can do. What about that caterer you said you've been working for?"

"Milos? Yeah, I've filled in on a few jobs for him. The money is great."

Reminder to self: Open savings account before this week is over. Prego jar is overflowing.

"Why don't you do that full-time?"

"Because it's waitressing, Buckley."

"And what you're doing at the ad agency is so much more fascinating?"

"Absolutely." I nod so vigorously a blinding pain shoots through my poor hungover head.

"It's fascinating yet horrible," he says, with a nod. "That makes a lot of sense."

"Buckley, leave me alone!" I swat his arm. "I'm too fried to be philosophical right now. Just go get me my coffee, and maybe we can talk."

"Now she's giving me orders," he says, shaking his head. "Okay, I'm going. I just have to get changed."

He starts to pull off his T-shirt.

I quickly shut the door.

I study myself in the mirror in Buckley's bathroom—which I can't help comparing to Will's spotless, Lysol-scented bathroom. Buckley's sink has beard shavings and soap scum in it, the toilet seat is left up, and there's a week's worth of towels hanging from the hook on the back of the door.

There's also a stack of magazines on the back of the toilet. *Sports Illustrated, The New Yorker, People*… I love it. A man who reads in the bathroom and doesn't try to hide it.

Personally, I always read in the bathroom. Will once said that he thinks it's a disgusting habit, which is why I never do it in front of him.

I help myself to the latest issue of *Maxim* from Buckley's personal library. Read a fascinatingly smutty article about how to score with women at weddings and funerals. Brush my teeth using toothpaste on my finger. Take a shower.

When I get out, I towel off and put on the clothes Buckley gave me.

He's right. I do feel better.

As I pull on the well-worn T-shirt with its faded Abercrombie and Fitch logo, I inhale its distinct scent: fabric softener and some vaguely masculine aroma that isn't cologne.

Will's clothes all smell faintly of his cologne, but Buckley doesn't seem to wear any. From what I can tell, he's a no-frills kind of guy.

I tell myself that Buckley is the kind of guy I should be with.

I tell myself that it would be so easy to stop loving Will and start loving Buckley.

But the truth is, it wouldn't be.

I can't make myself fall in love with Buckley any more than I can make myself stop loving Will.

I'm swept without warning into a tidal wave of longing, missing him so badly that I physically ache. The pain is worse than any hangover; worse than the heart-pounding, chest-tightening sensations of last night.

More than anything, I want to be in Will's clothes, in Will's bathroom, in Will's apartment.

I want everything to be the way it...

The way it never was.

I realize with sudden clarity that the whole time Will and I have been together, things have never been settled. Will has always been leaving.

He was gone long before he packed his bags for summer stock. He was always gone, in the way it really counts. He has always been pulling away even while I'm trying to grab on, to hang on to some tangible part of him. The whole time Will and I have been together, we haven't been totally together. I've always been...slightly single.

It's been a struggle from the start. Back then, when we first met, the excuse—his, and mine—was that he had Helene. The hometown girlfriend.

After that, there were always classes, and studying, and exams to take. Auditions and rehearsals and performances. Trips back home to Iowa, trips to New York City to find a job, an apartment.

We could have taken those last trips together; I was moving here, too. But he came alone. Found a job on his own, found an apartment where he would live alone.

I never really expected us to live together right out of college.

But the thing is...

I don't know if Will expects us to live together ever.

Or am I getting carried away?

Will, after all, is with me. He's been with me for three years now. If he didn't want me in his life—if he didn't love me—then he would have broken up with me before now.

Why would he keep stringing me along if he didn't think we had a future?

That question…

Sara asking, *So why does he keep her on a string?*

Me answering, *Because his ego needs to be fed by her blatant adoration. He gets off on seeing her so into him, and knowing that no matter what he does, she'll be there.*

But that's not me and Will.

That's Mary Beth and Vinnie.

We are not them.

I am not her.

I didn't get married too young and saddle myself with two kids and a mortgage. I'm not living out my life in Brookside, laid off from a teaching job, pathetically, perpetually in love with a man who no longer loves me.

Mary Beth has baggage.

I don't.

Mary Beth is too afraid to find her way out of the trap.

I'm not.

I was brave enough to come to New York City by myself and make a life here.

Or was I?

Maybe my coming to New York and Mary Beth's

staying in Brookside are the same thing. The cowardly thing.

She stayed in Brookside to be with Vinnie.

I came to New York to be with Will.

No. That's not the only reason. I wanted out of Brookside long before he ever came along—

A door slams.

Buckley's voice calls my name.

"I'm in here," I tell him.

I shove thoughts of Will aside.

It isn't until later—much later—that I allow him back in. Later, after I've called voice mail and left Jake a message saying I need a sick day and then spent the morning watching trashy talk shows with Buckley and the sunny afternoon meandering down to my apartment.

My disgusting clothes from last night are rolled up into a tight little ball, crammed into a white plastic D'Agostino's shopping bag and stuffed into the bottom of my big leather bag. I'd have thrown them away, but I happen to have been wearing a newly discovered old pair of pants I haven't fit into in over a year, and I can't quite bring myself to trash them without getting more use out of them. It feels too good to pull them on and feel the zipper glide up effortlessly—to pinch an inch or more of excess fabric at the waistband.

Yes, I walk home. Even though my head still aches and my stomach is still vaguely upset, and my legs aren't quite steady.

I could've taken the subway, or even a cab, and I certainly could've done the walk home in less than an hour. But I revel in the freedom of this weekday afternoon not spent at a desk in a cube. Yes, the city is dirty, and crowded, and the hot, humid weather makes everything and everyone smell disgusting. Yet it's glorious. I'm liberated. I take my time making my way downtown. I buy *The Post* and sit on the steps of the palatial Forty-second Street New York Public Library to read it. I stop for an Italian ice from a cart in Union Square Park and slurp it as I walk, until it's so drippy I have to toss it into an overflowing wire trash can. I buy two bottles of mineral water, one just so that I can clean up and the other to drink. I poke in and out of stores, looking at skimpy, sexy summer clothes I'll never be able to afford or be thin enough to wear.

Or will I?

If I keep losing weight…

If I keep saving money…

Well, you never know.

Inspired, I remind myself that the first thing I'm going to do when I get home is the Jane Fonda workout tape. I've been doing it faithfully, almost every day. It might be wishful thinking or my imagination, but I feel like my thighs bulge out less right below my hips—like there's a smoother line of flesh there. And I'm positive there's less jiggle and thigh-chafing when I walk.

When I get back to my apartment, the Jane Fonda

workout tape has to take a back seat to the answering machine.

Because the message light is flashing.

As I reach out to press the play button, I want it to be Will.

Yet I know without a doubt that it's Jake, calling from work. I'm positive that he's figured out that I'm not really sick. I didn't sound genuine in the voice mail message I left him. Or somebody saw me out and about, and reported me to human resources.

It's Jake.

I know it's Jake.

But it's Will.

"Tracey. I'm sorry I had to hang up on you before. Are you okay?" A pause. "Are you there?" Pause. "Pick up if you're there." Pause. Sigh. "Okay. You're not there. Where are you? It's midnight. I'll call you again."

With that message, hope rises.

It isn't much.

No "I love you," much less an "I forgive you."

But at least he called.

And he'll call back.

Sixteen

Will doesn't call back Thursday night.

Will doesn't call back Friday night.

Will calls back Saturday morning, as I'm getting ready to rush out the door.

"Hello?" I say breathlessly, snatching up the receiver.

"Tracey? It's me."

My heart stops. "Will."

"Are you in a rush?"

"No…"

"Oh. Because when you picked up, you sounded like you were in a rush."

"I'm just…I'm going to Brenda's wedding in a few minutes."

Silence.

I picture him, blank-faced, trying to remember who Brenda is.

"She's my friend from work."

"Oh, right. The wedding you're bringing Raphael to."

"The wedding I was supposed to bring Raphael to," I say, taken aback that we're having this perfectly conversational conversation, under the circumstances. "But he canceled on me. The Czechoslovakian ballet dancer is history—"

"Huh?"

"Didn't I tell you about him? He was into S and M, which isn't Raphael's scene, and anyway, now he's seeing this new guy, Wade, who invited him to his beach house in Quogue for the weekend, and you know Raphael. He had forgotten all about the wedding until I called him yesterday morning to remind him. He was really apologetic."

"But he still dumped you," Will says. "Leave it to Raphael. So you're going to the wedding alone?"

"Actually, no."

"Oh." A pause.

And I like this.

Despite everything, I like knowing he's searching his mind. Trying to think of another gay male friend I might be bringing. Maybe he's even jealous, wondering if I could possibly have a real date.

"You're not going alone? Who are you bringing?" he asks.

"Buckley. He's a friend of mine. I met him at Raphael's party. I told you about him. Remember?"

"No, but...." He doesn't sound concerned. Or jealous. "Well, if you have to run..."

I check my watch. I do have to run. The wedding starts in an hour and a half, and I have to meet Buckley and get all the way to Jersey.

But Will is finally on the phone, and I'm not letting him get away this time.

"I have a minute to talk," I tell him, carrying the phone over to my closet and digging out the shoes I'm going to wear.

"Look, Trace, I'm sorry I had to hang up the other night. But I had to get back to the show..."

"I understand...."

"And I thought you had been drinking. If you hadn't, I'm sorry."

"It's okay."

"So you weren't drinking?"

I'd love to tell him that I wasn't. But something tells me that a lie won't make the situation better. Because this isn't just about the other night. This is bigger than that. This is huge.

"I'd had a few drinks, yes," I admit cautiously, lighting a cigarette and hunting down an ashtray. "But I called you because I was in trouble, and I needed help. You were the only person I knew I could turn to."

"What kind of trouble?"

"I don't know... It was some sort of attack. It was like I couldn't breathe."

He digests this. "Are you okay now?"

"Yes."

After all, it hasn't happened since. But I'm afraid it will again. I don't know what's triggered the last few episodes, so I don't know how to stop another one from coming on.

"Was it a panic attack?" Will asks.

"A panic attack?" I repeat slowly. I take a drag on the cigarette. Exhale. "I don't know. Maybe."

"Helene used to have panic attacks. Her heart would race and she'd feel like she was going to die. She had an anxiety disorder."

"This is different," I say quickly.

And it is different.

Because I don't have an anxiety disorder.

If I had an anxiety disorder, I would be...

Well, I don't know what I would be. But I don't have one.

"This was a physical thing, not a mental thing," I tell Will, shoving my feet, clad in sheer black stockings, into a pair of black sling-backs with low heels. "It was pain. In my chest. Like I couldn't breathe."

"That's what used to happen to Helene."

Helene, his loony, overweight ex-girlfriend, whom he dumped.

"It wasn't a panic attack," I insist. "Anyway, the point is, I needed to talk to you, and I had no way of getting in touch. All I wanted to do was call the pay phone in the cast house so that we could talk.''

I walk over to the mirror carrying my cigarette and the ashtray. I study my reflection as Will says, ''Edward said it was an emergency call from home. I assumed it was my mother. I thought something horrible had happened.''

''Well, I'm sorry.''

''Okay.'' He clears his throat. ''It's just…everyone was asking me what happened. They saw Edward pull me out, and they thought it was serious.''

I feel sheepish, ashamed that I caused such a disruption.

Meanwhile, I can't seem to help noticing, as I look into the mirror, that I look damn good.

I'm wearing a short, simple black cocktail dress with a swirly skirt. I bought it two years ago, for my cousin's wedding. I wore it only that one time, and it was too tight. Now it fits the way it's supposed to. Maybe it's even too baggy around the hips and stomach.

Are you ready for this? I've lost twenty-three pounds—the last few, no doubt, thanks to the big vomit fest the other night.

When I started this diet, I thought I should lose thirty to forty pounds. That means I've got less than ten pounds to go until I reach the high end of my goal weight.

I wish Will could see me now.

"Will, I want to come up there," I say abruptly, stubbing the half-smoked cigarette out in the ashtray.

"I know. I want you to."

I'm not sure if I believe him, but my heart leaps anyway and I ask, "When?"

"I don't know…"

"I can come next weekend," I offer.

Please don't say no, Will. Because if you say no…

"That might work," he says slowly. "We're doing *Sunday in the Park with George.* It opens Friday night. I'm playing George."

"Will! You got your lead!" I'm stunned that he hasn't told me until now. He must have known for at least a week.

"I got my lead," he agrees. "That's why I haven't called. It's been insanely busy, trying to do *Grease* at night and rehearse for *George* during the days."

"It's okay. I've been busy, too," I tell him, reaching for my hair spray so that I can give my head another spritz. I'm wearing my hair piled into an upsweep—mostly because it's almost a hundred degrees outside with full humidity, and this is the only way I won't look like a drowned rat at the wedding.

"Yeah," Will is saying, "I heard you've been doing quite a few jobs for Milos."

I poise with the Aussie Scrunch spray aimed at my 'do. "You did? How did you hear that?"

"I was talking to one of my friends back in New York."

"Oh."

So he's been in touch with someone from Eat Drink Or Be Married.

That bugs me for a million reasons, not the least of which is that he obviously hasn't called me as often as he could. Not if he had time to chat with someone else.

Okay, maybe I'm being irrational.

And maybe I'm imagining things again....

But I can't help asking, "Who?"

"Who...what?"

"Who did you talk to? About me," I add helpfully, careful not to let the tension I'm feeling creep into my voice.

After all, it was probably John, or one of the other guys.

But it wasn't.

"Zoe," he says, and I'm sure I hear a reluctant note in his voice. "She says she met you."

Zoe.

Zoe with the Pamela Anderson body and the Catherine Zeta Jones face.

Right.

"Yeah, we've met a few times," I tell Will. "I didn't realize you were friends with her."

"Sure. I'm friends with a lot of people there."

Uh-huh. Will and Zoe are friends like Bill and Monica were friends.

"So you've been making some extra money, then, huh?" Will asks.

"Yeah, the money's great," I say absently.

Will slept with Zoe.

I know it.

Why else would he be calling her from North Mannfield?

Why else wouldn't he be calling me more often?

"Will…"

"You've got to go, don't you?" he says. "It's okay. I have to get to a costume fitting. Let's plan for next weekend. Okay?"

"Okay."

"I'll find you a place to stay. There are a couple of bed-and-breakfasts that are close to the theater. Esme's parents just stayed at one, and they loved it. I'll ask her about it."

Esme again.

Esme.

Zoe.

I hate the shards of jealousy that slice into my gut, but I can't do anything about it. Maybe if Will were here, with me…

Or maybe if I trusted him.

But I can't.

Why can't I? It's not as though I've ever caught him cheating on me. I've never even found solid evidence that he has.

It's just this instinct I can't ignore.

"So I'll call you on Tuesday or Wednesday to make plans," Will is saying.

"Okay. I'll see if I can take off on Friday."

"Don't do that. Just come up Saturday."

"But...that's only one night."

"I know, but Friday is opening night. It'll be crazy for me. Opening nights always are, and this time I'm the lead. Come Saturday. Bright and early."

What can I do? Argue?

No.

There's nothing to do but agree.

And hang up.

I take another look in the mirror, half expecting to see my old fat, frumpy, insecure self.

The thing is, I still look good. Better than I ever have before, in fact.

But I'm not nearly as exhilarated about my appearance as I was a few minutes ago, thanks to Will. Damn him.

I was planning to go to this wedding and have a good time with Buckley, who was surprisingly agreeable when I invited him. I only did it because I realized I couldn't possibly show up dateless after I'd already RSVP'd to the invitation saying I was bringing a guest. I've now worked enough catering functions to know that Brenda and Paulie would be paying for Raphael's uneaten dinner.

Anyway, Buckley said, "Sure, sounds fun" when I asked him.

And I was looking forward to it.

Until now.

All I want to do is stay home and mope.

But Brenda is walking down the aisle in a little over

an hour, and I've got to get my butt in gear or she'll never forgive me.

I rush to the Port Authority, where Buckley is waiting. It takes me a moment to recognize him, because he's wearing a suit. Somehow, I'm surprised by that, but I shouldn't be. After all, we're going to a wedding. I guess I just forgot amid all my despair about Will.

Now, though, I shove Will—and Zoe and Esme—firmly from my mind.

"You look amazing," Buckley tells me.

"So do you," I tell Buckley.

"Really? Because I was drenched in sweat, walking down here. I couldn't get a cab."

"I did, and it wasn't air-conditioned. The driver was drenched in sweat."

"Ick." He leans toward me and sniffs the air. "Don't worry, the fumes aren't clinging to you. You smell like honeysuckle."

"I do?" I *am* wearing honeysuckle. "I can't believe you know what it smells like."

He shrugs. "My mom has this honeysuckle bathroom spray."

Oh.

We take the bus across the river. I try to focus on what Buckley's saying as we go through the Lincoln Tunnel. But I start thinking about what happened on the bus home from Brookside the other day, and my heart starts to pound wildly.

Buckley doesn't seem to notice. He's telling me about his sister's wedding—something about how the band leader got food poisoning the night before, so his brother-in-law's cousin had to fill in and he only knew the lyrics to three songs.

The bus seems to be crawling through the tunnel even though there's no traffic. I look at the tiled walls, counting the lights as we pass them.

"Are you okay?"

I try to take a deep breath, but I can't. My chest is all tight again.

"Tracey?"

I look at Buckley.

He's looking at me.

"Are you okay?" he asks again.

"I don't know." I swallow, and the saliva seems to get caught in my throat. Why can't I swallow? I try again. It doesn't work. I'm over-thinking it. I have to think about something else.

But I can't.

"What's wrong?"

"I don't know," I say, and I can hear the note of panic in my voice.

Panic.

"I think I'm having a panic attack," I tell Buckley.

He picks up my hand and squeezes it. "It's okay. You're okay."

"I don't know…" I look at his face. I look out the window, at the tiles and the lights and the other cars.

"It's okay, Tracey. Tell me what you're thinking."

"I feel like something bad is going to happen."

"Like what?"

"I don't know. I think I might..." I look at him again. His face is so kind, and I want to tell him, but he'll think I'm crazy.

I'm not crazy.

Mental note: Stop doing this.

"You think you might...what?" Buckley nudges gently.

"Die," I say in a small, strangled-sounding voice. "I think I might die. I feel like I'm going to die. Or something."

"You're not going to die."

"I know." I exhale a shaky breath. "But I can't quite get my brain to believe that. It wants to freak out."

"Has this happened to you before?"

"The other night. The night I called Will, from the bar. When I was with you." I'm trying to focus on what we're saying, so that I won't panic. If we could just get out of the tunnel... "And before that, too. A few times."

I can't believe this whole bewildering, humiliating *Girl, Interrupted* deal is happening to me in front of Buckley—not that he seems to mind.

"What triggers it?" he asks earnestly.

"I don't know," I say, not really hearing his question.

Don't think about being in the tunnel. Don't think about the tunnel collapsing and water crashing in. Don't think about drowning. Don't.

The bus lurches a little.

I gasp.

Buckley squeezes my hand.

"It's okay, Tracey," he says. "I'm with you."

And after a while, it is okay.

The bus comes out of the tunnel.

The panic subsides.

And Buckley is with me.

Seventeen

"Tracey! Ohmygod! You look like Cindy Craw-ford!" Raphael shrieks on Wednesday afternoon when I meet him on the corner of Madison and Forty-eighth. We're having lunch today.

"Shut up, Raphael," I say through clenched teeth as several construction workers eating lunch on some nearby steps turn around, check me out and obviously conclude that I look nothing like Cindy Crawford.

"No, really! I love the hair slicked back like that. What'd you do?"

"I sweated like a pig all the way over here, so I just pulled it back with a clip I had in my pocket." A clip that happens to belong to Sonja. I forgot to give it to Buckley to give to her. Oh, well, her loss. It's a nice clip.

"Oh, Tracey, stop," Raphael says, draping his arm around me. "You look trés chic. I love the outfit." I have on a plain black linen sheath that actually does look pretty good on me this summer. Last year it was too snug in the hips and kept riding up.

"You look trés chic, too," I tell Raphael.

"Do you think? Oh, yawn," he says, looking down at his outfit. He's got on sunglasses with pink lenses, cropped khaki pants and some kind of vest without a shirt beneath it. Office wear, Raphael style. "I'm so ready for fall clothes, Tracey. Bright-colored sweaters are going to be all the rage."

"Really? Black is always all the rage with me."

"Mark my words, Tracey, you're going to be wearing colors one of these days," Raphael says.

"I doubt it." I take out my pack of cigarettes and put one between my lips.

"So hurry up and tell me," Raphael says, stealing a cigarette from my pack and taking my lighter out of my hand. "How was the wedding, Tracey?"

"It was great," I say as he lights my cigarette, and then his. We both inhale. "We were late getting there and we missed half the ceremony, but not the best part."

"The vows! Did you cry, Tracey?" Raphael wants to know as we sidestep a puddle left over from this morning's thunderstorm. The sun is out now, and it's a steamy summer day in the city, as usual.

"I cried," I admit. "But just a little."

"I always cry at weddings. When I have my commitment ceremony, Tracey, I'm going to be a mess. I'll probably collapse on the floor from all the emotion.''

"When you have a commitment ceremony, Raphael, I'm going to collapse on the floor from shock.''

"Tracey!''

"Raphael. Come on. You're just not a one-man man.''

"That's because I haven't met Mr. Right yet.'' We stop on the corner of Fifth and wait for the orange Don't Walk to change to a white Walk. "Are we still having sushi at that place on Forty-sixth, Tracey?''

"Definitely.'' Sushi is slimming.

"What was the food like at the reception?''

"It was delicious, Raphael. There were theme stations. A fondue station. A raw bar station. A potato station. Oh, and by the way, Buckley said to thank you for ditching me because he had a great time.''

"Tracey! I didn't ditch you!'' Raphael looks horrified. "I would never ditch you.''

"Sure you wouldn't.'' I pretend to be pissed.

"Please don't be angry, Tracey! I had forgotten all about the wedding and I had already told Wade I'd go with him to Quogue, and—''

"It's okay, Raphael. I forgive you. How was Quogue?''

"It was fabulous, Tracey. Kate and Billy came out and joined us for dinner. Wade cooked. He made a spectacular seafood risotto. I thought it was a little heavy on the oregano, but Kate really liked it.''

"What about Billy?"

He shakes his head. "Tracey, you've met him, right?"

I nod.

"What did you think?" he asks ominously.

"That I'd expect nothing less from Kate. I don't know him well, but from what I saw, he's superintelligent. Drop dead gorgeous. And rich as—"

"Tracey, I hate to say it, but Wade thinks he's an ass."

"Really?" Having never met Wade, it's hard to say whether this bombshell is meaningful or not. Maybe Wade thinks everyone is an ass.

We've made it to the restaurant. Every table is taken, but we manage to find two seats at the sushi bar.

"What did *you* think of Billy?" I ask Raphael as we wipe our hands with the hot, steaming wet towels the waitress has brought on a tray.

"To be honest, Tracey, I thought he was hot."

"Please. You think everyone is hot."

"I don't think he's hot," Raphael says in a stage whisper behind his hand, motioning toward the portly, unshaven businessman slurping miso soup on the seat to his right.

"That's a first." I place my hot towel on the tray and pick up my menu.

"Speaking of hot, Tracey, did Buckley come out to you on Saturday night?"

"No!"

"Oh." Raphael looks disappointed as he surveys the á la carte list.

"Raphael, Buckley can't come *out* because he isn't *in,* because he isn't gay."

Raphael gives a maddening shrug.

"Trust me, Raphael. He's straight."

"How do you know? Have you slept with him?"

"Absolutely."

Raphael drops his menu.

The portly soup slurper retrieves it for him.

Raphael thanks him with a kittenish giggle, then whispers to me, "You know, there is something enticing about him in a rugged, manly kind of way."

"Raphael, are you on crack?"

He gets back to the business at hand, clearly stunned as he asks, "You've slept with Buckley?"

"Yep." I nod vigorously. "In the same bed. Twice."

"Tracey! Why didn't you tell me?"

"Because it was no big deal. Unlike you, Raphael, I can share a bed with an attractive man with no sex involved."

"Tracey! I can do that."

"Only if the attractive man happens to be a blood relative, Raphael."

He nods in unabashed agreement. "Tracey, I haven't got all day here—" Which is bullshit, since Raphael is known at *She* for his three-hour lunches "—so hurry and tell me, when did you sleep with him?"

"The first time was last week, after we went out. I drank too much and slept it off at his place." That sounds suitably tamer than the stark, smelly, spewing, sobbing reality. "The second time was Saturday night, after the wedding. It was so hot when we got back to the city, and so late…and I don't have air conditioning. So when he told me I should stay over, I took him up on it."

"And nothing happened between you."

"Absolutely nothing."

"Tracey, I rest my case," Raphael says with his best smug Camryn Mannheim imitation. "He's just not ready to come out of the closet."

"Raphael, I have a boyfriend. *That's* why nothing happened with Buckley. We're just friends. The whole night was completely platonic."

And I'm telling the complete and utter truth…

Except for one thing.

At one point, we were on the dance floor at the wedding. One minute, we were doing the Electric Slide. The next, the DJ had gone into a slow dance.

It was this old song, "I Could Not Ask For More," by Edwin McCain. I told Buckley that I loved it, and he grabbed my hand and pulled me into his arms, saying, "Then let's dance."

Everyone else was slow dancing…the bride and groom, Yvonne and Thor, Latisha and Anton.

Buckley and I had already danced a few slow songs—but it was different music. Jazzier. Like "The Way You Look Tonight" and "Summer Breeze." We danced to those songs like I danced to them with my father and my uncle Cosmo at the anniversary party— jaunty steps, spinning turns, body contact limited to one arm around each other's waists, the opposite elbow bent, hands clasped.

This was different.

This was romantic.

Buckley just kind of wrapped his arms around me and held me close and we swayed with full body contact.

The way you do when you're in high school.

Rather, the way everyone else did when I was in high school. I was hardly ever asked to dance back then.

The thing about slow dancing with Buckley—aside from the fact that it became, let's just say, *obvious* he's at least mildly attracted to me—was that for a few minutes, I almost forgot that he wasn't my boyfriend. And when the song was over and I remembered, I found myself wondering what it would be like if he was.

Because Buckley is always so nice to me.

And Will...

Well, sometimes, he's not.

But that's because Buckley and I barely know each other. Will and I are in a relationship, and all relationships have problems.

Anyway, after that slow dance, the DJ played the Tarantella. Naturally, Brenda and Paulie made sure everyone joined in. After that, Buckley and I were right back to being platonic, and the mood lasted for the rest of the night.

We were especially platonic the next morning when I left for home and Buckley left for his Rollerblading date with Sonja.

I pick up one of the small pencils in a cup on the glass-topped counter to begin marking the boxes next to my choices. I opt for sashimi, which is slices of raw fish without rice. I'm down another two pounds and I'm determined to lose more before I see Will on Saturday.

"Did I tell you I'm going to see Will this weekend?" I ask Raphael after we've handed our orders to one of the guys behind the counter.

"No! Tracey, that's great!"

"I hope so."

"Uh-oh. What's wrong?"

"Nothing," I say quickly. "It's just that Will has been kind of distant since he left…and I'm worried things won't be the same when I see him again."

Actually, I'm worried that things *will* be the same.

But I don't want to admit that to Raphael.

Or even to myself.

I have to make things work with Will.

I'm not ready to let go.

I'll never be ready to let go. I love him.

After lunch, I go back to the office. Jake's left a yellow Post-it note stuck to my computer screen. It says *See Me*.

I go into his office.

"You're back," he says, not looking up from the yellow legal pad he's writing on.

"I'm back."

"I need you to make sure you keep your lunches to an hour, Tracey."

I check my watch. I was gone an hour and ten minutes. "Sorry," I say.

He nods.

He's been like this with me ever since the chocolate episode last week. I don't think it helped that I called in sick the next day. In fact, when I got back on Friday, he barely spoke to me all morning.

I guess he didn't believe my story about getting food poisoning from some bad clams. That seemed like a viable excuse to me. People get sick from raw seafood all the time.

Now Jake says, "I need you to run an errand for me."

"Okay…"

"I need you to go over to the Orvis store and pick up something I ordered. They just called and said it came in."

"Okay."

Another personal errand.

Latisha and Yvonne keep telling me I should stop doing stuff for him. They're going to give me a hard time when they find out about this. Brenda would understand, but she's off in Aruba on her honeymoon.

"I already gave them my credit card number over

the phone," Jake says. "So it's paid for. All you have to do is pick it up."

"Okay."

He doesn't even say thanks as I head out the door.

As I walk over to Orvis, smoking a cigarette, I think about the upcoming visit with Will. He hasn't called me yet, but I'm sure he will tonight. He'd better, because I'm working for Milos tomorrow and Friday.

When I reach the store and the salesman retrieves Jake's order, I'm stunned.

It's an enormous fly fishing pole.

The kind of fly fishing pole you can't carry down a Manhattan street without attracting the undivided attention of every oversexed construction worker, leering flyer hawker and various other forms of urban low-life.

The giant phallic prop I'm lugging is not lost on any of them. I get a flurry of lewd comments, assorted kissing noises, a couple of butt pinches, and an incoherent marriage proposal from a guy wearing a plastic visor and a sandwich board.

By the time I get back to my building, I'm livid.

I march toward Jake's office carrying the fishing pole.

Yvonne is just coming out of her cube. She takes one look at me and summons Latisha.

"This can't be happening," Latisha says, gaping. "This can't be happening."

"Oh, it's happening," I say, forging onward.

"Girl, you've got to put him in his place."

"That's what I'm going to do."

"Are you going to quit?" Yvonne asks.

"Quit?" I stop walking. "No!"

"Good," Latisha says. "You just tell him he can't get away with this stuff anymore. Tell him you'll report him to human resources if he doesn't straighten out."

"I will," I vow. But I've lost a little steam.

I was so angry I hadn't thought about what I was actually going to do about this.

"Go on," Yvonne says, giving me a little nudge toward Jake's office.

I start walking again, with a purpose. They're right. I have to stand up for myself. Jake is totally taking advantage.

I'm all geared up to tell him off—in a professional way, of course.

But when I get to his office, it's locked.

In my cube, I find a note from him saying that he's gone to a meeting at the client's offices and won't be back in the office until tomorrow. The note says that I should lock the fishing pole in the storage closet.

I'm tempted to leave it right out in the open and let Myron and company do what they will with it.

But it turns out that I can't.

I lock the pole into the storage closet.

And I leave the office at five on the dot.

I walk all the way home, swiftly.

I'm soaked with sweat when I get there. I strip off

the dress and toss it into the pile of stuff for the dry cleaner. I put on shorts and a T-shirt.

I put a small potato into the microwave. Then I cut it open, top it with leftover steamed broccoli and a piece of fat free cheese. I dump salsa all over the whole thing. It doesn't taste that bad when I use enough salt.

While I eat, I read a chapter of *Gulliver's Travels*.

Then I go through my wardrobe, trying on clothes and trying to put together a couple of decent outfits to wear this weekend. I come up with nothing. Half of my clothes are too baggy now—not that I'm complaining—and the stuff that fits looks really dated.

I count the money in my Prego jar. I still haven't gotten to the bank with it, but I will. This week. Definitely.

I've saved almost fourteen hundred bucks so far.

It won't hurt if I take some out for a new outfit or two. I deserve it.

I count out two hundred dollars and stick it into my wallet. Tomorrow, I'll go shopping during my lunch hour. Maybe I'll go over to French Connection.

Hmm.

I count out another hundred bucks.

Then, inspired by the thought of new clothes, I pop my workout tape into the VCR. Now that I know the steps so well, it's pretty much effortless. Fun, even… when I'm in the mood.

I'm in the mood tonight.

The phone rings just as I'm finishing the cool-down.

I leap for it, knowing it's Will.

"Hey, what's going on?"

"Buckley!"

I look at the clock. Will might be trying to call me. But I can talk to Buckley for a few seconds. I don't have call waiting, but Will will try back if the line is busy.

Of course he will.

And anyway, what are the chances that he'll choose this particular minute to call when I've been waiting at home for the phone to ring all night?

"Haven't talked to you since Saturday," Buckley says. "I've been on a deadline all week. I still am, actually. But I wanted to call just to say hey."

"I'm glad you did."

We talk about his freelance assignment, which somehow segues into a debate about whether Jimmy Stewart is dead. Buckley swears he isn't, and I'm positive he is.

"I know he died a few years back, Buckley."

"I don't think so. That was Donna Reed. They did a whole thing about *It's a Wonderful Life* on the news."

"Well, they did it when Jimmy Stewart died, too."

"It can't be, Trace. I just saw him on some talk show."

"So did I. Leno, right?"

"I think it was Letterman."

"Whatever. It was a repeat. I'm telling you, he's dead."

"I'm going to find out," Buckley says. "I swear to God. I'm going to show you that you're wrong."

"What are you going to do for proof? Show up on my doorstep with Jimmy Stewart?"

"Think you're quite the little Quipster, huh? Actually, that's exactly what I'm going to do."

"So who's going to help you dig him up?"

We both get hysterical, envisioning this whole scenario like something out of the movie *Weekend at Bernie's*. We're laughing so hard we both keep making this snorting noise, which makes it even funnier.

I guess you had to be there.

The thing is, I'm having such a good time talking to Buckley that I forget all about Will.

Then I remember.

Then I stop laughing.

"You know what?" I say to Buckley. "I've got to go. I'm waiting for this call...."

"From who? Will?" he asks.

I'm surprised Buckley remembers his name. "Yeah. I'm going up there to see him this weekend."

"Hey, cool. I guess it worked out, then, huh, even though—"

"I made an ass out of myself the night I called him? I don't know yet. I mean, he seems to have forgiven me, but I'm not sure he gets what was happening." I'm not sure *I* get what was happening. I need to change the subject. "What about you? How was your date with Sonja on Sunday?"

"So much fun that we went out again Tuesday."

Really? I thought he was on a deadline.

"Where'd you go?"

"To dinner, and then to this Learning Annex lecture on meditation. I was the only guy there. I can't figure out if it made me feel like Sean Connery or Just Jack."

"I thought you were on a deadline," I'm compelled to say teasingly.

At least, I meant it to come out teasingly.

But for some reason, I kind of bark it.

"Hey, man cannot live by copywriting alone," Buckley says lightly. "Okay, you'd better go. I know that Will—"

"Yeah, he's probably trying to call. So what are you doing this weekend? Seeing Sonja again?" I ask casually.

"Nah. This is her weekend to go out to the beach. She's got a half share in Westhampton."

Of course she does.

"So listen, have a great time with Will," Buckley says sincerely.

"I will."

"How are you getting up there?"

"How else?"

"You're driving up in your new Beemer?"

"Actually, it's in the shop so I'm taking a bus."

There's a pause.

I know what he's thinking.

"Trace, you'll be fine," he says quietly.

"I hope so."

"Look, if you have another panic attack, you should really think about seeing someone about it."

"Seeing someone? You mean a shrink?"

"A therapist. It can help. I have the name of someone who helped me a lot, after my dad died."

"I can't go to Long Island to see a shrink," I say, because I have to say something.

"Her office is here. On Park and Twenty-ninth."

"Oh."

"Just think about it, Tracey."

"Yeah, I will," I say quickly.

It's not that I'm embarrassed, because strangely, I'm not. If it were anyone else, I would be. But there's something about Buckley that removes all my defenses. I've been myself with him right from the start, not worried about what he thinks of me. And it's not just because I'm not interested in dating him, because I'm more comfortable with him than I am with my other friends, like Kate, and Raphael, and everyone at work.

Buckley and I just clicked.

And even though we've only known each other a few weeks, I can tell he's going to be a really good friend—someone I can confide in.

"Go," he says. "Will's probably getting a busy signal."

"How do you know I don't have call waiting or voice mail?"

"Because I've gotten a busy signal a few times

when I've tried calling you," he says lightly. "Have fun this weekend, Tracey. And listen…"

"Yeah?"

"Call me if you need to. Collect."

"That's crazy! I would never call anyone collect unless it was an emergency."

"So if you have an emergency, call me."

"Buckley, I'll be fine."

"I know, but if you're not, I'll be here, writing the cover flap for the latest installment in that talking parrot detective series. Trust me. No interruption will be unwelcome."

"Okay."

I hang up.

For a foolish moment, I hold the cordless receiver in my hand, looking at it expectantly.

It doesn't take the hint and ring.

Nor does it ring when I put it down and try to pretend I'm interested in a breaking news bulletin about a plane crash in Japan.

In fact, it doesn't ring until I'm dozing in front of Conan O'Brien.

"Collect call from Will McCraw," a robotic voice says.

And for a split second, I'm tempted not to accept it.

But of course I do.

"Trace? Did I wake you up?" Will's voice asks, unapologetic.

"Of course not. I always stay up till at least 1:30 a.m. on work nights. It helps keep me fresh."

At least he has the grace to say, "Sorry." Unapologetically.

There's a lot of noise in the background.

More noise than the usual cast house banter and giggles.

In fact, I think I can hear a live band.

"Where are you?" I ask.

"At this bar," he says. "We had a rough dress rehearsal today, and everyone needed to blow off a little steam. I completely forgot I was supposed to call you."

Normally, I would let him off the hook. But maybe I'm cranky because I've been sleeping. Maybe I'm not loving the image of Will blowing off a little steam in some bar with a live band. Or maybe it's time to stop letting him off the hook.

Whatever. I hear myself say, "Great. Thanks a lot."

"What are you talking about?"

"I just can't believe you could forget to call me when you know we have to make plans for the weekend."

"The weekend is still two days away."

"And you know I have to work for Milos for the next two nights. I won't be home till late."

"So what's the problem? I'd just have called you late."

"Obviously, that's no problem for you." I hate the way I sound, but I can't help it. I'm pissed.

"Why are you being so bitchy?"

I don't answer him. Because I can't answer him.

"Look, maybe we should just forget it," he says.

Stab of panic. "Forget what?"

"Your coming up here this weekend."

Oh. Thank God.

Not that I want to forget the visit, but I thought he meant the whole thing. Us.

"I don't need this right now. I'm under a lot of pressure to carry this show. I've got a lot riding on it, and I don't need…"

He trails off.

I'm tempted to prod him into finishing the sentence.

But I don't really want to hear the rest.

"I'm sorry, Will," I force myself to say.

Because I can't not go up there this weekend. If I don't see him this weekend…

Well, I have to see him. That's all there is to it.

"I'm just exhausted, and it scared me when the phone rang at this hour. I didn't mean to be a bitch."

He says, "Okay."

But not right away.

He pauses a few seconds, and I spend those seconds anticipating rejection.

He tells me he got me a reservation at the B&B where Esme's parents stayed. He says it's not far from the cast house. He also says that it costs almost two hundred dollars a night.

"Is that a problem?" he asks.

And I realize that I'll be paying for my own room.

Well, what did I expect?

He's not making much money doing theater this summer. Much less than he makes in New York, working for Milos.

And now I'm working for Milos, so I've got extra money.

I get his logic.

But there's a part of me that wishes he would tell me not to worry about what the room costs, because he's paying for it.

Or even, he's going to split the cost with me.

But he doesn't say that.

He says, "Is that a problem?"

And I say, "Of course not. I can't wait to see you."

Eighteen

When the bus pulls into North Mannfield, Will is waiting exactly where he said he'd be: on a bench in front of the little luncheonette that doubles as a bus station.

Naturally, he looks fantastic.

But then, so do I.

I'm wearing a new, body-skimming, short summer dress. Black, of course. I tried it on in more colorful shades, but I'm not ready for that yet. Black is slimming. And even though I'm slimmer than I used to be—I've lost another two pounds in the past two days, thanks to virtual starvation in anticipation of the weekend—I'm still not as slim as I'd like. I'm not as slim as Esme.

How do I know that when I've never seen her?

Trust me. I know.

I know in the same way I know that she's the one I have to worry about. It's not that Will has even mentioned her name more than once or twice in passing. But something about the way he's mentioned her name—or maybe just her name itself, *Esme*—piqued my girlfriend radar. I'm definitely on the lookout for her.

I hurtle myself into Will's arms when I get off the bus.

"Hey, where's the rest of you?" he asks, looking me up and down.

I know I should be flattered. He's noticed the new me.

But it's the way he says it.

Where's the rest of you?

I know it's a compliment, but it's vaguely insulting to my pre-summer self, who lurks closer than I want to admit. And I feel like I'm betraying her when I grin and say, "I sweated her off back in the city. God knew I needed to lighten my load."

"You look really good," he says, and now he's being sweet, and I don't even cringe when he hugs me. Usually, all I can think is that his hands are feeling the fat bulges around my bra straps. But this time, I allow myself to savor the feel of his arms around me.

He smells so intensely like Will that I bury my head in his neck and inhale deeply, wanting to get enough

Will scent into my nose so that I can keep it to take back to New York with me.

He laughs.

"What are you doing?"

"Sniffing you," I say. "Your cologne always smells so good. And you smell different now, too... like coconut lotion or something."

"Sunscreen," he says.

That's when I notice he's got a tan.

Will never gets a tan. He says it'll wrinkle his skin, make him old before his time, rule out roles that call for youthful-looking actors.

"You're tanned, Will!" I inform him.

"It's not real," he says with a grin. "Actually, I'm covered in number 45 SPF. But one of the girls uses this self-tanner stuff, and she's been putting it on me to give me some color."

Self-tanner stuff? She's been putting it on him?

I picture Will being lotioned by a strange girl—not woman but girl, as he oh-so-chummily put it.

Will picks up my bag, which I unceremoniously dumped at his feet when I leapt on him.

I notice that the air is far less humid than it was back in New York, and refreshingly cool. I could get used to this.

"How was the trip?" Will asks, leading the way down the street.

Well, I had a panic attack somewhere around Albany.

But other than that...

"Fine," I say breezily. "I got a lot of reading done."

We're walking now. Through a town that isn't all that picturesque. In fact, it's kind of dumpy. Besides the luncheonette, there's a Laundromat, a police-station-slash-post-office, a convenience-store-slash-gas-station, a bar called the Drop Right Inn and a bunch of old houses. Not charming-gingerbread-Victorians, old. Just…old. Crooked shutters. Missing spindles. Sagging steps.

"So what were you reading?" Will wants to know.

"*Gulliver's Travels,*" I announce.

I wait.

For what, you wonder?

Why, for his jaw to drop in awe.

He laughs. "*Gulliver's Travels?* God, why?"

"Because I'm spending the summer working my way through books I should've read long ago. You know, the classics."

In other words, I'm having the most boring summer of my life, while you're up here blowing off steam and getting lotion smeared on your loins.

Oh, hell. Why didn't I lie and tell him I was reading some bestseller? Or, better yet, that I haven't had time to read?

"That's great, Trace," he says. "I'm glad you're keeping yourself busy."

I'm glad you're keeping yourself busy?

I'm glad you're keeping yourself busy?!

That's the kind of thing you say to a recently widowed retiree.

"Insanely busy is more like it," I inform him. "Work's been crazy..."

"Really? What's going on?" he asks with what sounds like mild interest.

He's an actor, remember?

But he asked, and damned if I'm not going to tell him.

Naturally, I skip the part about the pilfered birthday chocolates and the fishing pole escapade.

As we leave the disappointing North Mannfield business district behind and walk down a tree-dappled lakeside country road, I tell Will about the deodorant-naming gig, making it sound as if the future of McMurray-White is resting on my capable shoulders.

"So far I've come up with a few possibilities that my boss really likes," I say.

"Yeah? You know what would be a good name for a product like that?" he asks.

Naturally, I cut myself off on the verge of spouting off my own ideas to ask, "What?"

"Maintain," he says, with a significant nod, as if he's just revealed with absolute certainty the name of the winner on the latest edition of *Survivor.*

"Maintain," I echo, trying to look impressed. "Wow, that's good, Will. I'll keep it in mind in case *Persist* doesn't work out."

Actually, it's not a bad product name.

Maintain.

I go on telling him how busy I've been at my glamorous ad agency job, and working for Milos. I don't linger too long on that topic, afraid he'll bring up Zoe. Instead, I move right along to provide a pumped-up account of my weekend travels, from the Hamptons to Brookside to Jersey for the wedding.

"How was that?" Will asks. "Did you have a good time with…what was his name?"

"Buckley."

Buckley, who remembers Will's name.

Buckley, who said to call collect.

"Yeah, we had fun," I tell Will. "That reminds me, is Jimmy Stewart dead?"

"Yeah," he says.

I notice that he doesn't ask me what reminded me of that. I wonder if he's even paying attention to the conversation. Or me.

And suddenly, I want to tell him about how Buckley and I were wondering about Jimmy Stewart. I want him to know how chummy we are. I want him to be jealous, dammit.

"Are you sure he's dead?" I ask Will.

"Jimmy Stewart? Yeah, he died a few years ago."

"Oh. Because—"

"There it is," Will interrupts as we round a bend.

And there it is. The Valley Playhouse. There's a freshly painted, hand-lettered wooden sign in front of a group of buildings that are set back from the road.

I don't know what I was expecting. Maybe a quaint,

scallop-shingled wooden structure, or even a deco-type circa 1930s place with a marquee.

Definitely not this cinderblock rectangle surrounded by what looks like a couple of Sears sheds and another lovely matching cinderblock dorm-type building.

I should probably be glad it's not a charming country haven upon which Will will look back wistfully in the future.

But what I'm thinking is…

He left New York—he left *me*—for *this?*

Instead of a marquee, there's a glass-fronted sign board on the lawn in front of the theater—the kind of sign you'd find in front of a church or school. It says "Now laying: Sunday in the ark With George."

"Looks like somebody's pilfered your p's," I tell Will.

"Huh?"

"The sign. The p's."

"Oh. Yeah." He grunts, unamused, shifting my bag to his other shoulder.

I feel compelled to apologize that it's so heavy.

Will feels compelled to grunt again.

"It seems kind of quiet around here," I comment as we approach the cast house.

"It always is, on Saturday. It's our only day off. Everyone's off running errands, doing laundry, stuff like that."

"Don't tell me you're going to have to wear dirty underwear for a week because I'm here," I joke.

"Nah, I got somebody to do my laundry for me."

"There's a laundry service around here?" Guess the town isn't as rustic as I thought. I never knew you could pay someone to do your laundry until I moved to New York.

"No, not a laundry service. A friend of mine from the cast said she wouldn't mind throwing my stuff in with hers."

"What a friend." I imagine Will's underwear whirling chummily in a steamy dryer with somebody's lace panties—perhaps Ms. Self Tanner Slatherer's lace panties.

"That's the theater over there," Will says, pointing to the cinderblock building that's not a Sears shed and doesn't look like a dorm. "This is the cast house."

We walk past some flowerbeds and up the steps. The door opens into a dim lobby-type room that I'd call a foyer if the house were more homey. In the foyer are the infamous pay phone, and beside it, a bulletin board with lots of messages tacked up.

"That's the bulletin board," Will points out.

Gee, good thing he told me, because I thought it was a drinking fountain.

"The cast leaves notes for each other there," he adds unnecessarily. "Like phone messages and stuff."

I nod.

It takes a second for that to sink in. By the time it does, we're in the big rec room off the lobby, and two scantily clad girls are looking up from the couch where they're giving themselves pedicures.

"Hi, guys," Will says.

The guys are buxom and wearing tiny spaghetti-strap tops that bare their concave tummies, and shorts the size of bikini bottoms. They have tans that are too rosy and freckled not to be the real thing. Apparently I'm the only pasty ghost in town.

Mental note: Finagle invite to Kate's beach house. Coat self in oil and sunbathe until golden.

"Hey, Wills," says the one with the straight dark hair and the slightly peeling red sunburnt nose.

Wills? I have to grin at that one. Last I checked, he wasn't heir to the British throne.

That my boyfriend seems to have acquired a ridiculous royal nickname here isn't all I have to ponder.

Will said the bulletin board is where they leave each other phone messages. Which means the pay phone can get incoming calls.

Assuming Will's telephone privileges weren't revoked before he even got here, he misled me. He could obviously have gotten phone calls all along. He just chose not to.

I'm steaming.

Yet, I'm proud to report that I muster a cheery, confident hello when Wills introduces me to the pedicure princesses, whose names escape me once I've duly noted that neither of them is Esme.

"This is Tracey," Will informs them.

He doesn't add the anticipated—at least, by me—"my girlfriend." This pisses me off even more. Has he even told anyone about me before now? Or is it like *Eat Drink Or Be Married*, where his co-workers treated me as though I had suddenly materialized out of a cave somewhere to stake my ridiculous Will's-got-a-steady-gal claim.

I am asked, "How are things back in New York?"

Which calms me a little, because at least they know where I came from.

"Hot," I say.

"I'll bet. I can't believe I was ever sucker enough to spend the summer there," says the girl who is painting her toenails electric blue, as opposed to the blood-red peds on her friend.

"Oh, it's not *that* bad," proclaims the only sucker in the room. Namely, me.

"All I know is that last summer in New York I was wearing sandals when it rained, and I stepped in a puddle and the next thing I knew, I was in the hospital with some disgusting bacterial infection," Blood Red declares with a delicate shudder.

Will gives her bare, sun-kissed shoulder a pat and says—no, not *and where were your galoshes, young lady?* He says, "That doesn't sound like fun."

She nods. "It sucked."

"Like I said, summers in the city suck," says Electric Blue with a laugh.

"Yeah, they're for suckers," I pipe up.

Everyone looks at me.

Oops, I guess that came out bitchier than I intended. Actually, I intended it to come out bitchy, but now that I've called attention to myself, I realize I'm not putting my best—unpedicured, I might add—foot forward in front of Will's new friends, so I just shrug like it was a joke and I'm totally in on it, and I say, "Trust me, next summer I'm outta there. So, Will, I want to see the rest of this place."

In other words, get me the hell away from these two girls who are looking at me like they're wondering why Will didn't just abandon me at the bus-stop-slash-luncheonette in the first place.

We move on to the big dining hall, which consists of several round metal tables with fake-wood brown tops. Beyond that is a kitchen. A lanky geek is there, cooking something on the stove. If I'm not mistaken, he's boiling his socks. Guess there's no laundry room on the premises.

"Are you making that cabbage soup again, Theodore?" Will asks.

"Oh, shut up, Will," says Theodore with such a flouncing flourish that I'm immediately aware that he isn't competing with Will for the fair Esme's attentions…as if his name, gold earring and Barbara Streisand concert T-shirt weren't evidence enough.

"This is my girlfriend, Tracey," Will tells Theodore, who drops his slotted spoon to offer me a limp-wristed handshake and tell me it's nice to meet me.

I tell him that it's nice to meet him, too.

Note that Will uses the dreaded G-word when introducing me to a male—and I use the term loosely, but still—and avoided it when introducing me to the twin temptresses in the next room.

As we leave the kitchen, he informs me in a low

grumble that Theodore has an eating disorder and lives on the cabbage-soup diet, which stinks up the cast house.

Naturally, fastidious Will doesn't appreciate stink of any kind—even imagined.

Mental note: Do not mention past ingestion of cabbage soup.

Getting back to Will's use of the G-word: as we make our way through the cast house, in and out of the dorm-like rooms upstairs, I keep an ongoing tally. It's not like he introduces me as his girlfriend to every guy, because he doesn't. He only uses the label one time other than with Theodore, and that's with another housemate who obviously is more interested in Will than he is in me. When we meet the two other guys— both apparently straight—and three other girls who are here, he just tells them I'm Tracey.

Everyone is polite.

I tell myself that I'm reading too much into it.

But when we're walking back downstairs, I can't help casually asking, "How come I haven't met Esme?"

And I swear it's not my imagination that Will is startled enough to semi-gulp before innocently repeating, "Esme?"

"Yeah, I've heard so much about her. I thought I'd get to meet her."

Actually, I've heard next to nothing about her.

But the two toenail-painters from the rec room are

just coming into the lobby, and when they obviously overhear my question, they shoot each other a look.

And that's enough to clinch what I've already suspected.

Will is screwing around with Esme.

"She's in town, at the Laundromat," Will says.

"Oh, is she the one who's doing your laundry?" I manage to ask from amid a cloud of swirling hysteria that threatens to touch down any second now.

"How'd you guess?" he exclaims, all golly gee.

"I'm taking a class in deductive skills at the Learning Annex," I retort.

"Really? My roommate took that class," Blood Red announces.

I shoot her a withering look. She doesn't notice. She's exchanging yet another long, meaningful glance with her friend. I'd be tempted to peg them as lesbians if I didn't happen to intercept the glance and realize that it clearly says, *We'd better scram before the obviously deluded Tracey makes a scene about Esme washing Will's undies.*

The two of them take off.

Will tells me that he's going to borrow someone's car to drive me over to the bed-and-breakfast.

He grabs a key that's been thumb-tacked to the bulletin board on top of a note that says simply, "Wills."

Wills. What's up with this? It's starting to get on my nerves—mainly because it doesn't seem to be bugging him.

I would never dare to call him Wills.

Once, when we first started dating, I teasingly called him Willy. Was he pissed. I thought he was kidding/pissed, but he was really pissed. Kind of like I am now, about the phone and the nickname and oh yeah, *Esme*.

As if I've let her slip my mind for even a second.

No. I've got a mission.

Mental note: Seek and Destroy Esme ASAP.

He takes me and my luggage out to the parking lot behind the cast house. There, we climb into a beat-up green compact car. I'm not good with cars so I have no idea what make and model it is, but I'm confident saying it's not a Mercedes or a BMW. I'm also confident in saying that it either belongs to a male, or to a disgusting pig of a female, which means despite her being on an intimate enough level with Will that she'd loan him her car, she's no threat to our relationship.

He wrinkles his nose and brushes off the driver's seat before getting in, then hunts for a napkin in the cluttered glove compartment so he can clean some kind of smudge from the inside of the windshield. The small back seat is littered with clothes, scripts, empty cigarette packs and fast-food debris. A Bic lighter lies handily on the floor at my feet, and there's a lovely ashtray overflowing with ashes and butts in the front console.

Which means I don't feel guilty lighting up.

Not until Will looks over at me and asks, "Can you please not smoke in here, Trace?"

"In here?" I echo. "Come on, Will, this is pretty much the Smokemobile."

"My throat," he says delicately. "I have to perform tonight."

"Oh. Sorry." I stub out the butt, inwardly grumbling. Then I ask, "How was opening night last night? I completely forgot to ask you about it."

"It went well," he says. "I want to stop and pick up the local paper on the way to the Inn to check the reviews. They should be out by now."

He seems to know his way around this place pretty well, I notice, as he maneuvers the green trash can on wheels over winding, mostly unmarked country roads. The lake keeps popping up, and he points out various local attractions along its shore.

I hate that this place is so familiar to him and it's so foreign to me. He has this whole life without me. He lives here, and I don't.

The thought that in a little over a month he'll be back in New York is no longer comforting. Not when I know I need to confront whatever he's been doing while we've been apart…and, possibly, whatever he used to do while we were together.

We stop at a little mom-and-pop-type store, the first place I've seen up here that's truly quaint.

I buy three packs of cigarettes, a Diet Raspberry Snapple Iced Tea, and the latest edition of *People* to read while Will is getting ready for his performance later. At this point, I'm pretty much *Gulliver's Traveled* out.

Will buys a newspaper called the *Lakeside Ledger* and whips through the pages as soon as we're back in the car. He finds what he's looking for as I open the Snapple and take a big gulp.

I realize I'm hungry.

"Are we going to stop for lunch anywhere?" I ask, thinking there must be a place to get a good salad up here. This is the country. Fresh vegetables. Home-grown lettuce. Deep red, sun-warmed tomatoes...

My stomach growls ferociously, unsated by the Snapple.

Greasy fries with tons of salt, vinegar and ketchup. A double bacon cheeseburger. A chocolate shake...

"Will?" I prod, weak from hunger.

"Shhh!" He's busy reading the review.

If we're just going to sit here without driving, I'm going to get out and smoke to take the edge off my appetite. I climb out of the car and light up.

As I stand there, leaning on the car in the gravel parking lot, looking around at the woodsy setting and the tourist types coming and going, I start thinking again about Will cheating. I picture him up here in the country, in the moonlight, by the lake, with somebody else.

Then I realize that I've smoked my entire cigarette and Will's still sitting silently in the car.

"That must be a helluva long review," I say, stubbing out the butt on the ground and poking my head in the open window.

Will is grim.

The page containing the review is crumpled on the floor behind his seat.

Clearly, it wasn't a rave.

"Are you okay?" I ask him.

He shrugs.

"What did it say?"

"See for yourself." He's looking straight ahead.

I climb back into the car and fish the review from a litter of ketchup-stained napkins and lipstick-stained tissues.

Will McCraw, as George, is a comely addition to the Valley Theater cast, but brings little energy to the challenging role.

Oh. No wonder he's upset.

I keep reading, my mind already racing for words of comfort.

His lackluster performance could not begin to capture the brooding enigma that embodies his character, a passionate artist. His thin, incapable voice frequently seemed to lack the necessary range. However, the dazzling Esme Spencer was perfectly cast as the beguiling Dot, who is head over heels over the career-obsessed George and must ultimately decide whether it's time to "Move On" in the show's most haunting musical number. To her credit, Spencer managed to consistently create convincing romantic sparks in her onstage moments with the hapless eye candy that is McCraw.

I feel like somebody just dropped a hair dryer into my bathtub.

The dazzling Esme Spencer.

So she's his leading lady.

So their onstage romantic sparks were convincing.

Don't do this.

That comes from a cautionary voice somewhere deep inside of me.

It's as effective as the *Patrons Only* sign on the rest rooms of the Grand Hyatt hotel on Forty-Second and Lex.

I turn to Will.

Will is now the brooding enigma that is his character, a passionate artist.

His arms are folded across his chest, his jaw is stiff, and he glares through the still-smudged windshield.

In other words, this probably isn't a good time to bring up our relationship.

But it can't wait any longer.

This has been building for the past few hours, since I got here.

No, the past few days, since he called me collect from a bar.

No, the past few weeks, since he left.

Oh, hell, it's been building since I've known him.

I take a deep breath and let it all spill forth at last, to my credit having the presence of mind to open with an obligatory, "Will, I'm sorry about the sucky review. But it's only one critic, and what does she know? The thing is, I've been thinking, and I've come to realize that I need to ask you a question, and I need you to answer it honestly for me."

He hasn't even flinched.

I wonder if he's even listening.

I rush on, "It's just this feeling that I've had, and maybe it's completely off-base. I mean, it might just be me—just my insecurity, and my imagination—but I need to know… Will, have you been faithful to me?"

Now *he's* flinching.

Not only is he flinching, he's turning on me in a rage. "*What?* You're asking me this *now?*"

My own anger bubbles promptly from the depths. My previously carefully controlled voice erupts into a shrill, "Well, when else am I supposed to ask you? You've been gone for a month. And you never call, so I can't ask you over the phone."

"I never *call?*"

"A couple of times, in the middle of the night. I'm supposed to work with that? Will, you're not being fair."

"*I'm* not being fair?" He gives a bitter laugh. "You're obviously celebrating Kick Will While He's Down day, and *I'm* not being fair."

"I know, it's not the best timing…and I said I was sorry about the goddamn review. But, Will, this is important."

"Tracey, right now, in my life, nothing is as important as this. Nothing."

"Including me," I say flatly, my insides churning.

He says nothing, just lifts his chin slightly and glares into my eyes.

"Take me to the bed-and-breakfast," I blurt, feeling the tears coming on.

He starts the engine.

But he doesn't take me to the bed-and-breakfast.

Sobbing in my seat, my face turned blindly to the open window, I don't realize where we are until we're pulling up with a violent jerking stop in front of it.

The bus station.

I turn to look at him, incredulous.

"Just go," he says, disgusted.

"You want me to leave...?"

"Looks that way, doesn't it."

"Will..."

But there's nothing left to say.

Nothing left to do.

Nothing but leave.

Nineteen

When the bus gets back to New York, it's raining. Thunder, lightning, torrential downpour—the works.

I descend into the depths of the Port Authority and find the dank, malodorous subway platforms mobbed with stranded passengers and the loudspeakers blaring with garbled, indecipherable announcements.

Rather than wedge my sobbing self and my oversize luggage into the fetid swarm of humanity, I robotically ascend to the street.

Even now, I barely notice the weather for the first block I walk after exiting the Port Authority.

My mind is a squall in itself, crackling with *coulda-shoulda-wouldas,* whirling with disbelief, sodden with wrenching grief.

But when I reach the corner of Forty-Second and Seventh, I realize that it's hardly a stroll-friendly summer evening.

The apocalyptic reality: arroyo-like gutters, steam rising from freshly baked pavement, cacophonous traffic clogging semi-flooded streets.

I've been walking blindly, lugging my bag, smoking a soggy cigarette that has finally been extinguished by the deluge from above.

The rain that soaks my hair and my clothes mixes with the tears that have been pouring down my face for the past three hours. My head aches almost as badly as the hollow above my eye sockets, and my cheeks feel raw.

I stop on the corner and I drop my heavy bag at my feet, into a disgusting, warm, polluted urban puddle that pools over my feet in their black summer flats and splashes up against my bare ankles.

This is it.

I've reached the end.

I can't go any farther than this. I don't care what happens to me now. If a wayward yellow cab hydroplanes me down, it will be a blessing.

Because Will sent me home.

Because Will hates me.

Because there's no way our relationship can be salvaged after this.

And the thing is…

There are two things.

The first thing is that this was inevitable.

The second thing is that I still want him.

I want him so badly that for an insane moment it seems logical to go back to the Port Authority, catch the next bus north and try to work things out with him.

I wipe my streaming eyes with the back of my hand as I've been doing for hours, and happen to glance down to see that streaks of black mascara and eye liner have stained my wrist.

Okay.

Clearly, at this point I look like Marilyn Manson. Somewhere in the midst of my misery and hysteria, I comprehend that going back to North Mannfield to win back Will's love is probably not a good idea right now. That it might, in fact, be a bad idea.

What I need right now is another cigarette.

Another cigarette, and a stiff drink.

Another cigarette, a stiff drink and shelter.

Another cigarette, a stiff drink, shelter and a shoulder to cry on.

I need another cigarette, a stiff drink, shelter, a shoulder to cry on, and...

Five golden rings.

No.

This isn't funny, not even in a bitter, dark, ironic way. But...

Five golden rings?

Uh-uh.

One golden ring?

Yes, that will do.

And the chances of one golden ring from Will—ever—are now slim to none.

Okay, none.

But you knew that, Tracey. You knew it all along.

Come on, Tracey...

Didn't you know that?

I'm walking again.

Uptown.

Because maybe this isn't the end.

Maybe it's a crossroads.

Meaning there's a path to be chosen...

And I've chosen my path.

Maybe what I truly need right now...

In addition to a cigarette, a stiff drink, shelter, a shoulder to cry on and one golden ring...

Is Buckley O'Hanlon.

Even if Kate or Raphael were available this weekend—which is unlikely now that Billy and Wade are on the scene—I'm not in the mood for *I Told You So,* or *You're Better Off Without Him,* or *Hey, Wasn't That Mascara Supposed To Be Waterproof?*

Buckley will comfort me without asking too many questions or offering advice. Unlike Kate, he won't do most of the talking. He'll listen in that quiet, guy way—a skill Raphael unfortunately lacks despite his gender.

Buckley will let me smoke and drink and cry, and in the end I'll feel better, and he won't have minded.

I know all of this instinctively, somehow, even

though he's been my friend for less than a month and my acquaintance for only slightly longer.

When I reach Buckley's apartment building it occurs to me that maybe I should have called first.

I press the buzzer next to his name and wait.

Buckley's voice comes over the barely functioning intercom, a single, blasted, inscrutable syllable.

Is he grouchy? Or is it just the intercom distorting his mood?

I hesitate only long enough to realize that I've outgrown ringing doorbells and running. I say, "It's me, Tracey."

The door buzzes open.

I make my way through the dimly lit, shabby vestibule and up three flights of stairs. The second-floor landing reeks of cruciferous vegetables. Apparently, somebody under this roof is on the cabbage-soup diet. In a building like Will's, cooking smells rarely make it past apartment doors. But Buckley's apartment building is only slightly more glamorous than mine, and I can always tell what every one of my neighbors is having for dinner as I pass their doors.

When I reach Buckley's floor, he's sticking his head out into the hall, waiting for me.

He looks rumpled, in too-generic-to-describe shorts and a T-shirt, and has five o'clock shadow.

"Tracey! What are you doing here? Are you having another panic attack?"

I shake my head. Strangely, I'm not having another panic attack. I didn't even have one on the bus on the way home. I push the thought from my head before a delayed panic attack can strike.

"Are you okay?" Buckley asks. "My God, look at you. You look like you fell into the East River."

I reach his doorway, open my mouth to tell him what happened and deposit myself, crying, into his arms instead.

Five minutes later, I'm on his couch, having spilled the whole sordid story. I'm tucked under a blanket, holding a Jack Daniel's on the rocks in one hand and a freshly lit cigarette in the other.

"I knew that if I came here, you'd help me." I sniffle. "I didn't know what else to do."

"I'm glad you came," Buckley says, sitting next to me with the bottle of beer he was apparently drinking before I materialized. "I figured something like this might happen."

"You did?"

He nods.

"Why?" I shakily inhale some calming tobacco smoke. "You never even met Will," I say, careful not to exhale in Buckley's face.

"I've heard enough about him from you...besides, just blame it on show biz. These things never last. Look at Bruce and Demi, Alec and Kim, Tom and Nicole..."

"Yeah, but Will's not a movie star!" I protest. "It's just fucking summer stock. This didn't have to happen! Oh, and by the way, Jimmy Stewart *is* dead."

Buckley doesn't blink an eye at that. Nor does he

ask me what I'm talking about. The nice thing about Buckley is, he always seems to know.

I'm off on another gale of tears.

Buckley pats my back and makes *There, There* sounds.

I am profoundly comforted.

Until the phone rings.

Until he answers it and I realize that he's talking to Sonja. He drags the phone to a distant corner and tries to lower his voice, but I overhear enough to know that he's in the process of breaking a date with her. I'm selfish—and maybe jealous—enough not to stop him.

When he hangs up, I ask innocently, "Who was that?"

"It was Sonja."

"Is she out at the beach?" I ask hopefully, thinking I might have been wrong.

"Nah, she ended up coming home early because of the weather. It's supposed to rain all day tomorrow, too."

"So you made plans with her for tonight?"

"We had plans, but I canceled. It's no big deal. We were just going to see a movie."

"Which movie?"

"Death Dot Com."

"Oh." I refuse to let myself feel bad about this. According to the reviews, I'm doing him a favor. Still, I offer, not very convincingly, "You can go with her. I'll be fine."

"We'll go tomorrow instead," he says with a shrug.

"It's too crummy out tonight to go trudging around in the rain anyway. Besides, I wouldn't leave you in your time of need."

"You wouldn't?"

"Nah. I'm a nice guy."

"You *are* a nice guy," I tell him. "I thought Will was a nice guy, but..."

Then again, did I ever really think Will was a nice guy? He's always been self-absorbed and distant and noncommittal.

"I know we probably have to break up," I tell Buckley, plucking another tissue from the box he so thoughtfully placed next to me on the futon. "I mean, this has been coming for a while now. Why does it have to be torture? Why do I feel like I'm in shock?"

"Because even when it's inevitable, it hurts. But it's good-for-you pain. Kind of like exercising. You have to feel the burn as your muscles grow stronger."

I give him a dubious look.

He shrugs. "The point is, you might be in agony now, and for a while, but in the long run, this is going to be the best thing that ever happened to you, Tracey."

I say nothing.

I am thinking that he's wrong.

"Someday, you're going to be grateful that Will dumped you. You're going to want to thank him."

"For dumping me."

"For dumping you."

"No offense, Buckley, but if that's the best you can

do, it sucks. Just in case you thought you were making me feel better, or anything.''

"Tracey, I'm serious.'' He puts his face right next to mine and looks me right in the eye. ''You're going to get over this. It's going to be okay. This is for the best.''

"This is for the best?'' I grab a pillow and shove it into his face. ''I came over here because I thought you were my one friend who would just shut up and let me cry.''

"Then I'll shut up and let you cry,'' he says, putting the pillow behind his head, leaning back and reaching for the remote control. ''You don't mind if we watch TV while you cry, though, do you? Because I've been sitting at the computer screen all day writing copy, and now I'm in the mood for some mindless trash.''

Curled up next to him on the couch, I continue to cry while he watches *BattleBots*.

But eventually, the tears stop.

Eventually, I start to laugh at Buckley's jokes.

And, as the Jack Daniel's builds a nice little fire in my belly, I find myself wondering what it would be like if Buckley were my boyfriend.

"Are you feeling better?'' he asks, looking over at me during a beer commercial.

I nod and check my watch. ''A little. I should probably go.''

"You don't have to go, Tracey. You can spend the night if you want.''

"No, that's okay.''

"You can stay," he says again.

"If I do, you might as well give me a slot in your toothbrush holder," I tell him.

"Well, I have four free, so that won't be a problem."

"What about Sonja?" I find myself asking.

He raises an eyebrow. "What about Sonja?"

Mental note: Shut up.

But the Jack Daniel's makes me ask him, "Is she your new girlfriend now, Buckley?"

He shrugs. "Not now. Not yet, anyway."

Terrific.

Here's Buckley, willing to acknowledge girlfriendly possibilities after a couple of dates with someone, as opposed to Will, who refuses to apply the label after three years with me.

"That's great, Buckley," I murmur.

"That she isn't my girlfriend?" he asks, looking surprised.

"Hmm? Oh, that's not what I meant. I was just thinking how nice it is for you that you've found someone again after going through a lousy breakup."

"That's what I was trying to tell you, Tracey," Buckley says. "This is a good thing, your breaking up with Will."

"But we didn't exactly break up," I point out. "He just told me to leave, so I left."

"So you consider yourself still in the relationship?" he asks.

"Until the breakup is official." Which it probably

will be the second I get home and check my answering machine.

Which is why I should probably stay with Buckley tonight, like he said.

It's better than being alone.

Anything's better than being alone.

At least, that's what I've always believed.

But I'm starting to wonder.

Twenty

Weeks go by.

Here is what happens:

July becomes August.

The weather grows hotter and more humid with every passing day.

The city grows more crowded and putrid and unbearable with every passing day.

Kate gets a new roommate. He is Billy. They are wildly in love.

Raphael gets a new roommate. He is Wade. They, too, are wildly in love.

Buckley is regularly dating Sonja. If they're wildly in love, I don't want to know about it, and he hasn't admitted it.

A glowing Brenda returns from her honeymoon.

A glowing Latisha meets a hunky single-dad mailman who adores the Yankees as much as she does, and she tells Anton to take a hike at last.

A glowing Yvonne is considering a green-card marriage to Thor.

The misguided Mary Beth and malevolent skank Vinnie are in couples therapy, talking about reconciliation.

As for me...

I lose another ten pounds.

I am not in the mood to shop, yet I buy a pair of size ten jeans. Just one pair. Just because I can.

When the weather cools, I will wear them. I will wear them with a shirt tucked in. Just because I can.

I continue to read the plodding *Gulliver's Travels*.

I fight off panic attacks, yet they still plague me.

But I frequently insist to Buckley that I don't need to call his former shrink.

I open a savings account and make regular deposits thanks to steady work from Milos.

I run personal errands galore for Jake, who informs me in passing late in August that the new deodorant— the one that lasts all week long—will be named *All Week Long*.

All Week Long.

Yes.

That's the name they came up with.

This news almost puts me over the edge, yet I remain curiously functional.

Functional despite the fact that apparently The Breakup That Wasn't...

Is.

I say this because Will hasn't called.

Not once.

Of all the scenarios I've pictured, this is the least likely...and, perhaps, the least welcome, although none were truly appealing.

But this...

This silence...

It's excruciating.

And there's nothing I can do about it.

Nothing.

But wait.

Wait.

Wait.

Twenty-One

It's ninety-five degrees on the Tuesday night after Labor Day. The city is still in the midst of a heat wave that hasn't let up in weeks. I would kill for a window air conditioner. I even took some money out of savings last week to buy one, only to discover that there's a shortage. Every store is out.

Now, after a blah dinner of steamed broccoli with melted fat-free imitation cheddar, I am sitting on the couch in front of the useless window fan, soaked in sweat and eating dessert—a store-brand fat-free lemon yogurt that is *so* not "luscious" even though the label promises that it is.

I am also trying to read *Gulliver's Travels* while watching one of those lame tabloid TV shows that is in the process of busting yet another smug, cheating Hollywood hubby who reminds me of Will.

But then, everything reminds me of Will these days.

The phone rings.

Everything reminds me of Will these days with the exception of a ringing telephone.

That's because, at this point, I'm long past thinking that it might be him.

I mute the TV volume and mark my place in *Gulliver,* wondering if I'll ever get past these goddamned Lilliputians and if the plot will ever pick up.

I lift the receiver and press Talk.

"Hello?" I wipe a trickle of sweat from the side of my nose.

There's a pause on the other end of the line.

Which means it's another one of those electronic telemarketing calls.

My dark mood grows darker.

But the voice that comes on the line doesn't belong to a computer.

It belongs to Will.

And all the voice says is my name. Tentatively.

All I say in response is his name. In disbelief.

Now it's his turn again.

"I'm sorry I haven't called," he says blandly.

I'm serious.

This is what he says.

After three years together and a summer apart…

After one fleeting encounter that ended with him

ordering me to get back on a bus and go back from whence I came, or whatever it was that he said...

After refusing to make the expected follow-up phone call to at least officially dump me...

This is what he says.

Blandly.

"You're sorry you haven't called?" I echo.

"We have to talk."

Is he for real?

I want to lash out at him, but he doesn't give me a chance.

"I just got back into town last night. Can you come over to my place so that we can talk?" he wants to know.

"Now?"

"No. Tomorrow."

"I have to work," I say in a bitchy tone reserved for self-absorbed actors who don't acknowledge that normal people work from nine to five—and who abandon their girlfriends while they are away doing summer stock.

"Tomorrow night, then?" Will asks.

No.

Not tomorrow night.

Not ever.

We're through.

That is what I should say.

This is what I do say:

"Okay."

"Can you come at seven?"

"Okay." Dammit, there I go again.

"All right." Will exhales, and I realize he may have been holding his breath the whole time we've been talking.

This should be comforting, but it isn't, because I've been holding my breath, too. The whole time we've been talking...

And ever since I left North Mannfield almost six weeks ago.

"I'll see you then." I hang up. I exhale.

I light a cigarette, shaking.

I dial Buckley's number.

"What now?" he asks when he hears that it's me. We just hung up from our nightly phone call ritual about a half hour ago.

"Will called," I croak.

"*Will* called?"

"He wants me to come over and see him tomorrow night."

"Did you tell him to go fuck himself?"

"Yep."

Pause.

"You didn't, did you," Buckley says flatly.

"Nope."

"What did you say?"

"I told him I'd be there at seven."

"Tracey..."

"I'm going to dump him, Buckley. I want to do it to his face."

"Tracey..."

"What? You think I'm going to be the dumpee, don't you?"

"No. I think he might try and talk you into staying with him."

"Oh, please." I give a bitter, incredulous laugh.

But inside, in the cold, brittle recesses of my jaded heart, something flutters. Hope. Buckley thinks there's hope.

"If he tries to talk you into giving him another chance, Tracey, be strong. Tell him how much he's hurt you."

"Don't worry, I will."

"Don't give in."

"Trust me, I won't."

But *I* don't trust me. If Will begs me to come back to him…well, there's no telling what I'll say or do.

What if he says he'll change?

"If he says he's going to change, don't believe him," advises Buckley-the-mind-reader.

"I won't."

"Because nobody can change."

"Right."

But is he?

Right, I mean. Is it true that nobody can change?

Look at me. I've changed. I've lost weight. I've saved money. I've eliminated clutter. I've read classics.

But for all of that, I realize, I'm still the same person inside. I'm still insecure, and afraid.

What the hell am I so afraid of?

Being alone.

That's what I'm afraid of.

"Tracey?"

"Yeah?"

"You were quiet. I just wanted to make sure you're still there."

"I'm still here."

"You're thinking about getting back together with Will, aren't you."

"No!" I say, as though he's suggested that I'm thinking of taking an elevator to the observation deck on the Empire State Building and stepping over the edge.

"I want you to come straight over here when you leave Will's apartment tomorrow night, Tracey," Buckley says.

"Why?"

"Because I want you to look me in the eye and tell me that you dumped him. That it's over for good. If you know you have to answer to me immediately afterward, you won't cave while you're with him."

That's what he thinks.

Whenever I'm with Will, it's hard to think about consequences.

"Okay, I'll come over," I say to appease Buckley.

"What time are you seeing Will?"

"Seven."

"Then I'll expect you here at seven-thirty."

"Buckley! Seven-thirty? Come on."

"How long does it take to dump someone and walk a couple of blocks uptown?"

"I'll get there when I can get there."

"Good. I'll be waiting. You can do it, Tracey."

And I probably can do it.

For Buckley.

For me.

It would be easier if there were some guarantee that if I dump Will, I'll find someone else. That I won't be alone for the rest of my life. That I'll meet someone fabulous, get married, have children, and live happily ever after.

If I knew all of that was waiting for me...

Then I could dump Will.

"You're going to be grateful for this someday, Tracey," Buckley says.

"I already am grateful, Buckley. You're a really good friend."

"Not grateful to me. Grateful to Will. For being an ass and giving you up."

That's what he said before. That Will's destroying our relationship will turn out to be the best thing that ever happened to me.

I wish I could believe that.

"I should go," I tell Buckley. "I need my beauty sleep if I'm seeing Will tomorrow."

"Tracey..." he says in a warning voice.

"Just to show him what he's losing," I promise.

"People like Will never know what they're losing,"

Buckley says. "Not when they're losing it. Sometimes not ever."

"That sucks."

"Yeah," Buckley says. "But just think, Tracey. The world is full of people who are not like Will. And if you're free, sooner or later you're going to hook up with one of them."

"Do you promise?"

"I promise."

"Because I don't want to be alone."

"You won't be. Not forever."

This is not as comforting as it should be. Because I don't want to be alone even for a while.

Maybe, I think irrationally, when Will and I break up tomorrow, Buckley and I will fall in love.

After all, you never know.

Which is why I'm going over to Will's tomorrow night with an open mind. I'm going to listen to what he has to say. And if I don't like it, I'm going to dump him.

If I do like it...

Well, like I said.

You never know.

Twenty-Two

The next day, on my lunch hour, I go to Bloomingdales and I buy myself new everything for tonight.

A slinky satin-and-lace teddy with a crotch that stays snapped. A short little black Tahari summer dress—a splurge even at fifty percent off, but it makes me look even slimmer than I actually am, and you can't put a price on that. Black sling-backs with a slightly higher heel, which means my legs look longer and leaner.

Yes, I bought all black.

What did you expect? Black is slimming.

Granted, I'm not as dependent on it as I used to be.

But I barely hesitated at the display of bright-colored, figure-hugging sweaters that are everywhere, as Raphael predicted.

It's still too damn hot to even think about sweaters.

Besides, I'm not ready to wear an actual color. Not yet.

Back at the office, I spend the afternoon preparing a deck for a new business presentation Jake is doing tomorrow in Chicago. He flies out at six o'clock tonight from La Guardia, which means there's no way I can get stuck at the office as I have more and more lately.

Shortly after five o'clock, Latisha sticks her head into my cube.

"I'm heading out, Tracey," she says. "Good luck tonight."

"Thanks. I'll need it."

"Be strong."

"I will."

Brenda comes up behind her, wearing sneakers with her suit and carrying her oversize purse and a Walkman. "I'm outta here, too," she says. "I told Paulie I'd make him stuffed shells tonight."

Stuffed shells. God, how long has it been?

My stomach rumbles. I skipped lunch today. Breakfast, too. I want to look as skinny as possible in that clingy little dress.

"Remember, Tracey," Brenda says, "if he tries to talk you into staying with him, think about how miserable he's made you."

"I will," I promise solemnly.

I hear a spurt of Binaca, and then Yvonne pokes her raspberry-colored bouffant over the wall that divides her cube from mine. "Whatever you do," she says in her raspy voice, "make sure that you dump the jerk."

"I will."

I look at the three of them.

"Really, guys," I say, realizing none of them trusts me to do the right thing. "I will. I'll dump him."

"Well, it's not easy," Latisha says. "Anton and I were so over by the time I gave him the boot, and I still had a hard time being firm when he begged me to take him back."

"Well, I'm not going to let that happen," I assure her, turning off my computer. "Tomorrow when I come in here, I'm going to be a free woman."

"What are you going to do until it's time to meet Will?" Brenda asks, checking her watch.

"Go into the ladies' room and make myself beautiful, what else?" I open my bottom desk drawer and show her the makeup bag and hot rollers I stashed there this morning.

The three of them wish me luck, give me hugs and are on their way.

I head to the bathroom with my makeup bag, hot rollers and shopping bags containing my new clothes.

Nearly an hour later, I return to my cube, knowing that I've never looked better in my life than I do right now. No matter what lies ahead, at least—

"Tracey? Good. I knew you hadn't left yet. I saw your bag on the hook behind the door."

"Jake?" I turn around to see him standing there,

looking impatient. "I thought you were supposed to be at the airport already."

"I changed my flight. I'm not going until tomorrow morning." He runs a hand through his stubbly hair, clearly having a bad day. "We have work to do."

My stomach lurches. "We do?"

"We have to redo the entire deck. Creative is going to take a new approach."

"Now?"

He nods briskly and dumps a sheaf of yellow legal-sized papers on my desk. "Here's the first section of the new deck. Start typing."

Start typing.

It's just the way he says it.

No, it's more than that.

It's the fact that he makes me do all his typing when he knows how to do it himself. None of the other administrative assistants do as much typing as I do. Their bosses all have their own computers so that they can do their own documents.

Not Jake.

"What are you doing?" Jake asks.

"I'm thinking about something," I snap.

"Well, there's no time for that. It's going to be a long night. Get busy."

The parking ticket.

The fishing pole.

Monique.

The chocolates.

"Why the fuck are you still standing there?" he barks.

That's it.

"I can't stay here," I tell him.

"What do you mean, you can't stay here?"

"I have to be somewhere tonight. I can't work late."

"Well, you don't have a choice. I need you to type this over."

"No, you don't, Jake. You know how to type."

"Typing isn't my job, Tracey. It's yours."

"Not anymore," I fling at him. "I quit."

"You quit?"

I don't even bother to answer him. I merely walk out, lugging my stuff.

Out on the steamy street, I fall into step with the throng of office workers and commuters.

What now?

I just quit my job.

What was I thinking?

Who cares?

I feel strangely reckless.

Strangely free.

I'll worry later.

Right now, I've got almost an hour before I have to meet Will.

If I walk across town, I'll be a limp, sweaty mess before I get to his apartment.

I figure it'll take me forever to hail a cab, but I've got time to kill anyway.

As luck would have it, I get a cab immediately.

It deposits me a block from Will's apartment building five minutes later.

Now what?

I could go over to Buckley's air-conditioned apartment and hang out with him until it's time.

Or I could duck into that air-conditioned little pub across the street and have a drink and some cigarettes to calm my nerves.

I opt for the latter.

The cigarettes and the glass of pinot grigio do calm my nerves. Sloshing into an empty stomach, the wine also makes me feel a little daring.

A couple of cute guys in business suits flirt with me.

They want to buy me another glass of wine, but I have the presence of mind to refuse. I tell myself that after I've dumped Will, there will be plenty of opportunities to accept free glasses of wine from cute businessmen.

I tell myself to believe that.

And I do.

Almost.

Maybe I won't be alone forever, I decide as I leave the bar and start walking to Will's, right on schedule. I light another cigarette, remembering that I won't be able to smoke once I get there.

I'm wearing my short black dress and my high black shoes and black sunglasses. Several men turn their heads to look at me as I pass. For added reassurance, a couple of construction workers on the corner make it clear, in an X-rated way, that I'm looking good.

I decide that once Will lays eyes on the new me, the ball will be in my court.

If I want to dump him, I can dump him.

But if I want to keep him…

Well, Buckley will kill me.

So will my other friends.

But maybe I don't have to keep him for good.

Maybe I can just keep him for a while.

Or just for tonight.

Because the thing is, I want him to look at me the way these horny strangers on the street are looking at me. After three years of never feeling like I'm attractive enough for Will, I want to see lust in his eyes.

I want him to see me in this little dress.

I want him to take off this little dress and see me in the teddy.

I want him to take off the teddy and see *me*. All of me. Me minus the lumpy thighs and hips and belly, minus the cellulite and drooping breasts and flabby gut.

And hell, I'll admit it.

After three months of celibacy, I just plain want *him*.

At his building, I take a deep, cleansing breath.

Then I breeze into the lobby.

"Yes? May I help you?" James, the doorman, doesn't recognize me.

This is flattering until I tell him my name and realize that he still doesn't recognize me. I remember that he never bothered to learn my name before. I guess I was invisible to him.

James calls up to Will's apartment, announces my name and gets the go-ahead from Will to send me up.

I step into the familiar mirrored elevator and press the button for Will's floor. I check out my reflection, not caring that there are probably security cameras recording my every primp. I look damned good.

Will is not waiting for me in the doorway of his apartment, peering down the hall, as Buckley always does.

I knock on Will's door, my heart pounding. I feel sick. I'm a nervous wreck. So much for the wine. All it did was leave me with a fierce need to pee.

Even though Will knows, via James, that I'm on my way up, it takes him a good minute to answer the door.

I'm not surprised.

Nor do I allow myself to take this as a sign.

When the door opens, Will looks gorgeous. Tanned, fit, healthy, with streaks of sun in his brown hair. He's wearing khaki shorts and a creamy yellow polo shirt, tucked in.

But I look gorgeous, too, I remind myself.

He looks me over. He notices. Well, how could he not?

''You've lost weight,'' he comments.

''Yeah.'' About forty pounds.

''You look good.''

Good.

Not beautiful.

Not even great.

I'm pissed at him all over again.

"Come on in." He holds the door open.

We don't hug.

I brush past him.

This hurts.

I was expecting it to be painful, but maybe I underestimated *how* painful.

It's pure agony to find myself here, in his familiar apartment, and know that it might be the last time I'll ever be here. The last time I'll ever see him.

"I made us a couple of drinks," Will says.

"You did?"

Maybe I'm wrong.

Maybe he's planning a romantic evening.

He nods. "Gin and tonic. You like gin and tonic, right?"

"Yeah."

He goes to the kitchen area, takes two glasses from the counter and hands me one. I immediately take a sip.

Then I set it on the coffee table. "I need to use the bathroom."

"You know where it is."

Yes. I know where it is. I know where everything is, here. And it's all just as he left it. Nerissa didn't take over. She didn't change things. She didn't make it difficult for him to come back, so that he'd find himself wanting to move out.

To move in with me.

Not that that's even a remote possibility now, after everything.

But still…

I go to the bathroom.

I wash my hands.

I study my face in the mirror.

I remind myself to be strong.

I remind myself that I'm here to dump Will.

I remind myself that I promised everyone that I would dump him.

Then I remind myself that if I happen to sleep with him before I dump him, that's my business. Nobody even has to know.

The truth is, I'm wildly attracted to Will despite everything.

And I can't help wondering if I was wrong about him. Maybe he didn't cheat on me. Maybe it was me, being an insecure girlfriend. Maybe I read things into our relationship—and into Will's relationships with other women—that weren't there. Maybe I falsely accused him.

The more I think about this, the more sense it makes.

It also makes sense that if he asks me for another chance, I should give it to him.

I exit the bathroom.

Retrieve my drink.

"Sit," says Will, on the couch. He pats the cushion beside him. Not too closely, I notice.

I sit.

Not too closely.

We sip our drinks.

"I'm sorry."

One would probably assume, given the circumstances, that Will said that.

One would be sadly mistaken.

I never cease to amaze myself.

Because I'm the one who said it.

I said, to Will, "I'm sorry."

Will looks at me.

One might expect him to be taken aback at my apology.

One might even expect him to respond with one of his own.

Two more sad mistakes.

Will says nothing. He just waits for me to go on.

Naturally, I do. Because I can't stand the silence. Because I want him to know that I'm giving him the benefit of the doubt.

"I never meant to stir up this whole thing when I came up to visit you, Will," I tell him, in between sips of my drink.

"You had lousy timing, Trace," he agrees.

"I shouldn't have brought anything up after that horrible review…oh, how did the show go?" I remember to ask.

"It was okay." The expression on his face tells me that he doesn't want to talk about it.

"It was just that you were so out of touch all summer, and I started getting these crazy ideas. I started thinking that you weren't being faithful to me.''

Will says nothing.

He listens.

So, of course, I continue to talk.

And drink.

I drink because I'm nervous, and because I'm thirsty, and because I can't smoke, damn Nerissa.

"I started convincing myself of all kinds of things," I tell Will. "I was sure you had had an affair with Zoe from Eat Drink Or Be Married."

Will says nothing.

I find this ominous. "Then, when I heard you talking about Esme—and when I read the review, about how convincing your romance was onstage—"

"I'm an actor," Will says grimly. "She's an actress. You should know better than to ever be jealous of what happens between me and another woman onstage, Tracey."

"I know. And I'm sorry. It was just…"

But I'm watching him.

And there's something in his eyes.

Something that makes me ask, just to be sure, "So you and Esme never…?"

He doesn't answer.

That's when I know.

It wasn't my imagination.

None of it, ever, was my imagination.

"You slept with Esme?" I ask, my voice trembling.

He nods.

This can't be happening.

I knew it all along, and yet I didn't know. Not really.

"But not until after you came up to see me," Wills says quickly, defensively. "Before that, I was trying to stay away from her, until I could tell you—"

"Until you could tell me?" I cut in, feeling delirious, amazed that I'm coherent. "You mean, you invited me to come up there so that you could tell me you wanted to see other people?"

"I couldn't do that over the phone." He is sad and noble.

I'm speechless with shock and grief.

"But after you left—I was pissed, Tracey. I was hurt. I couldn't believe you would treat me that way. I figured we both knew at that point that it was over."

"You never called me," I say, crying now.

"I know. And I'm sorry. I didn't know what to say. I didn't want to do it over the phone."

"So you're doing it now. In person."

He shrugs.

I can't let this happen.

I can't let him dump me.

I'm frantic. This has slipped beyond my control, somehow.

I have to be the one to do the dumping. But not until after we sleep together. Because this is my chance to let him see the new me. Maybe that'll change his mind.

And if it doesn't...

Well, it might be my last chance to have sex. With anyone. Ever.

"Will, don't do this," I hear myself say.

"I have to, Tracey. Esme and I—well, we have more in common."

"Esme? You're still together?"

He nods.

"She's in New York?"

He nods again. "She's working for a caterer in between acting jobs—he's much bigger than Milos. Handles more celebrity affairs. It'll be great for networking. Esme's getting me a job there."

Incredible. He's not just dumping me. He's dumping Milos, too.

How can he be this way? What's wrong with him?

What's wrong with *me?*

What's wrong with Milos?

Why aren't we enough for Will?

He reaches out to touch my arm, but I jerk it away. "Is Esme the only one you've...?"

He hesitates.

Oh, God. The pain is excruciating.

"Zoe, too?" I ask him.

"Just once," he admits. "But it didn't mean anything."

Not like Esme.

"Just once with Zoe," I say, sobbing openly now. "Did you go to see *Flight of Fancy* with her?"

"What does that have to do with anything?"

"Did you?" I shriek.

He shrugs.

"Fuck you, Will," I hurl. Then I ask, "Who else? Who else were you with?"

"Don't do this, Tracey."

"Who else?"

"It doesn't matter, Tracey. You and I were wrong for each other. You always wanted more than I could give. You never saw me for who I really am. You wanted somebody who would love you and marry you and settle down with you. I couldn't give you that."

"I never asked you for any of that!"

"But you did. Every time you looked at me, I could see what you were thinking. I couldn't take the pressure, Tracey. It wasn't fair to me. And it wasn't fair to you, either."

"I hate you!" Hysteria makes my voice harsh, hurting my throat as I force the words past the aching lump. "I hate you! You used me!"

"I never used you."

"Yes, you did. I fed your ego, all this time. You kept me around because I was as crazy about you as you are about yourself."

Oh, God.

I am Mary Beth.

How could I not have seen it until now?

I am Mary Beth, minus the house and separation agreement and the children.

At least she has those things.

I have nothing.

Will is leaving me with nothing.

"Tracey, don't," he says wearily. "This is useless. I'm going to put you into a cab, and—"

"No, you aren't," I say, plunking my empty glass on the table.

I'm going to walk out of here with my head held high.

I'm going to walk out of here alone.

And dammit, I'm going to be fine alone.

Because I don't need him.

I stand up.

I take a step.

Just one step.

And then the world swirls and goes black.

Twenty-Three

It's cold.

Why is it so cold?

I fumble blindly for a blanket and find one somewhere by my feet.

Huddled beneath it, I slowly open my eyes.

It's morning.

Sunlight is streaming through the window of my apartment, along with a chilly breeze that would ruffle curtains if I had them. But I don't have curtains.

Because this apartment is only temporary.

I glance at the clock.

It's almost noon.

What day is it? Thursday?

What about work?

Yesterday comes back to me in a rush.

I quit my job.

I wait for regret.

There is none.

Only the knowledge that I'm free.

Free…

Will.

Last night rushes back at me like a serial killer lunging from a closet, yet again, in a bad thriller.

I remember awakening, dazed, on the floor, with Will hovering over me, a worried look on his face.

"You passed out," he informed me.

I passed out.

Was it the liquor landing in an empty stomach?

Or was it the sheer horror of what was happening?

I still don't know.

"Are you okay?" Will asked, worried.

I told him that I was.

But I wasn't.

Not then.

Not when he held my arm all the way down to the lobby, ushering me past a curious James, who hailed us a cab.

Will rode downtown with me.

He insisted.

And so we said our final goodbye with the meter running.

"Stay in touch," Will said.

I didn't answer him.

So.

Am I okay?

I glance around my apartment.

There are no curtains.

There should be curtains.

Gulliver's Travels is poking out of the top of my bag, which lies just inside the door where I dropped it.

My new clothes are in a heap on the floor beside the futon.

The phone is off its cradle—I took it off the hook last night, not wanting to deal with Buckley.

I'll call him later, I decide, getting out of bed.

I shiver.

It dawns on me that the heat wave has broken.

I look down at the street. There are pedestrians. There is traffic. Life is going on as usual, beneath my window.

Life will go on as usual, from now on.

No matter what.

Without Will.

I'll be alone.

My heart begins to pound.

A panic attack is coming on.

Oh, Lord.

But this time, I know what to do.

I wait.

I wait for it to pass.

I pace the apartment and I smoke cigarettes and I remind myself that I'm not going to die. And when the panic attack is over, I hunt through my bag for my

Palm Pilot. There, I find the telephone number of Buckley's therapist.

Before I can change my mind, I dial the number.

"Hello, I was recommended by a former patient, Buckley O' Hanlon," I tell the receptionist. "I'd like to make an appointment to see the doctor."

I wait for her to ask me what's wrong.

I wonder what I will tell her.

But she doesn't ask me what's wrong.

She tells me there's been a cancellation for tomorrow morning, and asks if I want that appointment.

I tell her that I do.

I hang up.

I feel better.

Better enough to take a shower.

The phone rings as I'm stepping out.

I screen the call, afraid it's Will.

But it isn't.

"Tracey? Are you alive? I waited for you all night last night. I kept getting a busy signal when I tried to call your number. Call me. I'm worried about you."

I will call Buckley.

Later.

The phone rings again as I'm shivering into my new size ten jeans and a black sweater that used to be snug last winter. Now it's too big. Much too big. I need new clothes.

I screen the call again, afraid it's Will.

But it isn't.

"Tracey? It's me, Brenda. I'm at the office. Did you

really quit last night? Please call me. I'm worried about you.''

I will call Brenda.

And I'll call Milos.

Later.

I'll give Brenda the juicy scoop on my quitting.

I'll tell Milos that I'm available 24/7 for catering gigs, from now on. I might not want to spend the rest of my life serving canapes at other people's weddings, but hey—it's a living. And maybe someday I'll run my own catering business. Or some other business. Who knows? Right now, I just want to make enough money to pay for the rent and the bills.

Oh, and the new clothes I'm going to need.

That reminds me: I have someplace to go.

I pick up my bag and I head out the door, leaving the phone that will undoubtedly ring again, and again, with callers who aren't Will.

Out on the street, the sun is glaring.

Am I okay?

I put on my sunglasses. A brisk breeze rustles the leafy branches of the block's lone tree overhead. I glance up, half-expecting to see that the leaves have turned color overnight. There is no dazzling canopy of red and orange and gold.

But there will be.

Am I okay?

I head down the block.

I find myself standing in front of a small clothing boutique. In the window, mannequins wear expensive, figure-hugging, bright-colored sweaters. The newest look for fall, Raphael said.

I walk inside.

Five minutes later, I come out.

I'm wearing an expensive, figure-hugging, bright-colored sweater.

It's red. I'm wearing red.

There are two more sweaters in the shopping bag I'm holding. One is yellow. The other is orange.

I want to go home and call Raphael. I want to tell him about the sweaters.

And about Will.

I want to call Buckley, too.

But I have another stop to make, before I can go home.

I make my way to the big furniture store I saw in June. The Grand Opening streamers are long gone, but the big oak sleigh bed is still in the window, its summer floral-print sheets replaced by flannel ones.

I think about the fact that I don't have a job.

I think about the fact that I don't have Will.

I think about the fact that I don't have a bed.

All I have is a futon.

And a savings account.

Am I okay?

I walk into the store.

When I come out fifteen minutes later, I still don't have a job.

I still don't have Will.

I no longer have a savings account.

But I have a bed.

A big oak sleigh bed.

They're delivering it on Saturday.

I'm okay.

Really.

I'm okay.

The shopping bags are weighing me down, and my black leather bag is heavy on my shoulder.

I shift the weight.

I walk.

I'm still okay.

On the corner, I impulsively take out *Gulliver's Travels*.

I deposit it into the overflowing trash can beside me.

Now I'll never know how it ends, I think a little wistfully as the light changes and I cross the street.

I always need to know how books end.

I usually flip ahead to the last chapter to find out.

But maybe this time, for a change, maybe I don't need to know.

Maybe I'll just learn to live with the suspense.

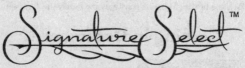
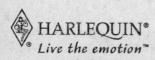

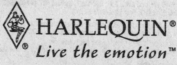